DANU VALLEY

DOUGLAS P. SMITH

KINGFISHER PRESS LLC

Danu Valley by Douglas P. Smith

The third book in the Fisher of Time series, after *River Forged* and *Shifting Ground*

Published by Kingfisher Press LLC

Fairview, North Carolina, United States of America

Visit the author's website at www.douglaspaulsmith.com

Cover by MiblArt

Print ISBN: 978-1-17373680-6-9

Dedicated to those who die, yet live again

CHAPTER ONE

The four warriors, carrying a hodgepodge of lethal weapons and proficient with them all, circled me and moved in for the kill. Unlike television battles, they all moved in at once, rendering a solid defense impossible. I could not dodge everything as they cut and gouged chunks from me. Lucky for me, their guns had already run out of ammunition. I needed to go on offense, but these guys had been practicing this for a thousand years. I was down a few pounds of meat and a quart of blood when Jen saved me by shooting two of them in the back with her last bullets. The third moved from me to deal with her, leaving me just one to tangle with. I roused myself and broke both of his collarbones, popped his knee backwards, and swept the legs. He grunted hard, but at least he stayed down. I watched Jen work on the last one. But he dealt her a killing blow just before I got there to assist.

The knife he had thrust at her was touching her neck when he froze it there. Her eyes got big as she knew she had just died. I hobbled back over and pulled my last opponent up from the floor. He was already healing and clapped me on the back, yelling something vaguely Scandinavian. Not clear if it was a taunt or a compliment, but he was kind of smiling. He and the guy that tapped Jen said something to her as well. The two on the floor Jen had shoot began moving, so the two talking to Jen went over and helped them up.

I was rethinking my strategy of asking these guys to attack us every day. I was glad we were all wearing the rune amulets that protected us from lethal blows during these "games" with Odin's einherjar. We needed the practice and improved weekly, but the barn and side building we had set up for the training attacks would not last much longer. I congratulated Jen on saving my ass, then we walked outside.

The two dozen attackers gathered together outside with what sounded like loud taunting and kidding among themselves. As the Farm people filtered out, most looking somewhat battered, they joined the attack group and grasped forearms, while a few traded high-fives. It was strange watching a hulking warrior killed two thousand years ago high-fiving a petite shapeshifting woman. A moment later, the good-natured attackers ambled off to their portal. I realized they were heading back to Valhalla to drink and carouse, and probably fight some more. I was proud that my far down-the-line descendants, most of them shapeshifters or friends, were adapting so well to the training sessions we had here at the "Farm," preparing for worse days ahead.

This craziness had started right after the New Year, after I had talked to both Michael and Henry about all the new threats we could be facing. Michael was my friend, sometimes mentor and employer, and one of the highest placed members of the Church no one had heard of, since he was the chief assassin and head of security. Henry was on old acquaintance and shapeshifter. Emphasis on the old as he was the oldest being I had met yet at somewhere around twenty-thousand years.

Henry and I had started sessions with the other Farm adults on the best way to improve defenses. I knew there were two people I needed to contact to up our security, although neither was exactly human. I made a "call" to Kal, my mentor and West Coast Bigfoot, and when he arrived, I gave him the thoughts and plans the group had come up with. He understood my ask and had some of his local "security representatives" join us the following day. It was like having the strangest board meeting ever, me and my people with six Bigfoots standing in the mountain woods in North Carolina. Or was that Bigfeet? I did not ask. They dwarfed me and the Farm adults, but we had a good meeting.

Since their telepathic communication was so fast, plus with their linkages to their network of their entire species, they came up with a defensive plan in a few minutes. They would have a few of their own on a nearby patrol to start, while setting up a network of organic sensors. I asked what those were but did not get a satisfactory answer. Apparently, they have some sort of passive communication with trees and large underground networks of fungi. The other part of the plan was a passive portal that they activated in our camp. The portal, once activated, would transport us to one of two safe spots elsewhere. I asked where, but only got "out west" for an explanation. After everyone else had left, Kal and I had some time together.

"I am a little unsure how this system works, specifically the sensors," I told him.

"The organic sensors are acutely attuned to their surroundings, and have been here, in or on the ground, for years or centuries. Your activity here is registering now to produce a baseline. Any future unusual vibration, pressure, metallic presence, or one of a few dozen other criteria will immediately alert my people. If there is a threat, it will notify you and yours in seconds. It will also activate the portal in case you need to escape. In case the worst happens, take everyone through, including the injured and dead."

"OK, that sounds reasonable. If something or someone odd shows up, we will know in less than ten seconds, right?"

"Yes. I suggest your people have drills to form defenses and lines of retreat. We can assist by timing false incursions most inconveniently, such as the middle of the night."

"We start that later today. What about the escape locations?"

"The first location will be somewhere near the Pacific coast. I cannot tell you where exactly, as the location changes. I tied it to one of my groups of people. As they move, the location moves. The idea is to get you to a group of my people to provide more extensive protection. Since the enemy cannot predict the location, it also helps prevent detection, unless one of their people gets through the portal.

"If that initial portal destination is compromised, once you arrive, my people will immediately teleport you away, or escort you to other portals. Any of those will take you to a sheltered valley under multiple layers of protection, including time barriers. I won't tell you where it is, as it is a closely guarded secret. If you don't know, you can't tell, regardless of the interrogation methods that the enemy might employ."

"I appreciate your thoroughness. I believe that should keep us safer by having both better defenses and escape routes."

"Yes, these measures should enhance your longevity. I trust you can also prepare your people to last long enough to repel the attackers or ensure enough time to escape."

"That is next on my list of calls. Thanks for your help, Kal."

Kal's people were absolute geniuses at setting up passive defenses. They were, however, completely non-aggressive, so the more I thought about our situation, the more I felt we needed more teeth in the system. I knew just the guy, or rather the god, to call and set that up both in place and in time, so he was my second "call." I just had to find Odin and figure out what he would want for payment, assuming I could persuade him to set up a system.

While I pondered how to contact Odin, I thought about the past few months, and how everyone at the Farm had progressed through the winter. Everything had gone better than I had imagined, which always worried me. The kids had progressed, and the adults were sharper than ever, while the borrowed Church operatives had also blended in seamlessly. Even a few romances were moving along without issue. In a few months we would have to recruit in new members, and even Michael had suggested bringing in a group from the Church to train with us. I stayed for as much of the training as possible, and since I wasn't in Europe, it was most of the time. Michael did not have any major projects for me but would occasionally ask about coming over for a visit, which I always declined.

I really did not need to since my house and apartment were being managed by a service. Thomas, my best friend in Amsterdam, also visited each place once a month to monitor them. He leaked that Anna may be pregnant, so I was waiting to hear confirmation, and I would plan to fly over after confirmation for a planned celebration. The one odd omission in my life was Jo. My mythology researcher, sort-of-wannabe girlfriend that could never be my girlfriend, colleague and commando that had recently saved my life after I saved hers. I knew our relationship was complicated, but she had gone quiet, and even when I asked Michael about her, he just said she was being kept very busy. I quit asking after it was apparent by her actions that she was not interested in keeping in contact with me.

I ended my procrastination and made plans to find Odin, first by putting together a list of places in the US that might offer the best chance of contacting him. I asked Kal one evening, but his suggestions were mostly those I had already considered. And those were not likely to work, as I didn't think that hanging out in Arlington National Cemetery at night to meet a god would go over well with the guards.

The next evening, I was at my desk working on supply lists, the budget, and searching for other locations of battlefield cemeteries with no guards. As Odin walked in, I looked up. I jumped up with a gun as I did not recognize him at first, since he was wearing a long cloak and hat, and carrying a large walking stick. I quickly remembered that was one of his "wandering" outfits.

"Hello Odin, and welcome. I'm surprised to see you here, but also glad since I have been working on a plan to contact you."

"Obviously you were, and that is why I'm here. That and to see what you have been up to since last we talked. I am always interested in new shapeshifters, especially since we have so few in Europe now."

"Would you like a tour while I prepare my ask?"

"I already know what you need, and I have made those preparations. My visit is to determine if there are any modifications needed."

"Thank you in advance, then. Will I be able to afford your offer?"

"The only payment I need is your assurance that you will keep these shapeshifters alive."

"That is my primary objective. Protecting them for now and preparing them for when they will need to wreak havoc. Ensuring that they and their families are safe afterwards; those are my objectives."

"And good ones at that, for those must be priorities when you lead a people. Now let us see what you have built here."

We walked out and went through the building and around the grounds. One group was in the classroom with Zena, the Church tactician and spook here on loan, learning something sneaky. Another group was in the field, training with Henry and Simon. Simon was also from the Church, a field operative and martial arts expert. Odin and I got a few odd looks, but nobody looked very impressed. We moved away from the buildings and toward the outside group. Odin stopped and stood still for a moment with his eyes closed.

"I sense the one you call Kal has begun the passive defenses."

"Yes, just as you came in, I got a flash that I had a visitor."

"Impressive. I have detected nothing until now. That will tie in nicely with my system. However, I believe there is a weakness if something arrives by air. I will have a flock of crows patrol to observe by day. I suggest you talk to Kal about having night coverage, probably by owls."

"Good idea, and I'll talk to him about the owls." I called out for Henry and Simon to come over, since they knew more than me about any other blind spots.

Simon and Henry jogged over, but when Henry got ten steps away, he stopped and stared at Odin, who reciprocated the stare. They both became still. Simon picked up on the atmosphere and I noticed the almost imperceptible change in his stance as he loosened his muscles to ready for battle. I wasn't sure what was going on, but it just got tense and dangerous.

"Henry and Simon, this is our guest, Odin, who is going to help us with Farm defenses." I slightly emphasized "guest" in that sentence. Henry picked that up and immediately relaxed, and Simon did a second later.

"Odin," Henry said, as he gave a slight nod.

"Wol," Odin replied. I thought that was going to require an explanation later.

Simon and Odin also traded nods of acknowledgement.

"I would like us to take a quick walk around the perimeter, as we need to discuss what we can do to improve the security and readiness of our people," I said.

Everyone agreed and off we went. After a half hour, we were back at the buildings. Odin had said little, but I could tell he was highly alert and could sense Kal's "sensors". We went into the less-destroyed barn and opened up beer, cider, and mead. Odin then explained what he wanted to do for us.

"Once an alarm passes through Kal's passive network, the einherjar, soldiers that have fallen in battle and residing in Valhalla, will issue from different sites along the periphery of the property. Since they are already dead and have been training daily for hundreds or thousands of years, they will be hard to kill. Since they were all originally soldiers, they know what to do, and do it with extreme prejudice."

"That sounds like a great plan," Simon said. "But if we have a sizable battle, how will the einherjar know us from the attackers?" Simon asked.

"Excellent question. They will instinctively know the difference. However, they are so fierce, mistakes could happen. Since the battle-killed all come to Valhalla, they may not be as judicious in separating out the mortals from enemies. No harm, no foul, once they join battle. I will furnish you with runic medallions that I suggest your people, as well as my guests, wear and not remove. That will protect you from all einherjar, as they cannot attack anyone wearing the runes."

"What about the cost?" I asked.

"That will be determined at a later date, but it won't be anything that you cannot afford. Each time the einherjar are called into battle on your behalf, you will owe me a favor. I can't tell what it might be, as that time has not come to pass. But it will be something easily within your purview."

"How many will arrive?" Henry asked.

"A minimum of twenty-four. They fight in groups of four, so there will be six kill teams, even if there is only one trespasser. If more come for the attack, multiples of twenty-four of my soldiers will arrive every few seconds."

"That sounds impressive," Simon said.

"The plan is to swarm any intruders before they can cause harm. The Kal network will allow my men to issue from portals nearest the point of incursion. I believe the terms are 'interactive' and 'real-time' in your vernacular."

Henry and Simon had a brief side conversation about practice training.

"Can we schedule the einherjar to stage attacks against us so we can practice our defenses and train our people?" Simon asked.

Odin considered, then responded, "Yes, that will be acceptable. The soldiers will consider it light duty, but will give them a chance to learn about your people and the grounds. Some will be happy to be back on earth, just as a diversion. But your people must wear the medallions at all times."

"That seems like a great idea, and a small price to pay for making us better," I said.

Shortly afterward, Odin left. We met and decided to begin the einherjar program the following week. It would be an exciting few days or weeks, we thought. We didn't consider how it would feel to "die" every day, however. But our people improved immensely after just two weeks of constant assaults.

We had our usual fire the evening after Odin left. I steered Henry away from the others for a few minutes. "OK, Henry, today was a little weird. Seemed like you already knew Odin, and he seemed to know you, at least under a different name. Pretty unusual for a regular guy from Oklahoma. Care to elaborate?"

"We once had a dustup out on the Bering Plains. He was chasing something toward us I didn't want around. We agreed to disagree about that plan, but we then worked it out by agreeing to kill that third party. Since then, we normally keep to our respective continents."

"That is... interesting? Possibly disturbing? But anyway, I don't think there is any place called the Bering Plains."

"Not anymore. The closest thing to it now is the Bering Strait."

"Damn Henry, that just opens up all kinds of questions."

"Yeah, but we can go over all that once you get back from Europe."

"I'm not going to Europe, at least not soon."

"Yeah, you are. We will talk then."

"A year ago, I was the oldest and most interesting person I knew. Now I'm surrounded by people, all of whom are older and more interesting than me."

"Yeah, well, hate to bust that bubble again, but you finally got something right."

"Ass."

CHAPTER TWO

All the Farm sessions continued going well, and some days we almost beat the einherjar. The students were still interested and improving in the classes and were learning to fight together in small groups, improving with each assault. Meanwhile, I continued having discussions with the adults about improvements we needed to make and recruiting the next crop of students. I wanted to have a good overlap between the current students with the new students. I didn't realize what a relief it was to have our security measures put up to repel or deal with most incursions. Late one night, it popped into my head That had left a huge loophole in the training. The next morning at breakfast, I tracked Henry down before he took a class out.

"Hey Henry, I just thought of something."

"OK, let me get a video going. Maybe call a caterer for a party. Although perhaps that should wait til I find out if it's a good idea."

"Smartass. I had a good idea, once. Although I'm rethinking the one about having an Ice Age Native American hanging around."

"I ain't."

"You ain't what?"

"Native American, technically. I predate all that geographical nonsense. I'm more Native Siberian, or Bering Plainsman."

"I don't even know how to respond to that. And since I have not gone to Europe yet, I guess you still won't tell me everything? Anyhow, my ancient Russian genius, we need to expand our training program to cover a new environment. We need to add water training."

"Hmm, that old brain of yours might be right. Also, perfect time to go on spring break. You thinking beach? Oh, your Europe trip is coming up in a couple of weeks."

"Already got cabins on Cape Lookout. Beach on one side, bay on the other. And I'm not going to Europe."

"I'm impressed. When do we leave? Better be within two weeks, since that won't interfere with your other trip."

I gave up in exasperation on denying the Europe trip. "Week after next. We need to do a lot of water exercises, but I think the kids will appreciate the beach time."

"That, plus all the amusement parks and shops."

I just smiled. "This island has nothing on it but the cabins. Not even electricity."

"They are going to hate you. I like it."

"Yeah."

A week later, I found myself immersed up to my neck in the bay, and the fish were schooling around me in a damned annoying way. It was to the point that was considering dropping a couple of quarter-sticks of dynamite in the water to drive them off. We were at Cape Lookout Island off the coast of North Carolina, south of the Outer Banks proper. The bay between the island and mainland was Core Sound. Mostly flat, shallow, and very clear. Very unlike the wild Atlantic Ocean, a few hundred feet on the other side of the island. Rough water, unpredictable currents, and marine life that reminded you that humans were not the top of the food chain in that environment. The bay was much tamer unless the wind picked up. The water was shallow enough that even a stiff breeze could generate waves of three feet in a few minutes.

I was here with all the people from the Farm, since I had come up with the idea of water training. None of the kids, and almost none of the adults, had spent much time on the water, so it made sense to get them used to it. Pools and lakes were not suited to do what we wanted. To provide that context, I rented the twenty cabins that were the only residences on the coastal island. We now had nearly ten miles of a scrap of land to ourselves, barely a hundred yards wide, between the ocean beach and the bay. The water was warm enough in the bay to use for extended swimming and water training exercises. We also rented a motorboat, a dinghy with an outboard motor, and several kayaks. All part of training for kids that had little to no exposure to big water or boat operation. Since big water was three-fourths of the planet, it made sense to train them here.

The bay was shallow and filled with clear water. There were patches of sand interspersed among the greenery of seagrass meadows, mostly eelgrass or shoal grass, that grew on the bottom. Although there were a few deep places, much of the bay was only four to six feet deep, perfect conditions for the vegetation.

It was easier to teach long distance swimming and water treading to the kids when they were not so worried about drowning or rapid hypothermia. Most could drop their feet and use their toes to keep their heads above water, and lightweight wetsuits provided enough warmth for two-hour sessions. Most surprising to me was how Emeline and Elendor, now called Em and El, took to water like they were born in a lake. But as mountain girls, this week was the first time they had ever been swimming outside of a pool. It should not have surprised me, as all the shapeshifters showed signs of being outstanding athletes.

What I also hadn't realized was that the entire group, from the teenagers to old Henry, all could have been world-class athletes that modeled part time. I was immune to all the bikini flesh, but I had conversations with Nan the first day about regulating, but not quashing, what I thought was about to happen. She reassured me that nothing would happen that had not already, and there would be no teenage calamities or fights.

"Stacey and Melissa are well past that phase. Em and El might be an issue with Ned and Jimmy, but like I said, nothing will happen here that hasn't already. And John Henry is too nice to get involved with any foolishness. He can't figure out whether to court Stacey or Melissa, or just concentrate on his studies. So quit worrying about that and enjoy your days as a fish attractor. And Simon and Jen are just fine, not that you care."

"OK, Nan, thanks for that. And the only reason the fish like me is cause I'm so perfect."

"No, that's not it. Aren't fish attracted to fermented products, like old chicken livers left in the sun?"

"Thanks again, Nan. Now take that perfect bikini body away from me far enough that I can't hear you anymore."

"It's so sweet you noticed my perfect body. You must be thinking about Jo right about now."

"Oh god, Nan, just please, go far, far away."

She laughed as she ran off to catch up with Henry and the guys to start the next drill.

Something else I didn't consider, because it never occurred to me, was how bothersome the damn fish would be. They didn't bother the others when they were in the water. But after I jumped in and swam for a while, they came in a schooled around me in rounded masses of fish bodies. It was so bad that I had picked up the nickname "chum" which Henry thought was a damn hoot.

After three days of being the star fish attractor, Henry asked me about it. "Either you ain't telling me everything, or possibly you don't know everything. But it gets damn weird every time we get around water, and this is half past strange."

"I don't know, Henry. I know there have been some odd things happening over the years when I'm around rivers, but I don't have a good explanation. Do you have any ideas?"

"Not really. Something about you seems to draw water creatures. I've heard tell of some things that can do it, but you ain't one of them. But might be best to take you fishing next time the guys go. You can splash around the boat while we just toss cast nets. Best you do not spend much time in the deep ocean, though."

"Yeah, a pod of killer whales might mistake me for fast food after they smelled me. Piranhas could get ticklish, too, down south."

We finished six days of water and boat drills, then lazed about on the seventh. That might have been a precedent somewhere. We had talked about having another einherjar sneak attack on the island, but ultimately decided against it. I sat on the beach in a corgi chair and watched the kids do all kinds of athletic things on the beach and in the water. I just had no interest in joining them, but they had issued a challenge to us old farts for a beach football match later. The chair was physically restraining me from getting up, however.

Michael called, as I was still basking in the sun on the beach. Since it was our last day, I considered not answering, but he normally did not call unless it was important.

"Hi Michael."

"Hello Senecus."

"I am lying on a sunny beach at the moment. How is the weather there?"

"Still rainy, foggy, with occasional sleet. You know, the typical weather here in The Netherlands. I'm at the Cottage instead of the Center this week."

"Sorry about that. What can I do for you?"

"Ah, straight to business. I assume you want to get back to your physically demanding beach lie-about. We have had a serious problem in Bangkok. We need someone familiar with supernatural events to investigate. This will not be an apprehension, but an investigation by a non-biased party. Any interest?"

"I could probably do that. I've been to Bangkok and Thailand a few times. What is the time frame?"

"Within a week would be good. The crime scene will keep, and they stored the bodies in the morgue until you get there."

"Wow, that just sealed the deal. Morgue bodies awaiting in steamy Bangkok sounds grand."

"Oh, since you have to travel halfway around the world regardless of which direction you fly, I'd consider it a favor if you could stop here for a day on the way."

"Damn him."

"Excuse me?"

"Sorry. Just thinking about Henry, he has been dogging me all month that I was going to Europe next week. Have you two been in contact?"

"Not at all. Perhaps he is prescient?"

"I would doubt nothing at this point. Anyway, sure, I will fly to Schipol, then hop over to Bangkok."

"Thanks. I'll arrange the flights. Enjoy your sand."

"See you in a few days."

That was strange, as were most events these days. I should have asked about Jo, but it didn't seem right to do so yet. I put it out of my mind and made my greatest decision of the day. Us old farts would take on the kids in a volleyball game rather than football.

We loaded up the gang, took the ferry over to the mainland, and began the long drive back. Everyone was tired but seemed happy. Something had been working around in the back of my brain for a few weeks. I volunteered to drive one of the vans first, and I got Henry to ride shotgun so we could talk.

"Henry, I have been thinking about something for a while, which could be important. But I want your perspective before I dig into this."

"Well, Chum, this should be good, since you've had a week of lying around thinking."

"Ha ha. But seriously, what is your take on what seems to be a real problem with Native American girls going missing?"

Henry was quiet for a minute and looked very serious. "It has not been as big a problem for us as it has been for others. But I think it is a genuine issue. When I put my predator hat on, it seems to me there are enough disappearances and patterns that make it non-random."

"I have been thinking the same thing. In fact, my initial premise is that a master vampire, possibly several, might be responsible, at least for some portion of the disappearances. I also won't rule out other monsters, most of which I probably don't even know about. But I thought you might shed some light on other potential perpetrators."

"I need to think a bit. Winnow out the likely suspects and how, or if, they are still operating. Most are gone now, but there are always some around. Like that pod of Uya that we took down in Arizona. But master vampires could fit that bill, too. I'll have something by the time you get back."

"Thanks for listening and thinking about it. I'm also going to give this project to Monk. If anyone can put that data together and come up with patterns, he could."

"That sounds like an excellent plan. He can run the statistical algorithms while we ground truth the output."

"Damn Henry, there you go again. From mammoth hunter to IT expert, complete with jargon."

"Can't help it if I'm special."

"Yeah, well, just glad you are on my side."

After we arrived at the Farm and unloaded everything and everyone, I drove to my Asheville house. I needed to talk to Monk and start getting clothes together for the Amsterdam-Bangkok trip.

"Hi Monk."

"Hello Senecus. How are you doing and where are you doing it?"

"Still in America, and I'm fine. I have a new project that I trust you can help with."

"Certainly. What do you have?"

"I need a search algorithm to check for patterns of missing people. Starting with Native American women, specifically in America and the Canadian border. The patterns I'm specifically interested in are disappearances, murders, and discovered bodies."

"That is a vast project. What are your specific parameters, or do you allow me to establish them based on the data I locate?"

"General parameters based on what I just mentioned, more specific ones should probably come from the databases, although I don't know how good they are. Pull any database you need, including all the law enforcement centers, despite the illegality. If that causes any problems, I'll get the Church to cover any problems afterward. This will be a scorched earth project, so take anything you need.

"Let me think, I believe it should model all missing Native American females over the past twenty years. Depending on the results, you might need to go back and add males, and expand to fifty years. If you can pull in any cases where arrests were made in similar mass disappearance or murder cases, it could add to the veracity of the model.

"I can forward several studies to you, or you can pull up your own that have the mathematics and simple algorithms for predation. Killer whales, wolf packs, solitary tigers, you get the picture. The hypothesis is that some percentage of the disappearances are attributable to one or more entities. If so, I plan to discover that perpetrator and end the cycle. How does that sound?"

"It sounds expensive, almost impossible, but then you came to the one that can solve impossibilities."

"That, plus you are also the humblest IT guy I know."

"Yes, I agree. I am the total package. But you failed to mention my good looks."

"It was implied. How long do you think it will take to put that together?"

"I should have it running in two weeks. Is that sufficient? I assure you that no one else could do it faster."

"That's just fine, Monk. You know where to send the bill."

"Of course. I look forward to bathing in bullion after this project."

"Yeah, now I have a disturbing visual in my frontal cortex. Thanks Monk."

"Goodbye Sen."

We hung up as I thought that if he told me two weeks, he'd have it done in five days.

I felt like getting some air and drove down to Asheville to walk around. As the sun had set, the crowds would be gone from the River District, so I should have the walk to myself.

CHAPTER THREE

Jo

The notice came in, and I quickly changed into ballistic armor and battle gear. I jogged down to the armory to pick up my auto rifle and pistol, and four magazines for each. Other members of the team began showing up to gather their gear. Various sniper rifles, short rifles, pistols, an RPG, and a crossbow. We formed up, jumped into the carrier, and drove to the local airfield. As strike team leader, I picked up a case-hardened computer and a special radio. As I trotted off, I heard the armorer yelling.

"Hey Jo! Don't forget this new helmet with the VR chip."

I ran back and grabbed it, thanked him, and caught up with my team. Intelligence and briefings started coming in through the radio. I understood the overall status of the mission, while the detailed information and maps we needed would be available for review on the flight.

Bandits on the Belarus border had kidnapped a small group of kids and their chaperones. The kidnapped were from a parish in Poland and had picked the wrong time and place to go hiking. Twelve hours after their abduction, and an hour after the first ransom demand, Michael had dispatched my team. We boarded a small Church jet, took off and arrived at a rural airfield within two hours, then we transferred to a fast cargo helicopter. A half hour later, it dropped us off five miles from the target zone, where we transferred to a car and three trucks.

My newest team had only trained together for a few weeks, but since everyone was a seasoned veteran, we meshed well. I had the least experience but made up for it with other skills. Sometimes I was the genius, sometimes I was the goon.

On the ride over, we tested the radio system and discussed the plans again for the fourth time. I sent them the latest satellite images, showing an older house, with a few small outbuildings, behind a fence. It was some distance north of Brest in rolling farmland. A forest was behind the house and a hill was across the road, with trees on the crest. Perfect conditions to place snipers both in front of and behind the house.

The bandits were a local rogue motorcycle gang that had gotten more ambitious since the Russians were playing more in Belarus. They were ever more brazen in their attacks and robberies in Poland. That was about to end. Because they primarily used motorcycles, we prepared for those in case they ran once the strike team engaged. There was also the van unaccounted for from the Polish group. I factored that in, and I set the plans.

We closed and barricaded the road to either side of the house with fake construction signs and strung ropes across the road at about neck height for a motorcycle rider. Beyond the ropes, caltrops filled the road in case anyone was smart enough to duck, or if they were using the van for a getaway. I don't know which would be worse: getting clotheslined off a motorcycle by the rope or going down on the asphalt after the tire exploded, skidding across the surface of the road and getting pin-cushioned by all the caltrops along the way. Either way would be a fitting end to this scum. If they used the van or another car instead, a sniper would administer a headshot before they left the property. We did not expect prisoners from this action.

When everything was set, a burly team member named Wenz changed into a utility uniform, then drove to the front of the house and got out with his clipboard. He knocked on the gate and called out. He stood there politely, waiting to see if anyone in the house would respond. Meanwhile, two teams of three each came in from both sides of the house, staying in cover. I had moved through the ditch along the road, and now was behind the car that Wenz had parked. A markedly undernourished-looking fellow wearing leather and flashing rotten teeth opened the front door, walked halfway across the yard and started yelling at Wenz. The tone suggested he was telling Wenz to leave, but Wenz yelled back about a utility bill. I believed everyone in the house was probably engaged in watching the argument.

The teams on the side of the house went in through the windows after I sent out the signal. I popped up and shot the skinny guy in the front yard, then as Wenz and I sprinted for the front door, I handed him his machine rifle. I got there first, went to the side, then Wenz, never slowing down, barreled through the front door as I immediately followed behind him. Four leather-clad men were down with various injuries from the side strike teams, mostly shots to the head. No triple taps for these guys, both because my team was that good, and since they might have been wearing kevlar pads under the leather. A lot of the gangs were wearing those inserts now, and we could not afford a bad guy surviving and shooting a machine pistol in that small house.

Another of mine kicked in a door to a back room and it was full of scared adults and children. They broke down in relief once we identified ourselves. The smell of blood and gunpowder, along with the gore, was sickening to me. But the looks on the faces of the hostages were worth what we had done to the gang members.

We heard engines starting up from the direction of an old garage off to the side of the house. Three motorcycles blasted forth and shot to the road. Two went one direction, the third went the opposite way. We had the passive anti-motorcycle system set up, so I had already radioed the team to not fire. No reason for excess bullets flying around.

The rest of the team, two each in a truck where the road-closed signs were set, later showed us the video of the attempted escapes. One solo rider hit the rope as planned. The ambulance that responded had to search for his head to put in the body bag. The other duo fared little better, as the first hit the rope, while the second guy, riding behind, ducked. Then his front tire hit the caltrops; he went down and rolled and skidded through the rest. He was not wearing a helmet. The ambulance that picked him up had to crowbar the metal spikes out of his skull before they put him in the body bag. The operation was brutal, violent, and entirely successful, as the gang had no chance to harm the hostages, and they were forever out of action.

Two vans pulled up after we cleaned up on our end. We had rented them to take the former hostages to the local police station, then home. We left our local contact to deal with the police and the report, then the rest of us got in the vehicles and started the journey home across the multiple carriers. On the jet, we had a mild celebration and took off the hot armor and vests down to our T-shirts. I noticed Frederick looking at me. Not suggestively, more like a questioning look. My sweaty clothes were clinging too tightly to my body. But I was glad that he said nothing. He was the only married one of the bunch and had three kids. Dammit, he knew, or certainly suspected.

After the long day, I was back at the base, and had eaten and showered. I spent an extra minute in front of the mirror. I used to do that as I was getting used to my new body; now I did it hoping to not see the newest iteration of my body. The body, or rather what was in it, that kept me constantly worried and awake at night.

How the hell could this happen? How? More importantly, what the hell was I going to do about this? Not that there was much anything to do. Regardless, this will still be the biggest thing I've ever done. I just never wanted it to be like this. I circled back around to the how of everything.

Michael had been understanding. He had even noticed before anyone else. And I was so lucky that he had, since I was about to get an exam and DNA test. But Michael talked me out of having a regular exam, and instead had the DNA sample sent to our lab anonymously, just in case. It was like he was expecting something. But neither he nor I expected those results when they came back. Nobody in the world could have expected those results. How could this happen? It was the repetitive theme in my brain now, echoing every five minutes. All my synapses were on endless repeat.

I need to calm down again, at least until the cycle started again. A nice cuppa and a long walk. No, a run, because walking will just let my mind relax enough to restart the questions again.

I went down the hall to change for a run. I checked my phone again to see if Sen called. That is the second most repetitive thing I do now. Even if he called, what would I say? I'm pregnant? I need you to be the father? Or, as Michael said, more of an uncle? How could I even explain all this on a phone? No, I can't tell him when I don't even know how I feel about him, or even guess about how he would feel about this baby. My baby. I never thought I would utter those words. How could this hap-. Stop. This question roundabout has to stop.

I felt the phone vibrate. It was Michael, checking in. At least he's trying to keep me sane, as he's the only person to know my secret. Not about being pregnant. That would soon not be a secret, anyway. You can only keep the bump hidden for so long, especially when training. Now it was past the hiding stage, and at least one person on the team was noticing. No, the real secret would have me revered as a goddess or killed as a demon. Maybe both. Thank God for Michael's quick thinking and intervention on the DNA test submission.

I answered finally. "Hi Michael."

"Hello Jo. From all reports and video, your operation was successful. Excellent job."

"Yes, it was, at least for us and the kidnapped group. Not so much for the gang responsible."

"They got what karma, or fate, had readied for them. I regret the extreme nature of the rescue, but it got the hostages released unharmed."

"I fully understand. Sometimes I wish it could be less violent. I doubt, however, that the gang took that into account before they pulled their stupid crime."

"I agree. Now, how are doing since yesterday?"

"Still on this endless bloody loop. 'How did this happen' plays out every five minutes. I know I need to get past that and now get to considering how to do this."

"Understandable. I confirmed with our lab that all test results went unrecorded or missing. It is still only you and I that know. Now that it is time for ultrasounds and other tests, there is no further reason for anonymity. Because of that, I recommend telling Sen when you next see or speak to him. Obviously in person is best, and soon."

"Of course, but it's not likely to be soon. Can't you just get him over here for a job?"

"Not that simple right now. His stubbornness about coming back to the continent, and also his schedule, are both contributing to complications. How are you doing physically?"

"Still the same. Eating everything in the pantry, twice over. I should have gained two stone by now, but still not an ounce added onto my fighting weight. I have odd dreams, but nothing too bothersome. All those weird symptoms, including passing nausea, that I thought were part of my transformation, have eased off. Now I guess I really am transforming. Just not into what I was expecting, pun intended."

"Let me know if those dreams change. We are in completely uncharted waters. I'm not worried about your weight, since with your physiology, you may not gain any other than the child's weight itself. You knew it was a girl before the test. Any reason for you to think that?"

"The dreams. Since that first night I dreamed I was pregnant, the dreams always showed me a little girl. When I look inward when I'm awake, I also see her."

"Interesting, and we need to know if those dreams change or worsen."

"I shall let you know. I need to go get a run in. Talk tomorrow?"

"Yes, usual time, and I dare say, usual topic. Oh, can you get over to the Cottage tomorrow? I have a feeling you might need to be here for a few days."

"OK, I can do that. Do I need to bring anything special?"

"No, just yourself."

We hung up, and I changed clothes. I looked in the mirror, which I now did multiple times a day. Maybe there was a bump showing? Yes, there was. I was not normally so body conscious, but I had just gotten used to having an athletic model's body that seemed to be the envy of everyone I worked with. And now I was having a bump right in the middle of it all. A bump that would turn huge and keep me in everyone's sights. Damn Senecus. I couldn't decide whether to love him or kill him.

I thought back to our time in Finland. I'd never let go like that before, never even imagined it. And no shame or guilt, either. That was a first, but before I could even enjoy that, the nausea and revulsion set in. His actions gave me the most wonderful experience I had ever had, then the worst. Damn Senecus. I thought about how to tell him. Michael and I had gone over several scenarios and role-playing exercises. No matter what, it was going to be difficult.

How could I tell him I was carrying a baby, that was sort of his? And that no one could ever know the real secret. And that he would have to play along at being a dad to keep us all safe. It just wasn't a conversation I felt I could ever have. But I absolutely had to. I was supposed to go with Michael at Christmas to tell him. But I turned tail and ran instead, as I could not imagine or foresee a successful conversation. I had let Michael go alone. I secretly longed for Michael to have told him, but he had too much integrity. Now I would have to find my own way to do it. Damn Senecus.

So now I was pregnant and about to be exposed to the world. Michael would leak that Senecus was the father, but we'd had a falling out, and he was staying in America. I needed to tell Senecus before all that happened. And then tell him his damned DNA, which he'd given me to save my life, was so full of weird fish and amphibian junk, that I'd become pregnant by parthenogenesis.

It was such a strange word that I vaguely knew from science classes. Self-fertilization of an egg by the mother's own DNA. Humans could not do this, and no known mammals could either. Other creatures, like fish and birds and amphibians, could do it. Perhaps I was no longer exactly human, and that also made me worry about my baby. But worst of all was that I now was the new Mother Mary, birthing a child without a father. Which made me a new saint and my child a new messiah, or made me the mother of the antichrist, depending on which faction of the church interpreted the event. Either way, my life, and my daughter's life, would be over, whether they killed us or worshipped us - which would be a kind of imprisonment - by the Church's doctrines and bureaucracy. Which is why no one could know, and Senecus had to be the father. Nothing else made sense.

He kind of was the father. I thought at first, he was, when I first felt something was off and the test came back positive. But the timing was too far off. Therefore, in the traditional sense, the child was not fully his, but she would share much of his DNA that he had passed to me. I needed him regardless, as he had to help me protect this child. I was having premonitions that our secret would get out, and it would take both of us to keep her safe.

Enemies inside the Church, and outside, would need to kill her and me. Although the reasons for the two different factions wanting us dead were very different, we would still be dead.

Damn Senecus. I could not do this anymore, so I picked up my phone and texted Michael to get me to America on the next available flight to Asheville. I had to go, and if I didn't do it now, I never would. Time to rip off the scab and staunch the bleeding. Was I the scab, or was it Sen? Hell, I didn't know anymore.

Michael immediately called me. "That was fast. You must have had a plane on standby," I said as I answered the phone.

"I think I have some good news on that front as I just got off the phone with Sen. He is on his way to Ireland to hunt down some rumors of his origin. I believe you should meet him there instead of flying to America, worrying all the way. From the Cottage, you can get to our plane and be in Cork in an hour. Much easier than the intercontinental flight."

"That is good news." While I said that, I was also cursing under my breath. Both because it was going to happen, and because it was even sooner than I expected.

"Should I let him know you will meet him there?" Michael had obviously picked up on my hesitancy.

"Yes, please let him know I'll be coming, and ask where to meet. At least I won't have to pack too many jars of olives and Greek yogurt, then spend time in the lavatory tossing most of it back up on that short of a flight."

"Interesting. Olive and yogurt cravings and morning sickness. My wife went on an odd fad, but for her it was figs and anchovies. Together. Thankfully, that did not last long. I'll text you the time and location for Sen. He said he would be free later tomorrow, so we will send you on our plane to make the trip easier."

"Thanks Michael. Any last words of wisdom?"

"Just be yourself. He loves you, and that will continue, despite the surprise you are about to unload on him. He has been alive long enough to absorb this in stride."

"Thanks, I'll talk to you later." I did not feel nearly as confident as Michael that Sen would be amenable to being an instant dad. Or worse, what if he wanted the whole family thing, a wife and a child? I just could not handle that right now, either. Damn Senecus.

I arrived at the Cottage but had nothing to do there. It was driving me crazy, so I drove down to Woerden just to walk around the cute little town. It had nothing to do with being Sen's "hometown" either. As I walked through the cobblestoned lane in the shopping area, I noticed a storefront. The decorations included some colorful onesies in newborn to six-month-old sizes for babies. There was also a baby carriage full of stuffed animals. I broke down crying right there in the street. I had not cried like that in years, and never in public. Yet here I was, the epitome of the weepy preggo mom-to-be. Humiliating. When I regained my composure, I kept walking, and somehow felt much better. These hormone shifts were going to be the death of me. Damn Senecus.

I made it to Cork the next day without incident. I went early in case I needed to spend time in the pub loo to throw up, before meeting Sen. Although my morning sickness was declining, my nerves stirred my insides. It was a beautiful day, unusually nice this time of year, so I sat upstairs by the one of the two windows to enjoy the breeze and watch for Sen. I caught a glimpse of him coming down the sidewalk. Just before he got to the door, some beautiful woman kicked him, and they both vanished into some kind of conjured door. That bitch. She just walks up and ruins everything when I came all the way to unload my secrets. I ran downstairs and outside, but there was nothing to see. I called Michael to tell him the news.

His response to my story was most unusual. "Jo, I know this looks bad, but you should wait there for an hour. I suspect that he will be back, and mostly unharmed, quite soon."

"How can you say that? You don't know who that was, or what she or they will do to him? He could be dead soon."

"I doubt that. I just came into some information that, based on the location and the timing, applies to this situation, and I believe he will be fine. Just as you have your secrets to reveal, he also has one to tell you. I think that secret will help explain this situation. Just be patient a little longer. If he is not back in an hour, I will have a strike team meet you there in ninety minutes."

"OK Michael, I'll trust you and stay here."

"Good, I'll talk to you soon."

Well, that was damned odd. Sen just got abducted by a sorceress or witch or whatever, and Michael was not bothered. Secrets and weirdness were everywhere. The thing that she did out there put her on a short list of beings I knew about, and none of them were good. Now she had taken him, just when I needed him. Damn Senecus. Damn her too.

I waited, worried, fidgeted, checked my phone a dozen times. I just wanted this over. Finally, I was feeling comfortable in my new body, and after all the training, I was now the baddest bitch on the block. Except, maybe, for that one that just took Senecus. But that must have been some sort of magic. I didn't much believe in it, but after all the myths I had studied, I knew there was the possibility of strange events, like I had just witnessed. The woman that had taken him was also gorgeous, not that I much noticed. I swear I saw her glance up for a split second with an evil grin. If she wanted to mess with me, she'd need all the magic she could get before I ripped her face off.

These thoughts and feelings were also new. More aggressiveness, thoughts of kicking ass, slugging through problems, and rolling over opponents. Something because of my transformation, or hormones from the pregnancy?

Perhaps both, and having missed breakfast? That reminded me, my lunch was now late. Sen better have a good explanation for this, and better take me somewhere good for lunch. This pub didn't even serve food. I rummaged in my bag to see if I had any snacks. Nothing really, not even biscuits, so I would have to starve. He now owed me a very large and very good lunch. Now what was I thinking before the hunger pangs? Oh right, kicking the evil witch's arse all over Cork.

Then there was movement below, and Sen reappeared on the sidewalk, alone. I looked down at him, furious for no real reason. Damn him. But I was also thrilled to see him. Not for the first time, I wondered how it was possible to feel such disparate feelings for the same person.

Now I just had to persuade him to be a father to a child. A child that was not his, not exactly. Unfortunately, I had to do it on an empty stomach. Maybe I could get through this and get him to be a dad before I had lunch and then killed him.

CHAPTER FOUR

I was standing on another bridge, staring down at another river. It was a familiar site since I had been here a few times before. Looking at the water, feeling the breeze, breathing that river essence, I began thinking about Jo. I should have known better than to let my concentration slip. Rivers had always been full of surprises for me and this one was about to prove it was not different, even if it was in America. But I never expected to meet a fairy harbinger on a cool night on the French Broad River as it flowed past Asheville.

I was by myself on that bridge until I wasn't. He was standing too close for comfort. Not a big guy, but that didn't make him any less dangerous. My extra radar wavelength was not giving me any threat notice, but he was also constantly changing aura colors like a disco ball. Mostly nonhuman and decidedly squirrelly. I readied myself for attack just in case he was camouflaging his intentions. Something clicked in my brain, and I realized I had seen him before. A while back on a bridge in Inverness, looking over the River Ness, I had briefly seen this same strange guy. I turned to face him and was ready for action, since it was obvious he had been tracking me.

"Now love, no need that," he said. "No killing the messengers."

"What?"

"Not here for fighting. Just talking."

"So, talk. Otherwise, you are going swimming when I kick you through the railing."

"Been looking for you a bit. Right long bit, all over places old and new. You even blinked out a long time, nobody ever did that."

"Yeah, I remember you from Inverness. What the hell do you want?"

"That wasn't a fish you killed. No fish. The night you went into the river as a soldier. That wasn't a fish. You thought it was. You spent all that time at them uni's, running tests, learning about nothing. A smart guy. But dumb. Good ideas, but so dumb."

"What the hell are you even talking about?"

"That was no fish. I been tracking you since you come to light. Went back through your past. Everybody been hearing about you. But the fish story got some attention. Real interesting. About the time you show up way back then, we lost something. Real valuable. That was no fish."

"I'll ask you again before I choke you to death. What the hell are you talking about?"

"No fish. You killed Danu. You killed her, drank her blood."

"Uh, what?"

"Danu, goddess of the river. Mother of our people. You killed her, drank her. Now, some of you is her. I found you. Kind of found her. My people be happy, most of them."

I had nothing to say. Surprise? Disbelief? My brain was squirming with those emotions and a dozen more. Part of my brain was in defense mode, but the little guy was no threat. My silence goaded him to continue, as he felt my confusion.

"You not believe. You been on rivers, around water. Strange things happen? Lights in the water? When you in the water, you no drown, right? Water your friend. I not turning you in. But others will come, some good, some bad.

Beware Morrigan. No telling what she does, keeps her counsel underwater, never in the open."

"I'm not sure you have the right person."

"That river you fell in, when you killed her. Is still a river? Or dried up and gone?"

"It's mostly gone, more of a canal in most parts."

"No Danu to protect it, no river there now. Without her, it nothing but a bog ditch. But you be him. Slayer of Danu, at least the Danu in them parts. But you don't glow right. Should be white, but you be more silvery, maybe ocean-tinted. Be strange. But definitely Danu pouring from you."

"I still don't think I'm a Danu, or part Danu."

"Don't matter what you thinking. You Danu, sort of. I found you, now I'm gone to home. Give them the word."

"Wait, even if I'm part Danu, what does that mean?" As I asked that, I looked down at his strange shoes, a sort of old-style boot-sandal hybrid with open toes. Toes that were webbed. Hmm, that seemed familiar. Henry had found tracks like that on the Arkansas River after we fought off the Great Serpent, then we found similar prints after chasing something away from the Farm. I was about to ask the little guy about that when he winked and hopped over the rail. I glanced down at the water but didn't see him or hear a splash. Well hell, that put a twist on my evening, and most of my existence.

If this bugger's story was true, did that mean I'm also Irish? Or am I now somehow related to all the Tuatha? What exactly were the Tuatha, or the fae? I remember from both my and Jo's research that they were Irish and probably fairies, with all unique personalities and specialties. Are all my descendants now cousins of the Irish Tuatha? So now, am I Fish-Irish? Surrogate mother to the Irish fairies? The name Morrigan sounded familiar, but I couldn't remember why.

This was weird. The idea of moving to the American southwest with no rivers for hundreds of kilometers was becoming more appealing. How many times in your life does a strange man insist that you are the essence of a river goddess? I needed to think about it, however. Too many times in my life I had assumed something, sometimes for years, that was not true. And lately I had seen a lot of things that had been around thousands of years that I never even knew about.

I knew my previous research on fish proteins had provided a weak hypothesis that could explain some of my condition. To conclusively prove it, I needed to submit a blood and tissue sample to a well-equipped protein and DNA analysis laboratory. I still had great misgivings about doing that. Besides, was it more plausible my condition was due to some sort of magically acquired Danu essence, or fish proteins? A year ago, I would have bet on the proteins, but now I'd have to go with magic.

But how could I even research, much less prove, that I was part Danu? And who or what the hell was Danu? My only remembrance of that name was a reference to the Danube River and possibly a connection to Irish mythology. Finding out more would be my first task. I thought about calling Jo, but I hesitated. It wasn't like we were close anymore, or even in contact lately.

Then I thought of Erin and Davis, the selkies that I had worked with in Inverness. They might have some knowledge on my potential condition. But was it specie-ist to assume water creatures knew all other water creatures? Was specie-ist even a word, or even a category of prejudice? Was I going to continue asking myself stupid questions? The answer to that question was obvious. I was not sure whether selkies were also part of Danu's offspring groups, but I needed to start somewhere.

I remember them asking me about what the fish was that I tangled with and killed back in my past, when I became what I am. Perhaps they picked up something about me I was not aware of. Seemed important, but we got off topic with more important issues before finishing it.

After Inverness, I knew they were going to Ireland on the next assignment, and that was where Erin was from. I could ring either Michael or Simon to find the location. If they were not actively surveilling a target, then maybe I could travel over to visit with them. I was worried about the answer they would give. I was sure I had never considered a river goddess essence causing my condition. If it were true, what would that even mean? Back to the useless questions. Time to clear off the bridge and clear my mind. I walked around the dark town for a while and tried not to think about river goddesses. Or any goddesses, or near goddesses. Which, of course, led me right back to where I started, thought-wise, when I first walked onto the bridge tonight...

When I called Elias the next day, he told me that Erin and Davis were in Ireland. I asked about a visit, and after he checked with them, they gave the OK. I jumped the next flight I could get on to Dublin. I also called Michael and left a message to let him know I would be in his jurisdiction for a day or two. I assume Elias had informed him, but better to give him notice.

Ireland was always a pleasure to visit. Scenery was good, and some of the best people I had met in the world. Better yet, they knew how to cook. Breakfast was fabulous, if a little odd around the edges. Baked beans first thing in the morning? But the rest of the food and the tea made for a memorable meal.

I took the train to Cork and outside of town I found the place easily enough. A gorgeous small cottage, about as homey a place as I had ever seen, obviously cared for and loved by its owners. Placed on a small bay above the rocks, with a trail leading to the water behind the house. A wicker and driftwood fence surrounded a small vibrant garden full of plants and herbs. The house itself was a mix of stone and pale-yellow stucco, with sea green shutters. I could not decide whether to take a picture and make a poster, or just move in. Moving in without notice might be a little inconsiderate, however.

I had already texted them on the way, so they knew I was close. I knocked on the wooden door. It opened, and both Erin and Davis greeted me. I went in, accepted an offered cider, and we sat to catch up on events. They had been on a couple of jobs, the first of which was entrapping the wealthy men trafficking kids we had uncovered during the Inverness operation. Then on to another project to surveil a suspected master vampire, which turned out to be another false trail. Their latest effort had been fruitful, however, when they were assigned to another master vampire suspect. It turned out to be a real one, which Michael's teams had apprehended in Turkey. I had not heard about that one, so I guess Michael was keeping as many secrets as I was. Then it was my turn.

"You both remember back when we were in Inverness, and I mentioned my experience the night I became my current self. When I encountered a large fish or something in the river?"

They both nodded affirmatively.

"You seemed to think it was important what kind of fish it was that night. Lately, I have reason to suspect it is important, and wanted to get your perspectives on what that might mean."

"Fish and other water creatures play a big role in our lives, as you might imagine," Erin said. "Similarly, they also factor into our myths and religions as water dwellers. Your story of fighting something, then becoming immortal and physically enhanced, sparked a remembrance of an old rumor. One of our important deities, or at least one of her essences, went missing about the same time as your story, in the general area of northern Holland."

"I can cut right to my questions then. An odd fellow with webbed toes found me on a river recently. He told me I had killed Danu that night, and I now carried her essence. Is that feasible? If so, what does that mean?"

They both looked at each other, and not happily. They also were not saying anything. "Erin, you need to tell him," Davis said, finally. "There's no other explanation, and he needs to know in order to protect himself. If the Tuatha knows this already, they will come for him."

"Yes, I know. Senecus, I don't have all the facts, just pieces of a story. But I can give you some background that may help you understand."

"Sure, go ahead. Right now, I know little about any of this."

"Stories have mentioned Danu many times, but there really are not any complete descriptions or sagas of her. When the Christian priests and monks came to this land, many of the stories were lost or suppressed, since they were oral histories. The monks recorded a few stories, but they ignored many. Those that were written also suffered from mistranslations, or wholesale reinterpretation by the writers.

"One fragment of a story we know is that Danu grew weary, perhaps a result of her great age, and several millennia of conflict. She slowly transferred her essence to several water creatures and disseminated those in many locations to protect her old territories. But the effect of spreading herself too thin resulting in her primary sentience breaking up and no longer being a powerful goddess. But that may have been her intent. It was not physical suicide, but perhaps a slow version of mental suicide."

"The Danu creature I killed was one of many, not a whole goddess?"

"Yes, but regardless, she was a direct manifestation of Danu, so being exposed to the creature and its blood, tissue, and DNA would be just like being imbued by the whole of the goddess. Her essence has joined with you.

"Many have hunted for the versions of Danu, as tales were told that killing and eating her would imbue that person with great strength and longevity. But we do not know of any other instance besides yours where it may have actually happened. However, that myth lives on and could be part of the attraction for eating raw seafood and caviar."

"The little guy on the bridge gave a warning that his people may come after me and implied that could be good or bad. He also said that Morrigan may come for me."

"It is possible. There are many and various types of her people, especially here in Ireland. Some could be great friends, yet others are highly dangerous."

"What can I expect?"

"We don't know Morrigan very well, as she is a land dweller. She is also a direct descendant of Danu. Her reputation is that she is unpredictable. She may kill you and eat your spleen, capture you as a slave, marry you, or never bother you. Other beings in her realm run the gamut from harmless to problematic. But Morrigan is definitely dangerous."

"It seems Morrigan might be the primary threat. What form does she take?"

"Usually she is a beautiful, dark-haired woman with pale skin and blue eyes. But she can take any form. And she has many others working with her or for her, so you will probably not know who is after you. Also, the closer you are to Ireland, the stronger signals you put out, likely drawing them to you. I would suggest learning what you can about the Tuatha as I expect you will have interactions with them. They can be allies or enemies, and they are fractious enough that they can be both within the same day."

"Great. More family, and it sounds like they come built-in with problems."

"Just know that you are entering a different world, with many threats and just as many potential allies. Nothing is what it seems, and things are always shifting. Most of the stories about them are wrong, but some are factual. With all their issues, we choose to live on the fringe of our society and stay away from court politics."

"Well, this is a lovely spot and worth staying away from the crowd you just described."

"We feel strongly that this is the place for us. Will you stay for tea?"

"Thanks, but no, I need to leave soon. However, if you have a few minutes to show me around outside, I'm most interested in your garden and the waterfront."

"Sure, let's walk out."

I spent a few minutes touring the grounds with Erin, then Davis joined us to walk down to the water. Overall, it was one of the nicest places I've visited. But I had to get back to reality. I drove back to Cork, and realized I was once again driving on the wrong side of the road.

CHAPTER FIVE

M y phone rang as I walked around Cork, getting to know the city again. It was Michael, so I answered it, rather than my usual practice of ignoring calls on nice days.

"Hi there," he said. "Staying out of trouble?"

"So far. But plenty of time left for that to change. Say, I may need to go ahead with sending a sample to get a full workup of my DNA and protein profile in your lab."

There was a moment of silence. "Well, that is unexpected. I suppose you uncovered something unusual on your current trip?"

"Yes, my origin is getting more complicated than I originally thought."

"Possibly related to that odd chunk of fish or amphibian DNA you are carrying?"

I was too surprised to respond for a moment. "Did you sample my DNA when I was in the hospital?"

"Absolutely not. But you are not the only one carrying your DNA now, and not the only one with questions. And complications."

Ah, so that was it. Something had prompted Jo to get tested. "Perhaps you already know something about the physical portion of my ask, then. But that wouldn't likely explain the supernatural aspect of that DNA."

"No, but I sense there is a story there."

"Yes, apparently the odd DNA came directly from Danu, with all the baggage that now entails. The Tuatha know and are considerably interested. They found me in America and the consensus is they are looking for me."

Silence on the other end. "Again, most unexpected. That... complicates matters."

"Were you implying a minute ago that Jo is having problems?"

"Nothing that is dangerous to her health, if that is what you are worried about. But other issues have arisen."

"Once again, you are telling me something with an inscrutable riddle voice. Now, while you get to ponder all the possibilities of me being a Tuatha target, what was the purpose of your call?"

"Oh yes, since you are still close, Jo needs to see you. Your proximity makes everything more efficient, saving her a trip to America. I can have her there tomorrow. This is important as it pertains to the complication you need to know about."

Now I was silent. "It must be important then, and I suspect from your lack of explanation the last few times we've talked, and Jo's silence the past weeks, it is something quite dangerous, even if it isn't affecting her health."

"Yes, most important and dangerous."

"OK, I'll be in Cork through tomorrow. I'll head over to the Sin é pub and meet her there. She can text me a meeting time."

"Good. I would strongly advise you to tell her what you just told me. But let her talk first and keep your wits about you."

"Damn Michael, this sounds serious. But of course, I will listen to her. I still have powerful feelings for her."

"I know and keep that in mind tomorrow. We should also talk afterwards."

"Great, that isn't ominous at all. Anyway, I know you won't tell me, so let's talk tomorrow."

We hung up. Fantastic, another chunk of some crazy ass piece of life was about to get flung at me. I should not dwell on it but kept wondering if Jo's transformation had turned bad. I'd find out tomorrow, whatever the news was. And if her DNA was from me, maybe she was going to end up on the Tuatha list as well. Some consequences I just could not predict, much less manage.

I spent the day wandering and went to the University College Cork campus. One of my favorite places, the grounds were beautiful and peaceful. Which I realized was exactly what I did not need right now with my overactive imagination. Were Jo and I to end up as Irish fairy royalty? She would know a lot more about them than I, so I should get her to teach me about them. This should be a fun conversation.

The next day, I walked down to Sin é to grab a cider and wait for Jo. As I approached the building, I could see she was already there. I stopped a second to admire the side of her face in the upstairs window. It was such a nice day, rare for this time of year, that the window was open. Or maybe so she could get a shot off at me without breaking the glass. With that thought, I continued to the entry door. A step before I got there, I noticed a striking dark-haired woman exit the building next door and walk toward me. The place she had just exited was a funeral parlor, oddly enough.

I turned my attention to her as I got a weird ping from my extra sense. I started a defensive pose when her hands made a strange but incredibly quick gesture, then she rushed me faster than any human could. I did not even get my arms up before she kicked me and I fell back into nothingness, as she came with me and wrapped my wrists together in some strange substance that was like a cross between silk and fish mucus. It hardened to an unbreakable state before I even landed on my back, with her on top of me. It seemed we were in a cavern, with a stone floor. In a different context, I might have enjoyed a beautiful woman tying me up and landing astride me. But I felt this was not that context, and when she slapped me, I put my thoughts back into proper context. She stood up, and I got a good look at her legs under the dress. She kicked me. It was almost as if -

"Yes, maggot, I can read your thoughts," she said.

I immediately put up my protection, which I had leaned with slant.

"Impressive but blocking me won't save you. In fact, that just gives me the pleasure of now torturing you a bit. This is going even better than I expected. Ah yes, a delicious morsel. Shall I render you down and take back the essence? Or keep you here for centuries and slowly draw it out of you?"

"Morrigan, couldn't you have just said hello, and we could have had drinks in the pub? I'd happy to give you several doses of Danu's essence. I have it prepared and it's in Amsterdam."

That put her at a stop. "I have gone to all the effort of grabbing you and tearing you away from your little girlfriend, waiting upstairs. She looked so shocked; it gave me such a thrill. Now that you are here, I will at least torture you and remove some appendages."

"Before you slice and dice, you should know that it is probable that Odin would frown on that."

She hissed. Very unbecoming on such a beautiful face. "What does he have to do with this?"

"I suspect he would not appreciate you harming his current business associate. I also have a contract with him for his protection." That was partly a bluff, but I reached up with my manacled hands and pulled out the medallion that Odin had provided to our group.

No hiss this time, just a piercing scream of frustration. "If you are lying, I'll render you down myself while you are still alive. Melt you in the fire cauldron, feet first. I'll keep you alive until I push your head under, and, with your last gasp, you drown in your own rendered oil."

"As wonderful as that sounds for both of us, you really need to chat with whom I presume is your daddy before mussing your new pet." I had a strong suspicion she was Odin's daughter.

She kicked me again, then a crow flew in from somewhere and landed on her shoulder. They both vanished. What the hell was it with this family that they had to kick me all the time? And what was it with the birds? Did they watch Hitchcock movies?

I sat in the stone chamber or cave for a few minutes, then Morrigan and her pet chicken reappeared. She had the look of teenager when daddy had denied her the car keys. After a huffing sound and a wave of her hand, the hand binder stuff liquefied into mucus and poured down to the floor. She was waiting for me to speak, but I refused. She relented and grudgingly said, "I will release you now."

"Before I go, I stand by the offer of the Danu essence."

"You would do that? But wait, what do you want in return?" Her surprised look quickly turned into a calculating one.

"We should meet again soon. I'll give you the essence and an explanation of how to use it, and we will talk about a simple treaty. Basically, you and yours don't harm me or mine, and vice versa."

"That is all?"

"That is all."

"I can meet you and discuss that. Here is my cell number."

"Good." I also knew that would give her time to come up with an agreement that benefitted her more than me. But it was a start. It shocked me that a fairy queen had a cell phone, but I guess a goddess gotta keep in touch.

She made more hand motions, and a door opened to the sidewalk I had left just a few minutes ago. She gestured toward it and I walked backwards, not turning my back on her. That earned a beautiful smile from her. "He learns quickly." I nodded and stepped back into my world.

After I blinked back into existence, I looked up and saw Jo looking down at me with a face made in a storm. My fate was to go upstairs and weather that storm, but I didn't know it was about to get all Bermuda Triangle-ish. I went in and walked up, where the room was empty except for Jo. She didn't get up, which was unusual. I sat while she fumed, then as the server walked by, I ordered a cider. I asked Jo if she wanted one, but she just responded, "water" which was odd for her. The server left, and the storm broke.

"What the hell? I'm sitting here watching that gorgeous woman kick your arse and blink you out of existence before I can even get out of the window. I called Michael, but he told me to be patient and wait here for you. What the hell is going on?"

"Hi dear, how are you doing? I'm fine, thanks for asking. Been a while. What have you been doing?"

"Oh no, strange things are going on that you are not telling me about. I'm going to enjoy my anger and frustration and sling a little your way."

"OK, fire away. I can take it. It's not like you haven't been acting odd the past few months yourself. I know the Finland thing -"

"Shush," she nearly screamed. "Finland has nothing to do with this. At least, not really. You, though, you have everything to do with this. You and that damned DNA you pumped into me while saving my arse."

"Jo, you aren't being very clear as to exactly why you are hating me at the moment. I need a little more detail. Michael said there were complications. Are you OK?"

She teared up she was so mad. "You dolt, you do not know what complications are. But you are going to find out."

She stood up and stared down at me. I was completely lost and feeling like I was missing something important in the conversation as I looked into her eyes. Then I glanced down, and the world shifted. Baby bump? Drinking only water. Mad at me. I closed my eyes and looked at her with my extra sense. Two comets glowing in my mind.

"Holy shit, Jo," was my intelligent, compassionate response.

"Oh, right, more than you know. "

I sat dumbfounded, my mind silently counting up the months. Damn, it was not quite right, but with our crazy metabolisms, still possible.

"I would ask how it happened, but I mostly know how it works."

"No, you really don't."

"What?"

"This is not your baby."

"Uh, what? I mean, what the hell?" Several crazy thoughts went through my head.

"No, it's not yours, you idiot. Your DNA, yes, but not your baby. Parthenogenesis is the fancy word of the day. I'm having a 'miracle birth,' which is quite a bad thing, considering who I work for."

"Oh, damn. But humans can't... crap. But right, fish and amphibians can. Oh man, unintended consequences on steroids. And some in the Church won't take it well, while others..."

"Yes, and now you see my problem. It is officially our problem, however, as I'm naming you the father. I have to do this to protect both me and the baby."

"I get it. I really do. And I'll help however I can."

She sat with her mouth open for a second. "Just like that, you accept the responsibility?"

"Yes, I do. It has to be this way for both of us, and for the child. Anything else is dangerous madness."

"I, uh, well thanks. That will be a big help."

"Sure. When are we getting married?" She turned red and was sputtering, then stopped when she saw me laughing. "Ok, let me think. Michael has this all planned out. You and I are on good terms, but I asked you to marry me, and you said no. We will live apart amicably, but co-parent. Something along those lines?"

"Yes."

"OK, I can work with that. Oh, oh hell, this just got complicated."

"Well, duh, already is. But what do you mean?"

"This child is about to have a whole slew of interesting relatives."

"You mean your people in America?"

"No, they are pretty interesting, but in a safe way. I mean, our new people here in Ireland."

"You are not making any sense."

"I know. Let me try to explain something I just found out in the last few days. You remember my origin story?"

"Of course. What about it?"

"That was no ordinary fish that I fell on and fought. It was Danu, the river goddess. At least one version of her. So, my legacy, now our legacy, is a bit more royal than I thought. That crazy piece of beauty you just saw is a long-lost cousin."

"Oh my god, no. It can't be."

"Yep, it be. And so now all our new cousins are fairies. Your baby is a girl, right?"

"Yes."

"Direct descendant of Danu, and the only miracle birth in at least two thousand years. Hail, queen of the fairies, and the next baby girl Jesus, all in one package. This is going to be a wild ride for all three of us."

She had nothing to say. I pulled out my phone. "Michael asked me to call him after we spoke. Since we are sitting together, this seems like a good time to call him back." She just nodded a yes and continued to look thoughtful.

"Oh, can you give me a crash course on the Tuatha? I need to know what kind of present I should bring to the 'dirty Santa' Christmas party next year. On the positive side, just think of all the cool presents you are going to get at the fairy baby shower."

Her response was a vulgar hand gesture.

"I believe I deserve more respect as your designated baby-daddy." I thought she was about to come across the table at me. "Hey, don't kill me. I am riding back with you, and you don't want me bleeding all over the pretty jet."

"What? I thought you were going to Bangkok, or back to America, or somewhere."

"I probably should, but I realize I owe Michael a debt from a thousand years ago. It is time to pay up. I should do it while I am here. Meanwhile, he is booking me on to Bangkok for a quick investigation. And, well, I would like to spend more time with you, at least the rest of the day if you have the time." She looked pleased for the first time today.

"I don't suppose you will tell me about what that debt is about."

"I should probably let him tell you instead. But keeping secrets is getting annoying and I have to be nice to my baby mama." The storm face was back, but then she laughed. "I need to take Michael to his son's tomb."

"Oh. I don't know what to say to that."

"Nothing to say. I just need to do it, even if it is centuries late. Now, on to matters more fun. Baby showers, clothes, a nursery, and some names. We've got all day to plan."

"You really are going to enjoy this, aren't you?"

"Yes. But we are both really going to enjoy this. You might be out of sorts right now, but this will go better than you think. Oh, before I forget, you might be my sort-of sister slash baby mama, but I love you."

She reached over and grabbed my hand on the table. "I think I love you too... Thanks for doing this."

I completed the call to Michael to give him the latest batshit news.

Chapter Six

Jo and I arrived at the Cottage, and she took off to do whatever she needed to do, as I walked around in the study. Michael came in with an amused look.

"Hi Michael."

"Senecus, good to see you. I am surprised to see you here so soon." That sentence came out somewhat sarcastically. "But I think you win the prize for experiencing surprises recently."

"Yeah, I had planned to take a long hiatus from here. But now that I am a new father to a miracle baby and a maternal father to the fairies, and god knows what else, figured I might as well hang around a few days and see what other kind of craziness my life devolves into."

"An interesting synopsis, but somewhat correct. Well, there is one other bit of craziness I need to add to your list, which is long overdue. But I would rather wait until later to discuss that. How long are you staying? Do I need to reschedule the Bangkok trip?"

"I would like a little time with Jo, then my stay depends on how fast you and I can get to Morocco, specifically Spanish Melilla. I owe you a trip and would like to take you there, as a solemn duty and vow I took a long time ago. Probably safe to bump the Bangkok leg back a day or so."

"Ah, I see. We are going to Asif's tomb, I think?"

"Yes. My recent brush with mortality has sped up some plans and reminded me of the need to close out old debts."

"I'd be honored to accompany you and will arrange the trip to take us first thing in the morning. I think we can be back tomorrow evening. Will that work in your schedule?"

"Yes. That gives me time to visit with you and Jo."

"Good. Should I arrange your trip back to America from Bangkok?"

"No, in fact, now that I think about the timing, I'll need to change things up. I'll fly from here to Bangkok, then back here to pick something up, then go to Ireland. I have a deal with the fairies, or the fae, and Morrigan in particular. Then I'll go on to America."

"That is possibly quite dangerous. Our few dealings with the fae have never been completely insane, but they have always been problematic. Are you prepared for that?"

"I'm good, I think. I give them something, then we talk. That's all. Plus, I'm protected somewhat. I have a prior deal and a protection agreement with Morrigan's father. She doesn't like it but will have to live with it."

"I see. That would be Odin and one of the few to command respect among the fae. That should keep you safe."

"It is what I have. But it was enough to have already kept her from harming me, although she really wanted to boil me down alive."

"I imagine you get lots of those kinds of threats with your charm and wit."

"Michael, I am shocked you would say such a thing. We both know how reasonable and agreeable I am in all things. And I never get involved in anything weird."

"Yes, of course, my apologies. What would like to do this afternoon, spend time with Jo? We can then have dinner afterwards."

"I'd love that. Kind of feels like home again for a day. And the weather's atrocious, so it really feels like home. I'm going to find her and start tormenting her right now."

I sat with Jo by the fire in the study. I'd rather have been outside in the garden, but storms coming in from the North Sea decided otherwise. We chatted some about her work, and what I had been doing at the Farm. She wanted to come back to visit us but work and her new condition had prevented that so far. I told her that if her schedule was slowing down because of her pregnancy, she could come to the Farm and teach more classes on the supernatural entities. I felt it was even more important now that we were going to have ties to the Tuatha.

Then we moved to more personal issues. She had not been home for a few months but felt the need to visit. Jo had not told her family about their new niece yet. She was a little worried about how that would go over.

"Jo, I would be fine with traveling with you to go meet them. Since I'm the designated dad, it makes sense to do that."

"Oh, I'm not sure about that. But I guess it seems logical. Let me think about it some more."

"Sure. After Bangkok, I have to go back to Ireland to give Morrigan something. I can do it then if you decide you want me to meet them. We can travel together, or I can meet you there, after you spend some time with them."

"Thank you for offering."

"Let me know what you decide. I'll get a mohawk haircut and some tattoos if you think that would help."

"I appreciate the offer, but you, as you are, will make quite the impression."

"Thanks, I think."

The rest of our evening went well as we had reached a simple state of comfort with each other. It would probably last until the labor pains hit her. We ate with Michael and continued our easy banter.

On the trip to Melilla the next morning, I brought up something to Michael that had been bothering me for a while. "Michael, I'm troubled that the microbiome technology could be mishandled. I know that making lots of people live for two thousand years is a problem. I doubt the earth's resources would last if the current seven billion people lived for two thousand years, plus the issue of a lot of spontaneous pregnancies. Yet what about the medical benefits from the healing aspect? If there is a significant benefit to humans, is it not incumbent for us to provide a cure for illness?"

"There has been a lively debate about that lately as we have a group at the Center looking into it. We need to develop the technology to procure the right genes and proteins for good health without the immortality and parthenogenesis problems."

"Glad to hear the Center is working on it. I figured you Church people would be trying to do the right thing."

"Yes, we need a little longer to finish, but it should be workable. Another real problem is how to keep the full technology away from the powerful and wealthy in the world. I see a demand from that group, possibly the type of demand that cannot be resisted. That is truly our greatest fear. Even among the devout of the Church, dangling immortality in front of a powerful eighty-year-old bishop is too much of a temptation."

"I agree. Some people would probably do about anything to gain that advantage."

"Yes, possibly requiring a return to my previous profession."

"That would be a terminal solution for those that cross that boundary."

"Distasteful, but necessary if someone insists on appropriating that gift for selfish or nefarious purposes. Speaking of past professions, how are you doing?"

"Nice segue. If you meant to ask if I have killed any humans lately, the answer is no. I think that between that and all the other activity I have going on now, I don't remember that last time I was feeling down."

"Good, that sounds like your life has taken a turn for the positive."

"Or at least a turn to the very busy."

Michael and I took a fast boat, that was dark and sleek, over to the island from a marina at Melilla. Even with a speed boat it took nearly an hour. We had to be covert on the approach, as the island was technically off-limits, and a small Spanish garrison on the middle island ensured no trespassing on their territory. It was not a rigorous patrol, but they would chase off boats that landed and spent time on any of the three islands.

Since we arrived from the west, the garrison could not see us coming. We found a likely place, actually the only place to get on the island easily. We scaled the hill to the top of the plateau, then climbed up the western rock ridge where I had left Asif. The area looked mostly the same, but the details were a little off, either because of my memory or a thousand years of weathering.

I found the area I thought was the tomb. I pulled off a few rocks and Michael helped. The pile seemed smaller than I remembered, and we quickly came to the larger cover stone. It was no longer completely covering the hollow underneath, and some smaller rocks had fallen into the space beneath. We continued moving rocks and cleared the spot in less than five minutes. The area was empty of any remnants of bones or cloth, and even when I took out a flashlight and examined the hollow, there was nothing. As I was pulling myself back out, I dislodged the larger cover stone, which slipped to one side and tipped into the hollow.

I sat and wondered what might have happened, whether someone might have removed the body, or age had shifted the rocks through an earthquake, and the body had weathered away or taken by animals. I was about to say that to Michael when I felt his hand on my shoulder. He had a very thoughtful look on his face.

"You brought me here to find my son's remains, out of respect for him. Instead, you have brought me hope, and a great mystery."

"Uh, I'm not sure about that." Then I noticed what Michael had been looking at. On the underside of the cover stone, now tilted up, was a scratching that looked like Arabic script. I knew what part of it said.

"Michael, I'm not sure what happened here, but I did not put Asif's name on that rock."

"No, I expect you did not, and you also did not know to add the secret family name as well."

So that was the second part of the script that I didn't recognize. "But Michael, I left his body here, and I was pretty sure he was dead."

He sighed. "I suppose we should have had this talk some time ago. But I always had reasons not to, which was my mistake. What you don't know about my family, including Asif, is that we are much like you in some ways. Even your description of the violence visited upon his body would likely have not killed him. But he would have needed a day, probably two, of extensive healing while asleep to recover."

"Damn, you are telling me I buried him alive?"

"In a manner of speaking. But putting him under that cover rock protected his body and should have allowed him to fully recover. Of all the actions you could have taken while thinking him dead, this worked out for the best. How long between his death and the burial here?"

"I think it was roughly twelve hours, maybe slightly longer."

"That would explain it. He recovered and then left."

I was too stunned at first to think. Then I asked the obvious question. "So, where did he go, and where is he now?"

"That is the great mystery. But I think our journey here is done."

"Seems like it since there is nothing here. And now time to figure out what the hell happened and where he is."

We got out of the small rock pile and stood a moment to observe the view over the water.

"When I brought him here, there were tents over there," as I pointed to the middle island. "And on the far side, I saw a few fishing boats pulled up to shore."

"I believe that could explain Asif's first steps off this island. It looks swimmable. He could have gotten food and a ride to the mainland." I nodded agreement. "Meanwhile, he probably thought the pirates, or the shipwreck, killed you and the rest of the crew. And if he had searched for you, he would not have found you, since you were in a coma somewhere in the Pyrenees."

"That is true. But it does not explain why he would not have traveled to Alexandria to find you and his family."

"If he had traveled directly there, he would have found us. It was nearly two years later that we left Egypt for good. But even then, friends and colleagues in Alexandria could have directed him to us or sent letters informing us of his arrival. Yes, definitely a great mystery, but in some ways, this has been a great day, for Asif could still be alive somewhere."

"I'm glad for you then. First thing I am going to do is start my computer guy searching for any shred of evidence of him in history. There has to be some sign of him over the past thousand years."

"I shall request the same of the Center's computer staff. Perhaps our efforts can find some clues."

There was a strange hum suddenly around us, more felt than heard. It was very uncomfortable, similar to strong subsonic waves pounding against our entrails and eardrums. The frequency rapidly increased, and the hum grew more piercing, even making the air around us feel wrong. A small blue dot, which I assumed was a laser, appeared on the ground near the tomb site, similar to a laser being sighted in from the air.

My reflex was to run as fast as possible, which I did even as yelled to Michael, "Let's get out of here. This can't be good."

We sprinted away and off the edge of the steep rocky ridge, falling meters at a time, bouncing off the slope with our feet. Then we jumped and did the same thing down the long hill to the ocean shore where the boat was tied up. It took only a few seconds to drop from the ridgetop to where we left the boat. Michael had stayed with me the entire time, satisfying my suspicion that, despite his age, he had enhanced physical skills.

We landed hard on the bottom shelf of rock by the water, which had just a little sand over it to cushion our landing. I wouldn't be surprised if I had stress fractures throughout my legs and feet. A brilliant flash, lasting less than a second, blasted the top of the ridge we had just left. It left a burning blue after-image in my eyes. Then a massive boom immediately followed, which hurt my ears. A hot piece of something landed in the water near my foot, producing explosive steam. I waited a moment, then pushed it out of the water with my boot. It was a piece of crude glass.

"Well, at the risk of stating the obvious, I guess we just avoided being vaporized or turned into glass statues," I said.

"It appears our presence was not welcome here. Or perhaps it was, but the trap was a moment too late."

"That flash, being that large, almost makes me think it was something like a space laser. Took a few seconds to load up, then blast down. But we don't have those yet, at least not that large and in a blue color, do we?"

"No, not at that energy magnitude. That was someone else."

"So, our brethren Sky Lords from the future possibly have something orbiting earth or in nearby space?"

"It is possible but would be difficult to find and prove."

I said nothing, but I had ideas about how to find something like that. And how to deal with it, and as soon as possible. The idea of that thing being up there and blasting the Farm gave me a bad feeling.

"Michael, I am moving that ship up on my priority list. I can't have something like that floating around and zapping the Farm."

"I understand. I don't know yet how to assist but let me know if you need anything. You may have faster results consulting your other friends. But I think it may not be an imminent threat."

"Why do you say that?"

"I think this was an attack of opportunity. You and I were here alone, with no witnesses. Blasting that laser in a populated area, especially one monitored by major governments, would be imprudent."

"Yeah, that makes sense. I worry about how they knew who we were and why we were here."

"I suspect there was some sort of sensor on that tomb site. Anyone looking for Asif, or just blundering into that spot, were likely to get blasted."

"Even adds more questions about why they would know about Asif's tomb and booby trap it."

We looked at each, but neither of us said what we were thinking. It was too difficult to utter that Asif's disappearance might have something to do with the Sky Lords.

"Regardless of all that, this seems like an escalation, if indeed that was a blast from the Sky Lords. Sitting in our space and interfering like that seems like a new provocation."

"Yes, they seem to have assumed a new level of arrogance. I would counsel you to talk to Kal, or Odin, or both. They have a friend in common that should hear about this and may help you. He, and I use that identifier loosely, has more jurisdiction off the planet than on it."

"That sounds like somebody I should meet, but really wish I didn't have to."

"Needs must. And this is a definite need. Now, let's start the boat and sneak away from here before the garrison comes over to investigate that lightning strike."

CHAPTER SEVEN

An hour later we were back in Melilla, then on the Church jet to Schipol. We had finished our daytrip to the Mediterranean searching for a tomb with no body and getting shot at by a space laser. Another day for a normal guy that was part river goddess and mother to the fae. I decided to go further down the rabbit hole and finish up a conversation with Michael.

"You mentioned earlier that you needed to tell me about some other piece of my crazy life. Might as well tell me now."

"I suppose this will be your month of discovery, where everything changes. This piece won't be any easier to hear than those other gifts of knowledge you recently received."

"OK, hit me. We've got two hours in this tin can."

"First, I will tell you about the knife that you gave me at Christmas, as I believe it is a significant part of this story. I can't explain all the details, as this is not my area of expertise. But the blade has its own internal black hole, incredibly tiny, that fuels an interdimensional energy generator. That isn't exactly correct according to our physics, but it will suffice for this explanation. But obviously it is a unique and powerful artifact that predates anything made by humans."

I was about to say something like 'Oh, of course, I should have known,' but I wisely decided to stay quiet. It was the most outlandish thing I'd heard in the past hour.

"The blade pulls in any negative interdimensional energy it encounters," Michael continued. "It sucks it in and spits it out somewhere that is unknown to us, perhaps into another dimension or the other side of the universe. What all that means is, if you stick it into an evil entity, it devours them and puts them outside our reality. For good, as far as we know.

"The corollary to that, in a way that defies understanding, is a tiny amount of different energy resides in the blade. Once the blade is placed into a positive entity, it transfers that energy to that entity. If human, that individual is given enhanced abilities and a longer life. Not greatly so, as it increases strength and speed by fifty percent, and adds something like two decades of lifespan."

"OK, Michael, if I stab a demon, the knife sucks it in and tosses it into some hell far away. But if I cut into a good person, they get stronger and faster, plus live a few decades longer than usual."

"Yes. That is partly how I and a few others anointed the few uninfected that were left of the Northern Legions after the vampires destroyed the rest of those armies in the mass outbreak just after 300 AD. Our task was finding and anointing those we could find as quickly as possible, so they could fight off the vampires before all of Northern Europe was overrun and lost. The blade also contained an engineered virus that instantly inoculated that person against the vampire virus, plus added other physical enhancements to the person. Strength and speed, by affecting specific areas of the brain, and a great boost to the immune system to speed healing."

"You say that you and some of your colleagues ran through northern Holland one dark and stormy night, trying to touch any soldier, not already a vampire?"

"Essentially yes. The daggers needed to break the skin to ensure good contact and introduce the virus to the bloodstream. Since it was such a cold and wet night, for anyone outside on duty, such as you, we had to target the face or neck. In the inns or barracks, it was easier, as we just tapped the arms, hands, or legs."

"Michael, are you telling me that my origin may also be some part of an anointing, like you had hinted sometime back? I'm part fish-Irish fairy and part angel's little helper?"

"I wouldn't put it quite like that, but I believe you have captured the essence of what you are. Because of the extreme increase of your enhancements and lifespan, I suspect it was me, and this knife, that did the inoculation that night. If it was me, I had no idea that you fell into the river as I would have pulled you out before speeding off to the next soldier."

"How long have you suspected that I was one of your anointed?"

"When you first told your origin story, I thought it might have been possible. But there was no reason to believe that the effect of the anointing would have provided the gifts you received, especially the lifespan, so I rejected the thought. I implied that you may have been anointed, in case you knew something, or it jogged your memory. But obviously it did not. When you gave the knife to me, it finally came to me. All the coincidences that have happened may have begun that night. I still do not know why, but it is likely."

"I need to think about all that for a minute." A lot of thoughts raced through my brain as I sat quietly and considered all the implications. "How did you guys even get permission to inoculate soldiers across an entire country?"

"All I can say is that we are sometimes allowed a balancing of the scales."

"I suppose most of my research doctorates were for naught. My ideas of environmental microbiology and fish proteins, which were admittedly a stretch, end up have no bearing on what I am, between the Danu essence and the anointing blade."

"The research may not directly apply to your condition, but you learned a lot about mud microbiology and protective fish proteins. It's the little things in life that make it worthwhile."

"Yeah, thanks, that really helps me put this into perspective. First, you infected me with a powerful yet positive virus. The blade also kickstarted things in me with some sort of weird energy. OK, sure, that makes sense. Then when I fell and sliced up that Danu creature incarnation, I sucked in plenty of material to expose my internal and external self to that DNA, plus have enough to move down into my intestines and establish a new microbiome. Possibly a synergistic effect of all that as well."

"I believe that is possible. Quite a series of events took place to produce something, or in your case, the someone, that is unique. Then your ability to transfer that to someone else was unexpected. And you know how unexpected that additional effect on Jo was, as I don't think anyone would have predicted human parthenogenesis."

"Oh, Michael, before I forget, you just referred to the virus as being engineered. So where did it come from, considering that was nearly two thousand years ago?"

"You caught that part, did you?"

"Yes, I did. Time for more transparency."

"We didn't have the facilities but knew from the Sky Lords that the capability existed. Because this was a re-balancing effort to counter the introduced vampire virus, external help was available. The friend of Kal and Odin that I mentioned after the island attack provided the virus."

"Sounds like an advanced entity. Possibly one that was around with the dinosaurs, but escaped the big rock splat?"

"Yes, and a good guess. Don't hold me to it, but the name is something like Chklatwaquensmokkim in our language. But that is an approximation, as their language is not based on consonants and vowels. Anyway, I'm sure you will determine a nickname that is much easier to pronounce."

"Yeah, definitely. OK, give me that name again." On the second pass, I decided he, or it, was going to be 'Smokey,' or similar if the appearance fit. "What does he look like?"

"He usually appears in a bipedal form, somewhat amorphous and constantly changing dark cloud, but I think that form is only to appeal to our primate bias. I do not believe his species was anything close to a bipedal primate, as none existed during their time on earth or for millions of years afterward."

"When I get back here, I'll get an audience with Odin, or talk to Kal when I get to America. Then either way, I'll have a conversation with Smokey."

"Good, that should help with this new menace from space."

We both quit talking for a while, as we had a lot to mull over.

"Michael, are you ready to tell me about you and your people?"

He sighed again. "I suppose I should. I definitely owe it to you, although I almost never talk about it. You probably have guessed some if it by now. But it is a long and complicated story."

"The short version is appreciated."

"The ones we called the Makers came to Earth after the asteroid blast. Their task was to replenish the planet with sentient life. They placed various types of First Peoples here over time, to determine which would adapt and survive. People, in this context that I am referring to, consisted of a very wide range of life forms, as many were not primate-based. Over millennia, there were several iterations of various species introduced. What we call modern humans were toward the end, after a great deal of trial and error. They gave the first humans some enhanced physical characteristics and longer lifespans to withstand the environment. Interestingly, different groups of humans got different enhancements, with the idea that the best would survive, mate with other surviving groups, so the essential enhancements dictated by the environment would prove out. Over time, the enhancements and long lifespans became dormant. The remainder survived and became today's humans.

"Those that came before modern humans, the 'immortals' you might say, remained to guide and assist the newest groups of humans to increase their chances of survival. I'm using the descriptor immortal, but no biological creature on earth is truly immortal; just very long-lived. The First Peoples that stayed within their own kind to mate continued to produce immortal offspring. Those few originals that remain are called Guardians.

"But as with every project lasting many millennia, with tens of thousands of individuals, plans sometimes went awry. Some Makers caused issues with interference in those plans, and some of the original First Peoples that were primate-based, bred with the new humans. One effect was that those unions produced children with shorter lifespans, as well as other problems with the offspring."

"Then I assume your family was of that original immortal human line with the great lifespan."

"Yes, we are one of the Guardian groups. My ancestors usually mated with their own kind, including my direct line. But over time, there were too few of us left to continue our line. If Asif was here, he likely would not find an immortal mate. And that is acceptable, as we have served our purpose."

"Would the Makers be another name for God?"

"Oh, absolutely not. While very advanced, they would not fit our version of God. But who is to say that they were not acting on behalf of God?"

"Not me, as I don't know. But what about angels, how did they fit into this network?"

"They do not. Angels were apart from all this, and that is a whole different discussion. In this context, some also bred with humans and caused problems. But angels are from a different dimension and had, and still have, different roles than the repopulation efforts after the cataclysm."

"Within all this complex repopulation system, where do the Tuatha fit in? I've heard there were four Tuatha cities where the fae came from before relocating to Ireland thousands of years ago. They brought magical advancements with them, but could those be technical advancements? Were those cities here on earth, perhaps on the continent of Atlantis, or from the future and the Sky Lord's realm?"

"That is an astute question, and one I can only partially answer. Both because I know little about their cities, and because with Atlantis, there is a secret there that I am required to keep. But what I can tell you is that the Makers established a few research and monitoring centers as they conducted their grand experiment to bring sentient life back to earth. I suspect those four centers could be the origin of those stories. The timeline may be off, since I know they kept the centers quite hidden, and all became inactive perhaps ten thousand years ago. But Maker technology could be the basis for the fae advancements."

"Those Makers, are they true aliens from another part of the galaxy, or were they the group that developed on earth and then left?"

"They would be the latter. I have had limited contact with them, however, but when you meet the one you are already calling Smokey, he should be able to continue that discussion."

"Thanks."

"No more questions, even though I revealed little?"

"No, nothing right now, I have plenty to digest. Unless you want to tell me about Atlantis."

"I won't be divulging anything about Atlantis. But overall, I think you now have better sources than just about anyone on this planet. You may get more information than you want if you ask the right people. Or beings."

"Yeah, that is worrying me. Why would I learn all these things unless something terrible is about to happen and I'm expected to stop it?"

"Another good question."

We just smiled at each other. I took a break and got some juice for both of us. As we neared Amsterdam, I asked Michael about the Bangkok trip.

"OK, the usual questions for Bangkok - what happened, and where exactly?"

"The what is a theft of some great importance, and the where is near downtown Bangkok, on the southeast side of town. I believe you have been to Lumphini Park before?"

"Yes, I have been there on business trips. I've walked through the park before and stayed at a nearby hotel. One of those places nice to visit, but I couldn't live there because of the climate. But for this project, you know that a theft investigation is not really my forte."

"It is not a typical theft case. The item is irreplaceable, the disappearance has supernatural implications, and some forty-million people are at risk until we find the item."

"That sounds like something valuable."

"Based on our intelligence, they orchestrated the theft with something unknown, but likely orchestrated by a master vampire, and the Sky Lords."

"Quite a combination. I should probably go in with lots of artillery then."

"I don't think you will need any special weapons for this, but I will have a couple of items sent and waiting for you when you arrive. There is no remaining threat we know of."

"OK. I would appreciate a driver when I get to Bangkok. Driving there is atrocious."

"You will have a driver waiting, along with our agent on site. His name is Chalawit. I will email you the details we have so far, and Chalawit will update you when you arrive with a printed folder, including photographs."

When we arrived back in Amsterdam, I decided to just stay at the airport hotel. It would be easier flying out early the next day. My bag to Bangkok was small, as the weather there was always warm and humid. I did not know many Americans and Europeans that would make a high fashion statement in Thailand; most wore T-shirts, shorts, and sandals their entire visit. I would be more presentable than that, but not by much. I did not plan to spend much time there, I felt I needed to be back with Jo, and finish my business with Morrigan.

CHAPTER EIGHT

I studied what Michael had sent with me on the long ride across the Asian continent. It seemed simple in the folder - a large jewel was missing from a temple. A couple of still shots from surveillance video was sketchy but appeared to show a large black smoke blob monster taking it. It became odd when the report stated the jewel was part of a system that provided protection for Bangkok and much of the surrounding area. It sounded crazy to me, but the system repelled typhoons, earthquakes, and tsunamis, for approximately forty-million people. Without the system, the population was highly susceptible to natural disasters. I did not have any logical or scientific explanation for how that might work, but from what I had experienced lately, I no longer ruled anything out.

I met Chalawit, the Church agent, in the airport, then we exited into a warm damp blanket of air, known as Bangkok weather. I had never been here when it was otherwise. The entire year felt like this, with two seasons ruling the warm climate: a lot of rain, or a whole lot of rain. Old Siam never wavered much regarding the weather.

"I hope your travel was good," he said as we got to the car. "If you like, I can give you a brief update on the way to the hotel, although there is very little to add. Or you can rest on the ride if you are tired. Also, please call me Gai."

I had to chuckle to myself at that. Every Thai I had met had a nickname. I only knew a few words of Thai, but I knew this one well; Gai was the Thai word for chicken.

"I'd rather just ask a few questions. Have you visited the site of the theft?"

"Yes, but there was very little to observe. The foyer was empty, and the temple room, still sealed, was empty as well."

"And you saw the video from that night?"

"Yes."

"What is your feeling about whatever took the jewel?"

"I have not seen or heard of anything that looked like what I saw on the video. Evil smoke is the best description. The quick update I can give is something we have kept quiet so far. We found the guards dead nearby the temple. There was no visible physical harm done to them, but an autopsy with lab testing suggests the men were scared to death."

"Huh, I didn't know about that. I would like to see the bodies if they are still available."

"Certainly. The police will release them to the families tomorrow. After you check into the hotel, we will visit the morgue."

"Good. Perhaps a meal after the morgue."

"Most preferable; eating beforehand could be problematic."

"Are you the Church's security officer for this area?"

"Not exactly, as we have few assets here. I'm more of an emissary working through our Buddhist colleagues."

"How do you get along with them, since the religions are so different?"

"I believe that is a misconception. I know leaders from both faiths have said the belief systems are incompatible, but those of us working together have a different view. The teachings of the namesakes of our two groups are similar at a certain level. It can be summed up as 'be the best person you can be, and never stop trying to be better' which binds us more than separates us."

"That makes a lot of sense."

"Perhaps someday the world will see it the same way."

The driver and Chalawit, now Gai, dropped me at the Muse hotel and waited as I checked in. This was not the Holiday Inn experience. Instead of lining up at a cheap counter, you must sit down at a wood and marble desk, drink fresh juices, pass pleasantries back and forth, exchange documents, wait some more, then finally receive a key. It was a process, and more than that, a tradition, one long past in most places. The hotel itself was like something built from a 1930s Hollywood movie, but with all the modern conveniences and comforts. Baroque architecture with ornate dark woodwork, polished marble where the wood ended, and all fixtures were brass or similar metal. I threw my bag in the room, then went back down.

As I walked outside, I once again encountered the warm wet blanket that passed for air in Bangkok. The forecast could be on autopilot, and it must bore the weather forecasters beyond imagining. I was sweating during the fifty feet to the car.

The driver pulled back into the traffic hell that passed for streets. Traffic jams persisted twenty-four hours a day, which is why I wanted a driver. There were always vehicles everywhere. Scooters with teenagers, mostly boys transporting girls, carts of various sorts, junk cars, Maseratis, the famous tuk-tuks. If it had wheels, it was on the streets of Bangkok, and barely moving. An hour later, after traveling two miles, we arrived at the morgue.

It was a two-story white building with little adornment. Double glass doors frosted for privacy opened to let us in the foyer, just a white room with a receptionist behind glass on one wall. Gai went into a lengthy discussion in Thai with the receptionist. After a few minutes, a guard opened the only other door in the room and motioned us in.

We walked past several doors until we entered a fourth and stood in a refrigerated room with the entire back wall full of small, stainless-steel doors.

Two attendants opened three doors and pulled out stainless trays, with a white sheet over stiff bodies. We ventured closer as they pulled the sheets down.

Usually bodies are just bodies, and I had seen many up close that I'd killed myself. But these three appeared to have died badly. All three had gone into rigor quickly since their legs and arms were twisted in rictus, and their faces frozen in what I could only describe as terror. The small veins in the sclera of their eyes had burst, turning the white mostly red. Petechial hemorrhages were obvious on their faces and necks, showing they were alive when exposed to what killed them. Scared to death was as good a cause of death as anything else, I thought, after observing the bodies. I had seen enough.

We left and Gai said he knew a good place to eat. Most people don't leave the morgue for lunch, but dead bodies no longer suppressed my appetite. Besides, I was looking forward to the food after a long absence from the country. Thai food sometimes looked odd but was always good. Red and green curries, containing just about anything imaginable, but for me, best with chicken. Mangoes, ripe and fresh from the tree, sliced and slightly chilled, placed on a bed of sweet sticky rice. A plethora of seafoods which I avoided. Now I wondered if my reluctance to eat seafood was because I was instinctually avoiding eating my cousins. Probably not, though, I just didn't appreciate the flavors and textures. A thousand other dishes that would take me forever to try but were probably worth the effort. The driver let us out in front of a small place as there was no parking. I told Gai we needed to bring a good lunch back for him.

Everyone in the place knew Gai, and the servers automatically started bringing out dishes, most of which I liked. While we ate, I asked him about the set of gemstones that Michael's information said protected the city.

"I can tell you what I know, but much of this topic is still secret after hundreds of years. When we go to the temple where the crime occurred, we will meet a priest that has the details. Have you ever heard of the Navaratna?"

"No, I can't say that I have."

"It is a set of nine massive gemstones; eight are set in a ring with the ninth in the center. The arrangement has mystical power said to derive from the Navagraha, or astrological bodies representing most of the planets, plus the sun. That description is incomplete and does not include the mysticism involved. What matters is that the gemstones, placed in a specific configuration produces a field that somehow protects everything in or nearby the ring from natural disasters, forming a protective cordon around Bangkok. Each stone is housed in a nondescript temple, within a sealed room, with a few guards overseeing the grounds and the surveillance systems at each temple."

"I have a hard time envisioning that a few jewels scattered around the city could provide such protection."

"I understand. The priest we will meet later is also the prime caretaker of the system. His explanation will be much better than mine."

We finished the excellent meal. I was happy to get my mangoes and sticky rice for dessert. Gai ordered lunch for the driver, and we took it out to him. He was halfway on the sidewalk, half in the street, typical parking for Bangkok. Gai told him to take the rest of the day off since the temple was close, and the hotel not far after that. We walked and sweated our way across several blocks toward the temple.

It was a small building, starkly white, with few adornments compared to most of the elaborately decorated temples in Bangkok. The general shape indicated a temple, but most would walk past it and not recognize it. There was a single door that was open to a small anteroom with a priest standing inside, wearing a golden-orange cloak. It appeared to be a modification of the Buddhist robe most priests wore. Gai introduced me to Surasak, and we traded greetings.

"You come highly recommended by Michael," he said. "I hope you can assist us in retrieving the item, and perhaps preventing any further thefts."

"I will do what I can, but I'm just not sure what and who I'm looking for yet. I'm hoping you can help me with that."

"The missing item is a very large pearl, much larger than any other. The thief and murderer, for it caused the death of three guards, is some type of air demon, although unlike any we have seen before."

"I heard that there was some video that had the demon on it that I could watch. I'd also like to know about the gemstones and their properties, specifically this large pearl."

"Of course. But first, these are not mere jewels and gemstones. We call them Mother Jewels. They are the largest known specimens of their kind in the world, and they appear to be sentient. Of course, it is difficult to tell, as crystals communicate much differently and on longer planes of time than we do. There are seven jewels mined from the earth, and two from the ocean. If one of the earth jewels had been taken, there is some chance we could replace it, given enough time. However, we cannot replace the missing Mother pearl."

"If you cannot replace it, that makes it the primary target to steal and shut down the protection system?"

"Yes. The Mother pearl is the size of a basketball, as are all the jewels. But the pearl came from a special oyster that lived in a unique place and time. Neither that species, nor that place where it lived, exists any longer. Making it irreplaceable. Now the resonant protective ring of Bangkok is absent, and we fear an imminent natural disaster will occur within three years, with substantial loss of life."

"These gems, in the right alignment, produce some sort of dampening effect that works on earthquakes and the atmosphere?"

"An exact placement of the Mother Jewels produces a resonance that extends several miles both below and above the earth. The resonance field wards off earthquakes under the surface, and also dampens atmospheric disturbances such as typhoons. The field encircles Bangkok, or rather, it did until last week. This protection that we in Bangkok, and the surrounding area, have enjoyed for hundreds of years is now gone.

"The complex ring system includes the remaining Mother Jewels, an emerald, diamond, blue sapphire, yellow sapphire, cat's eye, garnet, and coral, placed in temples exactly like this one, in a circle around the city at a specific location and distance from each other. The exact placement required to provide the correct resonance took many years to perfect. A ruby is in the center of this ring and housed near the Grand Palace and Emerald Buddha in the middle of town. Obviously, we are near Lumphini Park, to give you some idea of the placement distance between temples.

"We believe this theft was conducted to put the region at risk and has nothing to do with financial gain. The other gemstones are just as valuable as the pearl. The thing that took it had no problem penetrating the temple, so it could have easily taken some or all the other stones if it so desired.

"One last concern. Some of our people that study this resonance ring also fear that the pearl, if placed in a particular location out of the normal sequence, could produce a different resonance that could cause earthquakes in the region. Fortuitously, we have seen no sign that has happened. For these reasons, we must find the pearl, eliminate the perpetrator, and somehow prevent further thefts."

A woman walked in and acknowledged Surasak with the wai greeting. She moved like an alpha predator, but I tried not to react, since she seemed to belong here. She was attractive and simply dressed, but I couldn't shake the impression that there was much more to her, and she might be a shapeshifter. Surasak introduced us.

"This is Naam. Naam, this is Senecus, and you know Gai. Senecus, she will accompany you for the rest of your visit in Thailand, and we will assign her to you for your next visit as well."

"Nice to meet you, Naam. Khun Surasak, what is Naam's purpose regarding my visit? And do you expect needing me in the future?"

"Naam's purpose will soon be apparent. And I envision you will eventually be back to get something. As you may say in your culture, go with God. Good day, Senecus, Gai," Surasak said as he departed. I looked over at Gai, but he just shrugged. Naam had yet to say anything and stayed quiet even when I looked at her. Just another strange day in Bangkok.

"We should watch the video showing the theft," she said finally. She had a bag from which she removed a tiny video player that was mostly a screen. She held it up for me to view, as Gai had already watched it. It was a wide view of a sealed white room with no openings, with a pedestal in the center. The pedestal looked mechanical, and I realized it must be adjustable. A massive pearl, truly the size of a basketball, sat on top. Otherwise, the room was completely empty. A large black shape appeared, looking like greasy smoke. It moved over to the pearl, covered it, then moved away and the pearl was gone. Then the smoke blob itself passed on through the wall.

The video ended after those few seconds as there was nothing else to see. The jewel room was clearly on the other side of the wall where we were currently standing.

CHAPTER NINE

"Any thoughts?" Naam asked.

"This thing is insubstantial enough that it can move through walls when it needs to. Yet advanced enough that it can grab that huge pearl and then flex physics enough to take itself and the pearl back through the wall. My first thought is it must be able to manipulate matter or dimensions to both exist here and to carry the pearl away. Ever heard of anything like that?"

Both Naam and Gai shook their heads.

"Me neither. Even worse, I do not know how to fight it or prevent this from happening again."

"We should go. There is nothing else to be seen here," Naam said.

"Wait, a moment. Were the walls examined where that thing entered and exited?"

"Yes, they were examined and tested. There were no residues or structural changes that we could detect," Gai said.

"OK, I guess back to the hotel for now."

We walked across Lumphini Park to the hotel, sweating along the way. At the hotel, Gai stopped in at the bar to get water, and I went up to my room. Naam followed me into the elevator. She looked at me after I gave her a questioning look. "My assignment is to accompany you while you are in Bangkok. That literally means everywhere that you go."

"Everywhere, including my room?"

"Yes, everywhere."

"Naam, are you covering me twenty-four hours a day?"

"Yes, and within three meters. I will stay with you in your room. Together in bed, or anywhere else you prefer, but in your room. I will also be at your bathroom door."

This was going to be inconvenient. But she was adamant, and I guess I could give up a little privacy a day or two since it seemed important to her. I changed shirts as she stalked around the room and looked out the window. "Is your assignment to protect me from the smoke demon?"

"It is to protect you against any threat. All other threats I will fight off, but if the smoke demon appears, my job is to make you run, as that may be the only survivable action."

"Let's join Gai at the bar."

We rode back down and found Gai, then ordered fruity but excellent drinks.

There was some discussion about the entity, what it was, and how to deal with it. We did not come up with any solutions. The group decision was to move to the restaurant for dinner.

It was quite a walk across several major roads. We watched those super-charged motorized carts zip through traffic and even the crosswalks at insane speeds.

"What do you think of our tuk-tuks?" Gai asked. "Do you wish to charter a ride?"

"No thanks, I've been in one, just once. The drivers are a special kind of crazy, and you have to be insane to be a willing passenger. I'd rather skydive with a faulty parachute. At least then I have a slight chance of landing on something soft. In a tuk-tuk, you are just going to hit something bigger or skid across the pavement while leaving swaths of skin behind."

The restaurant was a very nice open pavilion on the river with several ornate "cabins" that were set up to seat anywhere from a few to many patrons. We were in the smallest and by ourselves. The food was excellent and in the typical Thai presentation, with many dishes of reasonable portions offered. As usual, I stayed away from the seafood. The red curry was excellent, but I didn't care about the green curry. Not surprising considering how many hundreds of varieties there were. We talked briefly about the temple theft, but there were no new ideas or leads to investigate.

After two rounds of drinks, Gai told us goodnight and left. I suspected Naam stayed as she wanted to talk about something privately. I still doubted that she was going to stick to her assignment. Constantly watching over me and spending the night with me seemed overkill as there were no threats. We took our drinks and walked outside and stood in the pavilion at the edge of the river.

"I sense you are not just one of the Church's human investigators," Naam said.

"I am not. I do not think you are only that, either. My senses suggest you are more like my selkie friends from Ireland and Scotland."

"Ah, no, not exactly. I am surprised you know of the selkies. There are only a few of them left. But you are in the right realm with your guess. I am of the Undine, which you may know is the European word for water nymph or sprite. The Thai version is Phi Phraya, but we are not ghosts, but shape changers. If I may ask without offense, what are you?"

"According to information that recently came to me, an incident many years ago infused me with the essence of Danu. Enough so that my physiology and DNA seem to correlate with that idea. The Irish fae have also determined that this happened, giving me some odd type of kinship with them. During that same incident, I got hit with a Church artifact that was designed to turn me into a temporary vampire killer."

Naam stared at me with wide eyes. "If true, and I sense it is, that would make you one of the most powerful water entities in our realm. We have long heard of the influence of Danu in Europe and Central Asia, and some of our oldest stories mention her passing through our region."

"I'm just learning about this, so I need to catch up on the lore around Danu. They lost much information in Europe, whether by accident or by intention, during the people's conversion to new religions."

"We have less of an issue here, as many of our stories and traditions were preserved. Although Danu was a powerful goddess, she resided a continent away, so I can't tell you much."

"That's OK. I have others looking for answers."

Naam moved closer. "I need to tell you something. I have a bad feeling about the thing that stole the Pearl Mother. It is something that Gai doesn't fully understand, but I think you might have some idea of its nature. I am sure, with all my senses, that the thing is not from here."

"Are you saying it is not from Asia?"

"No, it is not from this world, and possibly not from this time. I wanted to tell you because I don't think you have any chance of surviving that thing if you find it. That is why you must run if it appears."

"Thanks for telling me. I didn't pick up anything useful at the temple because it had been too long since the theft. But seeing the footage and visiting the guard's bodies makes me agree with you. I think your Pearl Mother is gone and, for the near future, is unlikely to be retrieved."

"I just wanted to warn you beforehand." She moved closer. "I don't want you to perish trying to retrieve the pearl." There was the distinct release of a powerful pheromone cloud from Naam, right into my face. I looked into her eyes and felt the pull from the pheromones but knew what this was. She leaned in further and I stepped back. She looked at me with surprise, but then smiled. "I see I am too late. But I wish her well."

"Uh, what?"

"None can resist the pull of a water sprite, except those already promised to another. I sense you feel nothing for me and have no interest in pursuing me, as that place in you is already filled by someone else."

"I don't think I have promised myself to anyone else."

"I would disagree. Whether you know it or not, you have given yourself to another. If you know it not, I suggest you determine your heart's keeper, for both of your sakes."

"There may be someone, but we can't be together."

"But you already are, whether or not you see it. And my warning still stands. Do not chase and attack this thing, both for your sake and hers. You cannot survive it."

"Thanks for letting me know. I will refer further action to Michael, as he can probably pull something together to deal with this demon, alien, or whatever it is."

"That is wise."

I walked with Naam to the front of the restaurant as they were closing. The attack came as we were leaving. Shapes rose from the river, and as they came closer, they looked like bipedal catfish. Their skin was light grey on front and dark grey on their backs, heads oddly shaped, like something between fish and frogs, with gill slits on the sides of the neck. The skin was slick and slimy. They brought with them the wonderful odor of sewage and wet dog.

"What the hell are these things?"

"Children of Namazu. But they should not be in Thailand. Do you have a weapon?"

"Just a knife and a baton that Michael had waiting for me."

"Are they silver?"

"I think so."

"Good, toss me the baton. It's my favorite for fighting on land. They will be hard to kill but are mortal." I threw the baton at her, then she pulled out another from her bag with her other hand. She moved like she knew what she was doing. Three of them went for her, and three for me. They moved ponderously so my initial response was hitting and kicking them, then spinning away. But they were tough and strikes anywhere on their bodies produced little result.

Their strategy was to gang up and grab us. I realized why when two of them boxed me in on either side, then the third one tried to spine me. It tucked its head, then folded it down again at an unnatural angle. That brought a wicked two-foot-long spine on the back of its neck forward, and moving straight toward my face. If this thing was cousin to a catfish, I knew I wanted nothing to do with that spine, as it was likely poisoned. I swung my knife at the spine and lopped it off, which brought the thing's head up as it croak-howled at me. I spun away from it and the other two. Then the injured one and another tried to corner me again, with another bringing up its spine.

By then, I was tired of this attack and that putrid smell. I checked on Naam and she was doing fine. She was much faster than them and danced around them with batons. Not doing much damage, but she was distracting the hell out of them. When one turned my way, she would smack it in the gills, which seemed to cause immense pain. She then jammed one baton deep into a gill slit, and that seemed to paralyze it. It stood without moving or making noise. She repeated the maneuver in another with similar results. The third backed off as it realized it no longer had a three-to-one advantage.

I waded into my three with the knife. I swiped my knife across the neck of the nearest one, from gill to gill, and damn near took its head off, while a gallon of thick blood spewed from the wound. The second and third went just as quickly. Then I swooped over to Naam's two paralyzed fishies and took out both of their throats. The last turned and was moving back to the river. It took three steps before Naam paralyzed it. Still wary of the spine, I stepped around and took out its throat.

"That was fun, but smelly," Naam said. "I know you don't like seafood, but would you like to take home a fillet? If you give me your knife, I can also whip up a sushi plate."

"God, that's just wrong. Man-fish marinated in sewage. I don't see that showing up on a menu anywhere."

"You would then be surprised at the restaurants I have visited. This flesh is a delicacy in some places."

"I don't want to know. Well, I guess this attack was easier to deal with than the giant space laser I nearly got zapped with recently. Although it didn't smell nearly as bad as these damn things do."

"You really have enemies all over."

"Yeah, I'm the lucky guy that all the weird things want to kill."

We dragged the bodies and pushed them into the river. Somewhere downriver there was going to be a powerful stink after these things floated a day in the sun.

"You said something about these things should not be here."

"They are a northern species, and never venture this far south. Normally, the Navaratna ring would repel their presence. I suspect they were brought here to attack you. The Pearl Mother theft investigation could be the reason for the hit. Or perhaps one of your many other enemies has put out a contract."

"Yeah, and some of the fae factions that are not happy with me could have set it up."

"That is also possible. You should probably stay away from rivers for some time. Now you know why I was assigned to you. Surasak expected something would attack you."

"I appreciate his foresight. Now I'm really hot and sweaty, plus I stink like these things. Let's get out of here."

We hailed a taxi as the roads were slightly clearer. The driver grimaced so I gave him some extra bahts to ignore his nose. At the hotel, Naam went with me to my room. I packed up my small bag as I had an early flight out. We took turns in the bathroom and shower, then both slipped into bed. I would not be rude and insist she sleep on the floor, nor did I plan on the floor. We'd already established nothing was happening, so we turned in. I was restless and unable to sleep, but then I got a whiff of pheromones. I realized these were different as they were sleep pheromones. What a great idea I thought... and went to sleep.

During the night, I woke up while Naam was still asleep. We were tangled up, so I carefully slid away. Even if she said I was promised to another, apparently my subconscious still gravitated toward a beautiful body in bed. But I didn't want to awaken to her beating my ass with those batons because I was too close.

In the early morning we grabbed a quick breakfast, then she rode with me in the car with Gai and a driver. She stayed with me right up to the security area. We said goodbye, and I kissed her on the cheek and wished her well.

Finally on the plane, I had an empty feeling about the entire trip. This case was not getting solved by me, at least not anytime soon. But I had a strong feeling there was a new threat in the world and that we would see it again.

CHAPTER TEN

Amsterdam was grey and chilly, a whole different world from Bangkok. I was there just long enough to pick up the vial set from the hidden refrigerated compartment at my house, then back to Schipol to catch the Church jet. I was in Cork an hour later and walking down the street where Morrigan had recently and rudely introduced herself.

I sat in the pub where I had met Jo just a few days before. It felt like months ago since so much had happened. I never imagined that re-emerging into an active life after so many centuries would be so complicated. I suppose I craved excitement, and dammit, now I had all I could handle. Yet it was good, as I did not feel depressed or have any urge to kill humans.

I had texted the number that Morrigan had given me, with no reply. A multi-thousand-year-old Irish fairy toting a cell phone. I guess everyone had to adapt. I wondered briefly if she also watched kitten videos on her phone. The cider I had ordered went down slowly, then not at all, as it was less appealing when warm. I saw Morrigan walking up the old wooden steps but heard nothing. That was odd. Those steps usually squeaked like a pig in heat. I was thinking she was as sneaky as a bog cat. She smiled slyly as she walked up.

"Yes, and this big cat sometimes plays with mice, and that play ends when their heads get cleaved from their bodies."

"Good day, love, I see you still read minds and try to intimidate the small folk. Although I was thinking 'bog cat' rather than big cat." She stopped smiling. "Please sit so we can have a pleasant conversation. Would you like something to drink?"

"I'll take whatever is the darkest and thickest draft they have."

"A hearty brew then. He will be up in a minute with it."

"What?" She looked slightly confused.

"Ah, you thought you were the only one here able to do that. I told him what to bring up after I read your mind."

"You're just a human. You can't do that."

"You might want to take another look at me."

She still looked mad, but then closed her eyes for a second. She pushed back from the table to have room to maneuver. "What are you? You were just supposed to be some human that had picked up Danu's essence somehow."

"Well, I guess the long explanation is that I am Danu, plus an anointed Church vampire fighter, and trained as a Tsul Kalu shapeshifter. Not sure what catalog that puts me in."

"You just let me take you the other day without a fight?"

"I saw no reason to resist. Sometimes that is the better way to begin a conversation, and maybe turn it into a long-term relationship."

"I see. Maybe, just maybe, I underestimated you. Odin said you were more dangerous than you looked, but I thought he was just goading me."

"Regardless of all that, you are a beautiful woman with a dangerous reputation. And I have brought you a gift. All I would like in return is a pleasant conversation."

"What impresses you most, my beauty or my reputation?"

"Many women can be beautiful. But none are as dangerous as you, I think. Dangerous is impressive."

"Well spoken. Now, ply me with your gift."

I placed the small black box on the table and opened it to show her the refrigerated vials. She looked thoughtful, and it looked good on her, compared to the "I'm mad and want to boil you alive" look.

"This vial is to be injected into the bloodstream. The second larger vial is a little more problematic as it goes directly into the colon. This third vial is the real problem, because of logistics and keeping it fresh. It contains fresh blood and saliva, which goes directly into the mouth. Placing all three simultaneously into a subject gives them the essence of Danu, both in DNA and in the microbiome. You know, that stuff living in your guts. Afterward, the subject has enhanced physical skills, with extremely fast healing capability, and a two-thousand-year lifespan. Two caveats with this treatment. First, females become self-fertile. Second, I can't predict what other effects it may have on those of your people if they already have residual Danu DNA."

"What do you mean by self-fertile? Women don't need a man to reproduce?"

"Exactly. If they don't want to get pregnant, they should stay on birth control, and at a high dose. Otherwise, lots of little ones that look just like mama, as they are a type of clone, although I hate to use that designation. The offspring are just children with a lot of the mother's DNA, not anything like a true physical and mental clone."

"You have aroused my interest with this unusual gift. I cannot decide whether the fertility component is a feature or a glitch in the treatment. For us fae, you don't know if there are other effects?"

"No, since none of you have tried it, there is no way to know. I doubt there are serious effects, but then I never considered that females would become self-fertile either."

"I must consider who to administer this to for a test. How many of these can I get?"

"Depends on what type of agreement we come up with. Of course, if your test goes well, then you can also use that subject to produce your own essence, theoretically."

"Most tempting. You have given me much to think about. You asked for this conversation and previously mentioned a truce. So what do you hope to gain from this?"

"I hope to have a non-aggression pact between our people."

"Who are your people?"

"I have an extended family of Native American shapeshifters from a previous marriage there, as well as other allied shapeshifters. I suppose, in some sense, they are distant cousins of your people. Also, as I learn of your people, with your consent, I would also invite you and your people to learn about us."

"Do your people have other powers?"

"What I know, which is not everything, is that they are promoters of life. Where they live and work, they enrich the lives of people around them with better health, the fields become more productive, and enemies disappear, due to my people's ability to destroy them."

"They sound worthy. Back to your proposal. I can promise a truce for you on behalf of those of my people that I control. But there are always about a third of them that don't recognize my authority, as we are a dichotomous society because of our fractious origins. Some are insane, some are stubborn, while others are intelligent and calculating for their own gain. I'm sure you are aware of the reputation of the fae for being fickle."

"Yes, basically acting like humans, but with additional powers."

"Quite right. To give you fair warning, there are small groups in our realm that think that if they consume you, they will gain the essence of Danu."

"I'll try not to get eaten. Ironically, that won't do them any good. So far, the only way to transfer it is by the means I just gave you."

"Don't use that reasoning when they come for you. Just run. Or get some friends and slaughter them outright. That would make my life easier, anyway."

"I recently ran across a band of walking killer catfish in Bangkok. Sound like some of yours?"

"The size of a man, grey, with arms, legs and spines?"

"Yes."

"Disgusting things. Smelly, slow, but determined. I am surprised that were near Bangkok. They are very distant cousins of us, and I suppose I should include you in that category as well now. No contracts were let from here, at least on my authority. I cannot vouch for the other third of the fae, of course."

"Of course." I also thought that gave her a nice out. If I had an unfortunate accident, she could always claim it was from someone external to her control.

Morrigan looked out the pub window and arched her eyes. She quickly grabbed my forearm before I could ask what was wrong. There was a strange feeling of falling and darkness for a half-second, then we were sitting in green grass near a short cliff overlooking the ocean. It looked like any part of the Irish coast between Cork and Galway.

"Great place for a picnic date, but we didn't bring any food."

She sighed. "I save your life, or at least prevent a lot of unexplainable collateral damage in Cork, and all you have is dull humor."

"You also have my thanks. By the look on your face, whatever was coming was unpleasant. "

"You are welcome. Unpleasant is a mild word for what was approaching. I must hasten my announcement of our truce. I would suggest you stay away from rivers and other bodies of water for a while."

"You are the second person in a week to make that recommendation. What was coming?"

"A truly stupid thing, but most dangerous. I would describe it as a house-sized flying jellyfish with an impervious membrane. During a fight, it might flounder around and knock buildings over just trying to find its prey. Usually, it is only a threat to large fishing trawlers. Its presence here means they sent it."

"OK, a great reason for me to avoid water. Do we have a truce?"

"Yes, we do. I would like to have more vials, if you can name your price."

"Let's wait until you try the first batch and determine if it works without side effects. If so, then we can barter for more."

"You would trade with us?"

"Makes for a better relationship than a purely transactional arrangement. And you did just save me from death, or at least embarrassment."

She gave her first authentic smile since we had met. At least I thought it was authentic. She whisked us back to Cork, just outside the airport.

"Goodbye Senecus. I will test your vials and then contact you with the results. What might you think to barter for future vials?"

"Something I would enjoy is a real picnic date with you on the coast, with a conversation about your people. I am curious whether our peoples are similar enough to interact someday."

"Easily done." She looked pleased, whether with the price that favored her, or the asking of date, I wasn't sure. I had no intention of a romantic interest, but I wanted to gain her favor.

I walked away as she disappeared back to wherever the fae go. I hopped over to Manchester to meet Jo, as she had met up with her family, and now it was my turn to be introduced. Sounded like fun, similar to a root canal with minimal sedation.

Jo had gone over a day earlier to prepare everyone. I didn't know how it went but would find out soon. She picked me up at the airport and drove me to town, where one of her siblings had a house. If I had the math correct, I was about to meet at least nine adults and nearly a dozen children. Quite a gathering based on all the cars parked up front.

Jo opened the front door, and the people inside surrounded us; two brothers, two sisters, their spouses, Jo's mum, and kids ranging from three years old to the early teens. It was loud and very British, but everyone was good-natured. I had a dozen partial conversations with a dozen different people for the first fifteen minutes. Someone placed a cider in my hand and then the food commenced. They loaded two tables with food and the tradition was to grab, eat, and talk while moving around. It was a good way to socialize and ingest liquids and solids. The kids had made off with most of the sweets and were outside, with one occasionally coming inside to grab more food or solicit a bandaid.

During all the conversations and information overload, I heard that Jo was considering Isabel as a name. Although no one asked me, I approved, as I'd always thought it was a great name. I also realized little Isabel was going to get swallowed up by a host of family, including a gang of older cousins. It made me feel good.

After a busy evening, the crowd began dispersing, beginning with the ones that had the youngest children. Jo and I stayed at her brother's house, as they had spare rooms. We were going to stay together as we didn't want to arouse any suspicion. We climbed into bed and read for a few hours, then we both slept. She took me to the airport that morning to get back to Amsterdam. Jo stayed for another day to visit and probably answer another thousand questions. Now that they had met me, I was a fitting target for inquiry. At least that would give her a break from all the questions they had for her.

On the quick trip back to Amsterdam, I decided not to go back to America immediately. Seeing all Jo's family made me realize I needed to slow down and take care of business in Europe. From my Amsterdam house, I called Thomas and left a message about setting up a dinner. Anna was next, and we chatted about her new pregnancy and lots of smaller stuff. She and Kate were definitely interested in meeting up the next few days.

CHAPTER ELEVEN

Jo's trip to see her UK family was over and she was back in The Netherlands the following day, so we made plans to meet at the Cottage. I walked into the study where a fire was burning, and refreshments were on the sideboard. Jo was waiting for me with a smile. We hugged for a moment. It was warm and comforting, with no self-consciousness or hesitation from either of us, or sexual tension. We sat by the fire, with tea, for pleasant conversation.

Jo started off. "As much as it pains me to do so, I have to quit the strike team. I was just getting good at it, and it was the most fun I've had in years, maybe ever. But the risk is too great. I can get shot or hurt, then survive and heal easily enough. But what if the baby takes a hit? I assume she can heal as well, but I won't take that risk."

"I understand and agree it's not worth the risk. We just don't know enough about how all this works, and not worth the risk to find out if she's bulletproof. I assume you will be on desk duty and still working with the teams?"

"Yes, and it is important work but not as enjoyable. What are you planning to do, go back to America to keep training?"

"Something that I have just recently realized, because I am so slow, is that I should stay here a little longer before going back to America. There is a lot I don't know and have not even thought about regarding you and the baby. I also should see my friends, especially since I have not seen Anna since she found out she was expecting. So, I'm delaying my trip back to America. We need to get with my friends, our friends, and celebrate you baby mamas."

"What did you call me?"

"That wonderful Americanism signifying the female of an unpartnered couple having a baby."

"You can keep that phrase to yourself in the future. Are you sure you are ready to do this? Are you comfortable coming out to your friends as a new daddy?"

"I have to do it sometime and might as well do it now. And since this is child number eleven, I have no qualms about announcing her to the world."

"OK, if you are sure."

"It will be a lively evening, but we will get through it. Who knows, maybe there will be dancing. But we should probably spend some time chatting about our cover story and plans for the future first. Especially since I have a history of embarrassing myself and others at these events."

"Yes, you do. Let's talk about it now. Then you can sit quietly during the dinner and keep everyone comfortable with your lack of vocalization."

"Very sensible."

The remainder of the day and evening went well as we drank tea, snacked, and talked about how things would go for the next few months. And a little fleshing out of our cover story. Although it no longer felt like much of a story.

The next night, I picked Jo up, and we proceeded to the same restaurant as our last outing. I had already called and gotten confirmation there would be a band and dancing that night. Jo was wearing a nice grey dress with a black cashmere stole wrapped stylishly over her shoulders, falling down her front and clasped together at her waist by her hands. It looked good and hid her bump. I was rather plainer in a dark blue wool jacket.

Thomas and Willem were already at the bar, and we met them and did all the hugging an air kissing an inch from the cheeks as required. Thomas was also stylishly dressed, with Willem a little plainer. I thought the theme of the night was one partner stylish and the other plain, until Kate and Anna arrived, and both were stylish and stunning. It was then I realized that Willem and I just did not have the style gene. I could not resist, so I whispered loudly to Willem said, "Don't you just hate it when everyone is more stylish than you?"

Everyone was standing in the bar and doing a fresh round of hugs and the trios of air kisses. During all that time, Jo did an excellent job keeping the stole across her middle and camouflaging her bump. We went to the table as it was ready and settled in. We ordered a fresh round of drinks and water, as well as a bottle of wine to start dinner. Anna and Jo declined the wine when poured.

We rapidly moved from all the talk about our recent lives to Anna's new pregnancy. Jo and I had questions for Anna. Everything was progressing well, and Anna showed us her brand-new ultrasound photo. Appetizers arrived and Thomas got around to asking me for my status.

"Sen, what's your news?" Thomas asked. "You said you had new things going on."

"I'm going to pause before answering that question, just for dramatic effect."

Jo pushed back from the table slightly as she draped her stole on the back of her chair and left her middle uncovered. It took a moment, but Anna was the first to do a double take, then Kate noticed. Then they traded glances with each other, then both looked at me. I just gave them a sly smile and said nothing. The look on their faces was priceless, and I couldn't tell which one was going to burst out with the first question. But I was wrong. They were playing the long game and stayed quiet. Thomas and Willem didn't even notice anything unusual. Kate and Anna sat quietly, and then Kate asked me, "Yes, Sen, what is new in your life?"

"Enough with the drama. What have you been up to?" Thomas asked.

We all burst into laughter, except Thomas and Willem, who looked at each other bewildered.

"What is so funny? What did I miss?" Thomas asked.

I reached over and grabbed Jo's hand. "My dear, would you like to enlighten this poor man?"

"Oh Sen, don't be so modest." Then she surprised me by reaching into her bag and pulling out a handful of cigars, passing them around the table. Thomas still did not know what was happening, but now Willem was looking speculatively at Jo. Then he smiled.

I leaned over and put my arm around the clueless Thomas. "My friend, I'm going to be a father."

"What? When? With whom?"

At that point, the entire table erupted into a belly laugh. Thomas finally glanced over at Jo. Sitting made the bump more prominent. Thomas turned red, then nearly yelled with delight, grabbing me in a bear hug. "Why didn't you tell me? This is great news."

The table fell into an excited confusion of chatter as questions and congratulations came in from everyone at once. Jo was getting new hugs from Anna and Kate. Everything was going well, and for once, I would not ruin it.

"Sen, give us some history here, and your plans." Thomas said. The table quieted down.

"Well, Jo and I are working out lots of details, as you might imagine. Typically, my mouth outruns my brain. But tonight, I am not getting drug outside by you Thomas, 'for a smoke' that we have never actually accomplished. I have been to this rodeo before and gotten thrown off and gored by the bull. For that reason, I am going to shut the hell up and sit here while Jo, the star of this show, gives you guys the details and answers questions."

Everybody turned to Jo, and she was not shy about giving me a dirty look. Yeah, I'd pay for this, probably later tonight. But she should have expected it, as I had already told her she needed to provide the story, and I'd support whatever she said.

"Sen and I had a sort of holiday in Finland a while back. It was obviously an enjoyable time together, with a rather unexpected but wonderful result. He has been in America for a while, so when I found out I was pregnant, I wanted to wait and tell him in person, but crazy things kept happening to delay that opportunity. But I finally got to surprise him."

"And were you surprised?" Kate asked. Everyone laughed at that.

"Oh, you have no idea. And now I am extremely happy. Which puts me back over here much more, even though Jo and I remain quite busy with work, and now planning for a baby."

Kate was first up. "Do you have plans yet on your... logistics, or have you had time to work that out?"

I looked at Jo, but she motioned me to respond. "We are still working on details. What I can tell you is that I will be an active father, so I already know I'll be back here, probably living in Woerden. It's a good place for kids."

"Kids as in plural?" Anna asked. She looked both at me and Jo when she said that. I then returned the favor and motioned for Jo to answer.

"To be honest, I don't know. This is all unexpected, even more so for Sen. We will work out the details, as he said. I had just started traveling extensively for work, but I'll now be postponing that. My residence choices will be Italy, because of work, here in the Netherlands, or the UK, since it is my original home. But I think it makes more sense to be here with this baby. I do not know about more babies, and Sen and I have not even talked about it."

Kate and Anna were looking uncomfortable as the answer unfolded, but then looked pleased at the end. Thomas was still too surprised to ask anything, and Willem, ever the sensible one, remained quiet.

I fended off any more questions. "OK guys, that was our news. Stay tuned for the details to come. Meanwhile, since I have not been out in a while, what else is happening with everyone?" Willem was next with his news. His company, large and privately held, was going public. He stood to make quite a bundle if the stock offering went well. Then, even more surprising, he announced he was moving in with Thomas. They were keeping both apartments for now, but he would spend more time with Thomas in Amsterdam, especially with his increased workload coming up. It was quite an exciting evening, with two pregnancies and a move-in. Dinner arrived and provided another break in the conversation. Predictably, the conversations diverged between the men talking about boring business happenings and the woman talking about maternity happenings.

At one point, after Willem had gotten up for a moment, Thomas leaned over so no one else could hear and said, "I know you well enough that you aren't telling us nearly everything."

"You are right. There is a lot more. Do you have a free day this week? I think it is time to tell you everything. Well, not quite everything," I said, looking at Jo.

"How about the day after tomorrow? Is that too soon? I have a slow day at the airport, other than a training meeting, which I would love to miss."

"That would be great. Let's meet at my place in Woerden for a late breakfast. This may take a few hours."

Willem arrived back at the table, and we went on to more small talk. After dinner, it was time for dancing. We moved to the next room, divided into pairs, and swapped off with each song. When it was my turn with Jo, I did not reenact our last dance. I had no intention of tossing a pregnant woman several feet in the air, or worse, letting a pregnant woman toss me several feet in the air.

I did whisper to her, "I have decided to tell Thomas most of my secrets."

"Are you sure you want to do that?" Jo asked.

"Oh, right, so there is an exception. I will not say anything about you or the baby. I don't kiss and tell."

"You'd better not. Even if kissing had no part in producing this child."

"Well, my dear, I'd be happy to ply you with kisses now. But you repel me too much, so we will just have to dance."

"I share your repulsion, sir. But dancing is nice."

Working around to everyone else as the songs changed generated the same general questions and series of quiet congratulations. Until I got to Anna. "I am so happy for you Sen. Jo seems like a great person. And I will keep your secret."

"Oh, what secret?"

"Thomas told me when you went to Finland. I have been a physician in my field for long enough to know that your timeline does not match. Don't worry, I won't say anything, but you need to work on your story. Sorry, I can see by the look on your face that you are surprised by that."

"Yes, Anna, I am surprised you caught on. But it's not what you may think."

"What do you think I think?"

"That the child is not mine, and that I don't know that."

"No, I don't think that. If you had ten children in America, you would know how everything works, and you would have a good idea if the child were yours. I think something else is going on."

"Yes, I definitely know about that topic. What would you say if I told you that the child is not mine, but sort of is? But that there is no other father involved."

"I would say that you are referring to some variation of in-vitro fertilization or parthenogenesis."

"Damn Anna, you are even smarter than the genius I thought you were."

"I can't imagine a reason for IVF. We all know that parthenogenesis is not possible for humans, theoretically. But I am betting you found a way around that."

"I will never play cards with you for money. To answer your question without giving an answer, though, is that there is indeed a workaround for every impossibility."

"Then congratulations on your daughter, Sen."

I shook my head in wonder. Anna was incredibly smart and also perceptive. Her kid would not get away with anything. The song finished, and she kissed me on the cheek. "I really am looking forward to seeing how everything turns out. Life is so much more interesting than most people realize."

"After the past two weeks, you really have no idea how right you are. Thanks, my dear."

The evening wound down, and we all left with lots if goodbyes and the wishing of well. I walked with Jo to the car, and I was quiet because I was so preoccupied in my head.

"What are you so deeply thinking about?"

"Anna figured it out."

"What?"

"About the baby."

"You mean she knows about the origin?"

"Yes."

"How in the world did that happen? You must have let something slip."

"No, I didn't. She is smart, perceptive, and possibly telepathic. I would have given a thousand-to-one odds that not even a pediatrician like her could have put that together."

"Do you think she will keep it confidential?"

"Oh yes, she will. Because of how smart and perceptive she is, she knows the stakes. Plus, on top of all those other categories, she is loyal."

"Somehow, Sen, you made good friends." She leaned over and put her head on my shoulder.

"Yeah, somehow, I did. And now they are your friends, too."

I drove Jo back to Den Haag and brought up the idea that she was welcome to come to America and spend time at the Farm or Asheville. She thanked me, but still planned to work with her team and the new leader before going anywhere. She kissed me on the cheek as we said goodnight, and I drove home.

Chapter Twelve

I spent some trying to decide when to go back to America, and how much effort I should put into trying to talk Jo into going with me. I knew her feelings about wanting to continue some contact with her strike team. Once you get that type of group assembled and running, it's hard to let go. A dire event was about to help me with persuading her, however.

After an urgent call from Michael, I drove over to the Cottage. He had a flat screen set up in the study, while he and Jo were looking at a printed report as I came in. Both appeared somber and subdued.

"Thanks for coming, Sen," Michael said. "We had an incursion at the Center a few hours ago. I wanted to you to see the footage since you've recently had some experience with this."

"Sure, I'll take a look."

Michael turned on the screen to show security footage of several rooms. The dark smoke shape came through the wall and crept through the rooms. People were in three of the rooms; as the presence entered, they appeared to go into immediate convulsions for a few seconds, then go still.

"We lost twelve good people today, plus one survivor that may not recover," Michael said. "The intruder, which we are now calling a demon, seems to overwhelm humans with fear, then robs the body of energy. I assume this is what you saw in Bangkok?"

"Yes, not sure if it is the same one, but definitely the same thing. Any idea of what it was doing at the Center?"

"Not yet. Based on its path, it did not seem to move toward anything in particular."

"Do you have any items of power or protective significance there?"

"No, those types of things are stored or studied elsewhere, not in that facility."

"What area was this, in terms of departments?"

"Two of those areas were my previous responsibility, before I moved to the strike team," Jo answered.

"I'm not sure whether this is an intuitive leap or an unfounded assumption, but I'm thinking this thing was looking for someone, rather than something." I glanced at Jo. "If it was looking for something, I'm sure the Church has much more interesting things in Rome and other places."

"Quite right, and I have to agree with your intuition," Michael said. "How are your defenses at the Farm?"

"Robust is the best word. Kal has provided the defensive capabilities, while Odin provided the offensive power. I'm also working on something to zap these demon bastards. Not sure if it will work, but it is worth a try."

"Good. Your Farm protections sound better than anything we have at the moment. Jo, I am temporarily assigning you as our liaison to Sen's group and be based in America. Beginning as soon as you and Sen work out the details."

"Do you think it might be after me?" Jo asked.

"I don't know, but the circumstantial evidence is too compelling to ignore. Regardless of whether it was seeking you, the Farm is a safer place for now. I'm also going to keep Simon there and, with Sen's permission, place a strike team there for training."

"Sounds good to me. Elias and his people would be a good choice."

"Yes, excellent idea. Do you have space for them?"

"We will make it happen. Have you got a talented scientist and engineer we can borrow as well? I could use help rigging up our anti-demon device."

"Jo, do you know of anyone at the Center that could assist?" Michael asked.

"Yes, we have a few possibilities. Sen, what did you have in mind? Would they need to be in America?"

"Right now, the idea is to try an electrostatic sprayer with metal ions, followed by an electrical discharge. But I'm betting it will end up something different from that before it's completed. I think your guys can research the concept anywhere, but I'd want them at the Farm as soon as possible once the system is ready for installation and testing. Or even before it's ready, as we can modify during testing as needed."

"OK, I can get a short list started tomorrow if the Center is running by then."

"Good. I'm also going to call Henry and see if he knows someone over there that can help with it. The faster we have prototypes, the better I'll feel, but we also need to test them. Michael, got any demon test subjects locked up we can borrow?"

"Sorry, all out of those at the moment. But containing them, if they can't be killed, might be a positive outcome of this research."

My phone rang. Jo and Michael were looking at my phone as I was, since it was glowing pink. Damn, this smacked of fairy magic. That plus the caller ID showing "Favorite Fairy" gave it away. I excused myself and went outside to answer the call.

"Hi Morrigan."

"Hello Senecus."

"Kudos for the pink glow and caller ID tag. Nice touch."

"I thought you might like that. Was your girlfriend jealous?"

"Fresh out of those right now."

"Hmm... I have a niece about your age. Nice girl if you like green hair."

"Thanks for thinking of me, but I try to handle my own dating pool."

"Oh well, your loss. When you tire of the same old mortal women, let me know. I can recommend several exciting options."

"Now that you have tried to sell me a car I don't need, how can I help you?"

"The gift you provided was given to a subject of mine. It has gone well, and I would like to try several more. I believe we may need the extra help soon."

"Why, heading off to a conquest?"

"No, we were attacked last night for the first time in centuries."

"Oh, didn't expect that. Say, would it have been a large, dark smoky thing?"

"Yes, it would. What the hell do you know about it? Did you set it on us?"

"No, not all. In fact, I'm sitting here with another group trying to figure out a way to kill it. My Church colleagues were attacked several hours ago with significant losses. My trip to Bangkok a few days ago was because the same type of thing attacked a temple there."

"Do you have a way to stop it?"

"Not yet but working on some theories. They seem to need some physical form to exist in our reality, so we are going to try hitting them with an electrostatic spray of aerosolized metal ions, then zapping them with electricity. We don't think it will hurt them, but it should distract them, maybe muck up their senses."

"I see, so you propose attaching conductive microparticles to the ephemeral portion of the being existing in our reality, then overload the creature with a current to stun or confuse it."

"I could not have said it better myself."

"I doubt you can generate enough current to accomplish your desired outcome. But... we have something that might work. We will probably have another opportunity to try this idea."

"Is it coming back for some powerful object, or for a particular person?"

"We have things that were brought with us from our origins, that are of great power and protect our people. Lucky for us, those items are not only heavily guarded but also portable and were quickly moved and hidden as this thing searched for them. But we believe it will come back for them."

"Do you know what this thing is?"

"Some idea. We have encountered them before, usually far underground. But they were never aggressive and have never even acknowledged us. This one is acting unnaturally, as if it is driven to specific goals."

"Yes, apparently a combination of master vampires and future humans has enlisted one of more of those things for their own purpose. So far, it has stolen a gem to disrupt the protective Navaratna ring in Bangkok, and now seems to be on the search for a particular person in Italy."

"That is not good news. Are they enemies of yours, this group?"

"Very much so, as they have been trying to kill me for a while."

"Then we would like to get those vials as soon as possible."

"Thanks for the vote of confidence. They have been missing their chances at me for decades, so I have confidence I can avoid them."

"Were they using these new creatures all that time?"

"No, that just started, and those creatures aren't after me yet. But I get your point. I also have measures set up to detect them. I'm going to set up my electrostatic shock system as well. If you have ideas or modifications for that, will you tell me about it?"

"Yes, consider it part of our bargain."

"Meanwhile, I can get you three more sets of vials. But I'll need a picnic lunch date to deliver them."

"A picnic is easy. Where and when?"

"I'll have the vials this afternoon. Meet me in Amsterdam, Vondel park, at 2 pm?"

"I look forward to it."

"See you then, my favorite fairy."

I went back inside as Jo and Michael gave me questioning looks. "Just my cousin Morrigan. We have a meeting later today, so I'll need to leave soon. But of interest to our conversation, they were just attacked by that same thing, seeking objects of power. She wouldn't tell me what the objects were, but I think I could guess."

"A spear, a sword, a cauldron, and a stone, or some representation of those things," Jo said.

"That would be my guess. She mentioned those things protect her people, so sounds like the Bangkok situation."

"This is a widespread attack on objects of power that provide protection, probably from natural disasters," Michael said. "At the same time, we know the other side has been working to cause natural disasters, tying these operations together. That gives us two ways to narrow the search for future attacks; either the objects themselves or the places where nature is tipping over into disaster."

"Yeah, I'd say your group in Rome, and melting glaciers are two obvious places."

"I'll go start the warnings and searches. Jo, please continue with Sen on the American plan. I don't want to rush you, but I'd feel better if you were off the continent as soon as possible."

"No worries then, just the bum's rush out of Europe," Jo said in a sarcastic voice. "But I agree this might be an opportune time to visit America."

Later, I picked up the small, refrigerated box at my house with three full sets of vials. I would need to produce more to keep enough stockpiled for emergencies. It was a beautiful day but still cool, so I walked to Vondel to enjoy the weather. I sat on a bench, knowing Morrigan would find me when she wanted to.

I noticed her from a distance. Long pink hair, a too-short sundress that was a few weeks premature considering the temperature and riding a bicycle with a large picnic basket on back. Very Dutch, very pretty, and, for a moment, my thoughts were very inappropriate. I suspected that was the effect she was aiming for. She parked the bike and plopped beside me.

"You are looking very Dutch today, but the dress may be a bit optimistic for this time of year," I said.

"I don't get cold, so the ride was briskly refreshing, especially with no underthings on."

"I really didn't need to know that."

"Didn't you?"

"Nice bike, though," I said, changing the subject. "Got a live chicken in the basket?"

"Oh no, that would be so peasantly. Instead, I have wine, fruit, cheese, and other goodies. Here, you take the bottle and pour us a glass while I set out the bounty."

We sat and enjoyed a few moments together while watching the very early spring crowd parade through the park. Morrigan got more than a few looks. She seemed to enjoy the attention.

"You fit in very well here."

"It's nice to get out of Ireland occasionally and sit in the sun. It's a welcome change, as we normally stay out of sight. Even when we are up and about, Ireland might be even cloudier than Holland."

"Do you visit America often?"

"Rarely. It is difficult for us to go there. We have a few that can travel there, but for reasons very ancient, it is not comfortable for many of us."

"Is it something to do with the old boundaries the Makers made for the First Peoples?"

"I'm surprised you know of that. But yes, that is part of it. Plus, we have less control there, and enemies are harder to detect."

"Are you the descendants of a group of First Peoples?"

"Close enough. Some Makers interbred with a group of First People, and we are their offspring. When discovered by other Makers, my people were banished and cut off from all contact with the Makers. Some Makers were upset about that decision and smuggled some of their technology to us."

"You have the long life of the First Peoples and the technology of the Makers?"

"We do have long life, yes, but I must admit it is tempered with poor wisdom. And the gifts of technology have been useful but limited. Otherwise, the Makers allied against us would have tracked those items and confiscated them. Although now the smoke demon is trying to take even those."

There was a disgusting smell on the breeze, and unfortunately it was familiar. Morrigan looked at me as she put our meal back in the basket. "I believe some of your friends are here."

"Yeah, I see them. My favorite catfish. Can you zap us out of here?"

She closed her eyes, then opened them in surprise. "I can't. They are suppressing me somehow."

"Well, can you just get us a little farther out, away from all these mortals?"

"Yes, just barely."

A second later, we were on the fringe of the old Olympic Park area, just west of Vondel Park. "It seems I have just enough power to hop us short distances. Oh damn, here come our enemies again."

"Can you get us to Woerden? I have weapons there."

"I don't know where that is. Show me."

"How?"

"Come here and kiss me, while you concentrate on where we are going." I grabbed her and kissed her hard while thinking of my apartment. We landed in a small canal in a pasture full of dairy cows, somewhere between Amsterdam and Woerden.

"Am I that distracting, or did you sneeze while blinking us away?" I asked.

Morrigan was very unhappy and sputtering curses until I kissed her again. We plopped into my apartment, soaking wet and on my sofa. I ran to my hidden armory while tossing Morrigan a towel. I put the box of vials on the table until we could take care of our man-fish problem. Twenty seconds later, I had several items I thought would prove useful in our upcoming fight. Two swords, my battle-axe, and two pistols. She scoffed at the guns and grabbed a sword.

"Can you take us just a short distance out into the wildlife reserve?"

"Yes, but you'll have to -"

I grabbed and kissed her again. We landed in a green field, near woods, underbrush, and a large lake. A pheasant skittered off into the woods. The area was mostly empty of people other than some distant hikers.

"I wanted to be out of town and in the open when these things show up. They will show up, won't they?"

"Yes, they will. As we left Amsterdam, I felt their master. He's an old adversary and well versed on following me through the links."

Right on time, eight of those catfish things showed up, along with a good-looking man.

"Ah, this is great, a two-for-one slaughter event," he yelled. "This will be a glorious day. They will write poems and sing songs about me after this victory." He was garishly dressed and wearing sunglasses.

I looked over at Morrigan. "Let me guess, this is a spurned boyfriend, or one of those people you have no influence over?"

"Lucky guess, as he is both," she answered.

"At least he is humble."

"Be wary, he is dangerous. You make sushi, I'll deal with him."

"Beautiful, dangerous, and funny. Got it going on, Morr." She flashed me a mean grin and went after the posh dude.

CHAPTER THIRTEEN

U sing what I learned when fighting these things in Bangkok, I knew I just had to be fast and slashy. Just for fun, I shot one several times, including the general area of the head. It slowed but kept coming. OK, back to the sword and axe. I floated quickly past each before they could close on me, whacking their gill slits with axe or sword. It took a few minutes, but I was never in real danger as they were just too slow. I had some time to watch Morrigan and her buddy. I realized the fish were just a distraction for the guy to sneak in behind and kill us.

They kept flashing in and out of existence around each other, trying to anticipate each other's appearances. It would have been entertaining if they weren't trying to kill each other. Morrigan got lucky as she spun low and arced the sword around and behind her, just as he flashed into existence, and he took the sharp edge across his right thigh. He disappeared immediately.

"Almost got your jewels that time, Oggie."

He appeared behind her and stabbed her with the large knife he was carrying. She took it in the right shoulder blade as she was already twisting away from him. They both disappeared as he yelled, "Nearly got your heart, but you don't have one."

The last fishhead was down, so I tried an experiment and closed my eyes. I could see a slight glowing outline of both of them, even though they were not visible to my eyes. As the guy moved into position behind Morrigan again, just as they both flashed into existence, I shot within an inch of Morrigan's head and through the guy's left eye. He dropped as Morrigan stared at me.

"You can see us, even out of phase?"

"Yep. But just discovered that, or I would have offed him before he stuck you. But he's not dead, is he?"

"No, it will take more than that to finish him. But he will be out of the fight for some hours. Plenty of time for me to take him back to my dungeon where I will play with him for a while. But where are my manners? Meet Ogma. If he were conscious, he would sing his own song. As he has many times, including some ballads, about our lovemaking."

"I guess that would be the ballad of Mor-Oggie?"

She gave me a dark look. "No, he was not that clever."

"Isn't he sort of related to you by marriage?"

"We are not a numerous people. At my age, just about everyone has been my boyfriend or girlfriend at least once."

"Oh, right."

"That is why fresh meat like you will be welcomed in our realm. I predict at least three centuries of rutting awaits you. Five centuries if you count the men."

"Well, that is tempting, but it might have to wait for a time. World to save and all that, you know."

"Now, who is the humble one?"

"Right, so no world saving. Just a little piece of it, with a group of people that like me for some strange reason."

"Your new expectations are more reasonable."

"How about you zap these fishies into the lake, take care of one-eyed Og, then go back to my place for a shower?"

"Thought you'd never ask."

She zapped the fish into the lake and then zapped Og back to her lair. When she returned, I grabbed and kissed her, then we were back in my apartment. Morrigan ripped off the rest of the dress and stood naked as she asked me to dispose of it. Then she padded off to the shower. She came out naked, of course, and I gave her sweatpants and a T-shirt, as it was all I had that was fairly close to fitting her size. She made them look good.

"Thank you for the clothes, but we need to work on your sense of style."

"A dollar for every time I've heard that," I said, as I kissed her on the cheek. "I really did not have to kiss you for us to teleport together, did I? We could just have touched hands or stood together."

"You are right. But I found it humorous. If you already knew that, why did you keep kissing me?"

"I found it humorous. And because we are cousins, after all. That's what we do with cousins in America," I said sarcastically.

"The same with the fae," she said, but seriously.

I gave her the vials, and she blinked away. It had been quite a day. I showered and dropped in my chair to figure out how my life had been hijacked by all kinds of things I had not even dreamt of a year ago.

Thomas arrived just after nine the next morning. I had some food ready, eggs and various breads and spreads, butter and jam. And lots of coffee. We'd need it for the conversation about to start.

"Thomas, I know what I'm going to tell you sounds insane, because it is my life, and it seems crazy even to me. But I can show you enough to prove my point."

"Like that illustration in the book you gave me. It really looks like you."

"It is me and my wife in America. And although it was two centuries ago, it was a recent chapter in my life. Oh, are you squeamish?"

"Not really. Why?"

I picked up a sharp knife from the counter and jabbed it through my hand with a loud "ouch."

"What the hell are you doing?"

"It's OK. It will be healed by the time we finish talking. I just need to show you how it is possible that what I am telling you is real. I will wrap a towel around this to keep the blood off everything."

"Are you crazy? That will take days to heal, even longer if it gets infected."

"True, for most people. For me, about two hours. It is part of how I have stayed alive for so long, which is much longer than two centuries. Let's take a quick walk out to the kerkplein. Oh, see this? It has stopped bleeding already."

"Amazing. Then what, the skin heals and everything is OK?"

"Mostly. There will be a pink scar shortly, then that will disappear tonight. It will be sore for a few hours, as nerves take a little longer to heal up."

We walked down and out to the kerkplein, the open square between my building and the old church. The Dutch Reformation turned it into the old town hall, and now it was mostly ornamental.

"You have been here before for Saturday markets and Christmas. You remember these large grey stones set in the cobblestones?"

"Yes, it marks the boundary of the old Roman garrison in Woerden. The old church tower over there is built from stones from that garrison."

"Yes, and that is one reason I still keep a place here. This was once my station when I was a Roman legionnaire, back before all this crazy stuff happened to me. Yes, that makes me nearly eighteen-hundred years old. Now, before you call me insane, let's go back in to look at some things."

We went upstairs, and I opened my secret vault. "These are weapons I have used and collected over the years. That gladius there is not my original Roman sword, which I lost in the river, but one I found and restored it some years later."

"Is that a stack of gold coins?"

"Oh, yeah, I forgot I had brought those up. I owe my computer guy a payment since our arrangement is that I pay in bullion. Safer for both of us that way, as not everything we do is entirely legal. Sometimes you have to break the rules to chase the rule breakers. Oh, look at my hand, the wound has turned into scar tissue already."

"That is amazing," Thomas asked as he looked at my hand. "So, are these weapons things you once used?"

"Yes. Some back in ancient times, a few in the Middle Ages, including the crusades. Those muskets were from the French invasion of Holland. Those other items are from my first days in America. That last set is from World War II, when I fought with the resistance against the Nazis."

Thomas had been mostly quiet since breakfast. It was a lot to take in. We sat in the living room and continued the history lesson. "I was a regular guy and decent Roman soldier in the Woerden garrison until one night around 300 AD. Then a serious vampire plague swept through this region. The representatives of the early Church anointed and inoculated the soldiers that had not caught the plague yet. Details are not important, but that not only gave us protection from the vampire virus but also enhanced physical powers to fight off the vampire hordes. And those vampires were not like what you see in the movies, but more of a rabid dog crossed with a fast zombie type of creature. Unfortunately for me, as I got hit with the inoculation, I fell off my guard post and into the river. This is where it gets even weirder. I fell onto what I thought was a large fish that I ended up killing. Now I've found out that it was an essence of the river goddess Danu, the same one the Danube River was named after. Apparently, I ingested and absorbed a lot of her DNA. That, plus the inoculation, turned me into what I am."

"Yeah, that is incredibly weird," cracked Thomas.

"Anyway, apparently the combination of those two things resulted in my long life, mostly through my self-healing ability, and I also got enhanced strength and quickness. I kicked about here for a few centuries, traveled some, and eventually settled back here in The Netherlands. I spend some time in America since, during one of those trips in colonial times, I started a family over there that I am still involved with. That is my short story."

"Unbelievable. And you are living in Woerden and Amsterdam like a regular person. It's an incredible story."

"I know. And I mostly am a regular person. It's just hard for me to die, although I am aging, but much slower than most humans."

"My god, you are like that movie character, the Scottish fellow that could not die unless his head was cut off. I remember that because they dressed Sean Connery like a Spanish conquistador."

"Yeah, I saw that one too. Superficially similar, but it does not pertain to my condition otherwise. My situation seems to be unique according to my research, but there are others that also live for extended times for different reasons. This past year, I've met several."

"Oh, that makes sense. That is why you are working with the Church now. I suppose they do have others like you."

"Not exactly like me, but close enough. And chasing some bad things has brought me into a realm of crazy things that I didn't know existed two years ago."

"And now you have old weapons, a secret room, and lots of gold. OK, I suppose I believe you. Where are you going with all of this?"

"I have become involved in efforts to oppose a group of less savory but powerful characters that seem intent on either running things or ending things. That introduced an element of danger in my life, and some creatures have lately been trying to end me. Obviously, they have been unsuccessful so far. The Church alliance, plus some other beings I've run across, have become allies. My biggest fear now is that people around me are in danger."

"What do you mean?"

"Last year, in a way that indirectly ties to me, but probably more a result of her Church work, Jo was shot."

"Yes, I remember you telling me, and that you saved her. Wait, just a moment. How did you save her?"

"Ah, you remember. The only way to save her life was to turn her into what I am."

"You can do that? What, did you bite her?"

"No, not at all. I'm the anti-vampire type. No biting, but I had to inject her with some things extracted from me, and viola, she recovered."

"She is now like you, basically immortal and all that?"

"Yes."

"Amazing."

"Yeah, it is, but still science, but tied up in some bizarre realities I used to call mythology."

"You should sell this stuff. Everyone will want what you have."

"Yes, that is the problem. Think of some recent and current politicians and oligarchs that would benefit from this. Enormous market for the Hitlers and Stalin's of the world."

"Oh my, that is bad."

"Yeah. What I would prefer to do is quietly put this out there in a very limited way. Scientists at the Church are trying to figure out how to turn this into a treatment to keep people disease-free, while not extending their lives by two thousand years."

"Well, good luck with that. If all that is needed is extracts from your body, then I guess you are a massive target for anyone that finds out."

"Exactly. And the same for Jo."

"Oh no, that's not good. And your child?"

"The same problem. All good reasons to keep this quiet. But I'm tired of living with secrets. I have a long history of withdrawing from society, killing humans, and keeping secrets. That led to depression and dark thoughts and actions. I have vowed to stop doing all of that. I'm already feeling healthier than I have in a long time."

"I am a good therapist, as you are finding out. I just find all this hard to believe. It may take me some time to digest everything."

"I know it's overwhelming. As you know, I had told you some things, and over time, I would have revealed everything."

"But now you've told me everything. Why? Is there something wrong?"

"Not much more than usual. But I have picked up a lot more threats lately, although nothing I can't handle. Mentally, however, I have to unload this stuff out of my head. I have too many things going on, from work, to impending fatherhood, and training my family in America to fight the bad guys. I felt I just had to talk, and unfortunately, you are the one I know best."

"Thanks for confiding in me. I guess you and Jo will be a couple now and raise your child, all while trying to be normal?"

"I would love that scenario, but once again, it's more complicated than that. Jo and I can't be a proper couple, because we discovered that when I changed her, our DNA is now too similar, and our bodies reject each other. This child is perfectly fine, however. Have you heard of couples that have problems because their Rh factors are not compatible?"

"Yes, I heard about that from Anna recently. She was helping a couple work through that."

"Right. Well, Jo and I have the same type of problem now, times ten, but our daughter is fine. We will stay close together and raise this child, but for now we won't be more than parents."

"I'm so sorry. I just assumed you two were a couple, especially with a baby on the way."

"I once thought it might be possible, too. But we are good with each other and resolved to what we have."

"Huh, I just realized something."

"What's that?"

"My buddy is a superhero." He laughed at his own joke as I joined in.

"Well, not exactly. More of a guardian angel, with not much angel left."

Thomas left after more jokes and banter. He had taken things better than I had expected.

I talked to Jo on the phone the next morning to start planning the America trip. She would need some time to reconfigure her team and get ready for an extended trip. Tentatively, we'd leave in two days. That would give me time to run a few errands as well.

I had stayed in Woerden as I had gotten a ping from Monk and needed to look at his report. It was only about a week since my request, although it felt like several weeks. I called Monk and asked to meet. We decided on Harmelen, a small village nearby. Possibly because it had an ice cream shop near the old church in the town center.

I rode my bike over, so I could ride past the wetlands and low fields to see all the waterfowl gathered. It was rapidly moving toward mating season, so the lakes and ditch canals and fields were full of all shapes, colors, and sizes of birds. In town, I parked my bike and set on a bench by the church, and watched Monk walk up.

"I gathered all the legal data, then all the illegal data, and sorted it in multiple formats," Monk said. "I applied the predator algorithms, then trained them further to look for what you asked."

"Sounds promising. What did you find?"

"Not much, so you will not like it. Based on the parameters of this project, there simply was not enough good data to draw conclusions about individual or group predators in specific locations. There were general patterns in several states, enough to that suggest something is happening. But without more and better data, I cannot give you a strong positive outcome for this model."

"Well, that is disappointing, but I know you did the best you could, and nobody could exceed that."

"Of course. And that is why I found you something specific. It just was not exactly what you asked for."

"I knew you were sandbagging me. What have you got?"

"I'm not sure what bags of sand have to do with this. However, I took the data and model and expanded it. I rolled another four decades of old data, expanded the age range, and added male disappearances as well. The algorithms were well trained and quickly spotted an anomaly. You have a super predator that had been active for decades in Minnesota. I can pinpoint the center of activity much finer than that if you are interested in that outcome."

"I am. It may not be exactly what I hoped for, but it is an activity that must be stopped. This goes back forty years?"

"Based on our previous work, where you've asked me to go back many centuries, I thought you might ask that. American records are weak, but I can establish that this predation has occurred since 1870. The prior records are too incomplete to give any definite activity before that time. Interestingly, the activity increased the past month, making it easier for the program to spot."

"Great work. This is definitely something of interest. Hopefully, in the next decade, there will be enough data to rerun that first model."

"It will be simple to do and take less than a day once I hack all the new databases."

"This second model. Will it work anywhere? For example, I'm thinking about here in Europe."

"Yes, with the right data to input, I believe you can use it almost anywhere."

"That is great. Over the next few weeks, can you start it for all of Europe, then throw in Russia and the Middle East?"

"Europe and Russia, I can promise, as I know their databases and security protocols. The Middle East will take much longer, as I need to work through each country, which will be slow. I could speed that up considerably by hacking Israeli systems, but that could cause problems. I'm too young and good-looking to go into permanent hiding. Oh, especially now that I'm rich, thank you for that. I'm thinking of moving to Laren and dating actresses."

"Oh, OK, that is a lot to unload. Yes, stay away from the Israelis, and rethink the actress thing. Perhaps you should aim higher. Won't the Princesses be of dating age soon? Or some of their cousins in other countries?"

"Probably too young for me, but I like the way you think. I must research and consider the options of marrying into royalty. They no longer have political power, but they still retain extensive business and property holdings."

"There you go. Yes, you do that. You can invite me to the spring ball if things work out."

"Of course. I will also invite you to the wedding."

I pedaled home the long way, as I was thinking about how to invade Minnesota. I would brief Michael before going to America, as he might need time to get some teams together. Although it seemed we would have considerable firepower at the Farm in another week. It was time to go back to America to deal with a genuine threat, if Monk's analysis was good.

Chapter Fourteen

J o and I flew back to America together. I was trying not to be too obvious about not letting her out of my sight. I also had time to think about our return to the Farm. Jo's condition should get the rumor mill going, but it would be good to have her around for a while. I had called a few days earlier to let Henry know we had several long-term guests arriving soon, and at least one of them needed decent quarters. He made a snide remark about me finally getting a date as he hung up. Hah, I looked forward to seeing his face when Jo and I arrived.

In Asheville, I took Jo to my house so we could clean up and spend a restful first night in full comfort. We went back out to forage for food. I realized quickly that I was doting on her, and she was chafing at my attention, so I backed off. We had an enjoyable meal and a pleasant evening afterward. I felt better staying at the house for the night rather that going straight to the Farm. I did not verbalize it, but I also felt better about moving around, not staying in one place too often. The smoke demons did not seem smart enough to anticipate human mobility, at least not yet.

At the Farm the next morning, we got the usual small greeting party, then people, mostly women, started noticing Jo's new physique. A minute later we were mobbed by the crowd, since they always were a subdued bunch. Henry and all his guys put bear hugs on me in succession as the younger ones were slapping me on the back.

"Guess you finally got that date," Henry whispered.

"In a convoluted way, I guess I did," I answered.

Then the crowd migrated, as all the women hugging Jo came after me, while the men went to greet Jo. The rest of the day was spent buzzing at the news, while I found a spare rune amulet and put it around Jo's neck.

The next day was back to business. We turned off the einherjar exercise for the full day and everyone moved to the large barn for my announcement.

"I want to take everyone to Minnesota and set up a short surveillance operation. Although we have not confirmed this is a master vampire, Michael will send his teams as well. This becomes an exercise if there is no master vampire. If there is a master vamp, then we will integrate into those teams. If it is too risky, we will pull back into secondary containment or support. I will print out the evidence that Monk the IT guy has provided later in this afternoon.

"But before we start that long ride, I'd like to take everyone for another spa day at Biltmore. Again, if you don't do spas, then go horseback rising or skeet shooting. Afterward we'll go visit the ancestor's cave west of Biltmore." I intended to give everyone a break from the Farm drills and einherjar attacks before we left.

Afterward, I called Michael to get any updates on the Minnesota excursion, and he told me Elias and his teams were already driving our direction. We were about to get crowded, so I ordered some large double walled tents just in case we needed storage, or to have extra covered space to move people around.

Next up was a Kal visit. I sent out a mental message, and he showed up ten minutes later.

"That was fast," I said.

"I was considering visiting anyhow now that you are back, so this was an opportune time," Kal said.

"Good. Kal, I have some video to show you of an entity that has become a problem, attacking a site in Bangkok, robbing the city of its protective barrier. It then attacked the Church Center in Italy and the fae realm. I need to know two things, if this is in your jurisdiction. Can your sensors detect this thing, or can we change them to do so? Also, any idea how we can repel this thing or fight it?"

Kal watched the few seconds of footage. "I will need to consult with someone that has more knowledge than I do. You may remember I mentioned you should meet an entity on the plane some time back. I believe the answer to your first question is yes, but I don't know the answer to your second question. There should be some remedy to contain or repel it."

"Michael also advised me to ask you to introduce me to someone I have been calling Smokey. Apparently, he has been around since the dinosaurs and looks like black smoke, so I assume it is the Ascended being you mentioned. Also, the description sounds similar to this thing on the video. What prompted Michael's recommendation is that we were nearly zapped by a giant space laser recently."

"Yes, it is time the same being and is time for that introduction, for the reasons you mentioned, plus others, including this video. When it happens may be problematic, as he is not on earth. Although once communication reaches him, he will respond. You are traveling soon?"

"Just to Minnesota for what I hope is only a week or less. Will that be time enough to set something up?"

"Yes. But meanwhile, I will ensure the sensor network is adequate to detect this entity. Your people also need to know of this, and not to approach it, if it shows up here."

"Will the einherjar have any effect on it if it shows up?"

"They will distract it, and they will not die like humans do when approaching it. But they cannot harm it."

"OK, but they can distract it long enough to give us adequate time to escape?"

"That would be the best course of action for now. I will also inform Odin of this recent development, so his soldiers are prepared."

"Thanks."

Kal disappeared, and I wandered out to find Jo.

She looked up as I found her sitting on a log and watching Stacey, Melissa, and John Henry playing football with Em, El, Jimmy, and Ned. It was good to see them enjoying some free time. "If you ask me how I'm doing again, I'm going to open your body cavity and remove your spleen."

"Uh, OK, so that's a new alternative to small talk. But I get your point, and I'll stop doting. In that vein, I hope you fall off that log and bruise your elbow." At least she smiled.

"This place is so different from England or The Netherlands. I like it here because it is so quiet, but also because there is a purpose here. You are doing good things, Sen."

"Thanks Jo. I have been trying to do better. Helping humans rather than hunting and killing the bad ones. Getting to know my family here. I think I'm better than I used to be."

"Probably so. Just don't get too full of yourself, or I'll thrash you before I turn into a pumpkin."

"Yeah, before too long, I can push you over and watch you roll down the hill." She pushed me off the log.

Elias and team had arrived at the Farm per Michael's instruction. I recognized several from the Arizona operation when I greeted them. He saw Jo and may have made a few snide comments about my family situation. I may have responded with additional smartass comments, mostly concerning his choices in farm animals. We were good, as always.

I was considering having the einherjar come in for an attack to give Elias' people a workout, but I had to check to see if there were enough rune amulets. Henry came by with a worried look, and soon I had other things to consider besides a training attack.

"Boss, maybe we should not do this."

"What do you mean?"

"That is dangerous country up there. Nothing good happens in that place."

"OK but give me more. What is giving you such a fit?"

"If you take all of eastern Siberia and all of North America, the one place we lost the most people was in that Minnesota territory. It was OK for us only when it was covered by a mile of ice and big frozen lakes. Hard to explain. It's just bad country."

"Any idea why that is?"

"You ever heard of talking rocks?"

"Not exactly. But I have recently been hearing about sentient crystals. Earth is supposed to have some big ones down deep, and they are organized enough to sling an asteroid at Mars in retaliation for one that hit earth. When I was in Thailand, they had a ring of mostly crystal gems that they said were sentient, providing a protective barrier around the city of Bangkok. So, talking rocks makes sense."

"Yeah, that sounds right, and just because something is sentient, and talks does not mean it is nice. The things up there are not nice. You remember that feeling in Moffett when the Great Serpents were near?"

"Yes, a general feeling, like something unpleasant, strange, or oppressive."

"My people strongly feel the same way up there. Not intense at first but gets worse the longer we stay. If we stick around after that, something bad happens."

"What kind of bad?"

"Could be storms, ambushes, nearly anything. Whatever is there, it seems to detect and react to my people more than humans. We can't even get on the water up there. Freak storms, rogue waves, just bad times. Lots of stories about monsters coming out of the earth, woods, and water. Kal's people also have stories and don't normally live there."

"Henry, you are making me reconsider taking our people on this trip. And you think this all goes back to the rocks?"

"I know there are big crystals, putting out waves of bad thoughts. Might even be using water to focus it more. If the resonance it right, could vibrate the water and form a type of lens. And the Great Lakes are pretty damn big. Lots of negative resonance coming up and out of there."

"That sounds like a reasonable and terrifying hypothesis. I'm also thinking about what that means for the larger picture. The lava events in India or Siberia that caused widespread extinctions might have been a way to regulate biologicals on the surface. Plus, that activity could produce more crystals. Puts volcanoes, earthquakes, ocean disturbances, ice ages, and global warming cycles in a whole new light."

"Yep, especially if that could be manipulated by some of our enemies. If the Sky Lords are doing all that time traveling, they could have opportunity to work on those crystals, maybe."

"What worries me right now is if our shifters will get the rock's attention."

"If we go there with our shifters, our welcome might be unfriendly. If we're hunting a master vampire, one in touch with the Sky Lords, things could get ugly to the point of getting a bunch of us killed."

"You can feel the animosity, and can tell if it's building up?"

"Yes."

"If we went as a group, how long could we stay?"

"Two days at the most is my best guess. Also depends on if those crystals are sleeping, or already riled up about something else."

"Do you think it's possible, priming those rocks?"

"Could be, if the other side has figured out something? Or get them smoke demons to piss them off before we get there."

"You think it's a coincidence that a master vampire is operating out of the middle of that area, and we just found out?"

"Nope, I do not. It's not a coincidence that we found him."

"Trap?"

"You betcha."

"Damn. OK, I'm going to check in with Kal, then let's meet up with Elias and start figuring this out."

"Sure thing. But if this is a go, we need a fast way out."

"We can definitely set that up."

I had a thought about trying to use the crystals to our advantage somehow, talk them over to our side. But I had no idea how to communicate or interact with something like that. A brief chat with Kal ended up giving me much of what Henry had already told me. This operation would not be easy.

I went to find Elias. He was joking with Jo and talking shop about a previous operation. I joined them and started telling Elias about Henry's unique perspective on what we were likely facing. His questions were thorough, so I quickly called Henry over to provide the original story. I could tell Elias was rethinking his initial strategy. He also was giving Henry even more respect, which was nearly impossible, as Elias had looked up to him ever since the Arizona operation. I was also rethinking our involvement and planned to dial back having any of our people on the front lines. Jo was looking less happy by the minute. She now had plenty of experience to know how badly this operation could go.

After Henry finished, I summarized what I had dealt with in Thailand. Sentient crystals were a real possibility, and we were heading to an area teeming with unfriendly rocks. I told them about my chat with Kal, which agreed with Henry's assessment, plus that Kal's people also avoided Minnesota and other places around the Great Lakes.

"This information is speculative, but important. The entire area is a nexus of negative power. It goes back to unfriendly sentient crystals of incredible age. Something about the Great Lakes also seems to focus on that negativity. Through conversations with Henry and Kal, it seems unlikely this master vampire is here by accident. This is likely a trap, and we are going to be outnumbered and on hostile territory."

"But what do we do about that? We can't just let this thing keep killing and eating people, plus all the other things it's probably involved in," Elias said.

"I know. But we can't do business as usual here, at least not be successful and survive. And those are two of my must-haves, since I'm fond of my folks and I've grown to like yours as well."

"Yeah, I noticed. I'm thinking you are going to steal some of them for yourself, like Zena and Simon."

"Probably. You can try to take Simon back, but you will have to fight Jen first. Zena is another keeper. Besides, she likes Asheville. Have you seen her new tattoos?"

"No, but I'm getting a feeling you have. But back to business - what is the game plan here?"

"I don't have any idea yet. What do you normally do when you are after something that is stronger and faster than you, has a bigger army, and in territory that is hostile and actively working against you?"

"Walk away and send in a nuke."

"As tempting as that is for dealing with Minneapolis, especially during rush hour, I doubt your boss will approve that action."

"Yeah, he disapproves of nuclear mass murder."

"Before we get windshield time, let's come up something to get us ahead of the baddies, with lots of contingencies."

We spent hours going over different scenarios and completely reworked the initial plans. We brought in nearly everyone with experience, including Zena, Simon, and Nan. Others in Elias' group came and went as needed. We needed all the expertise we could get to survive what we were about to try.

CHAPTER FIFTEEN

We moved north in a small caravan of cars and trucks. I began the trek with Elias, Zena, and Simon, but we stopped every three hours and had people switch vehicles. Elias and I stayed together, with Zena and Simon switching out trip legs with Henry and Jo. As questions came up, we had phone conversations with those in other vehicles as well. We convened at a hotel several miles from the target building in Minnesota.

We rested, then split up to start surveillance for a few days. Small teams rotated around the area to minimize the chance of getting noticed. Long range observation started, and we occasionally sent drones up but kept them just above the trees and a mile from the target. The target building was a basic strip mall, common to America and an insult to aesthetics everywhere, on the edge of the suburbs south of Minneapolis. It looked new and had 'for lease' signs in the windows rather than any business advertising. New asphalt out front, some brick accents, frosted windows, and a flat roofline. A big garage door in back, rather than a loading dock. Ugly, American style. It was on an untraveled street with nothing it, although there was a subdivision of medium-sized homes a few hundred yards away. Less chance of collateral damage, if it came to conflict. But ever since I had first seen this place, I thought it felt wrong.

Surveillance had gotten us nowhere. Twice, a small box truck arrived, backed into the oversized garage door on back, then left after a few hours. We followed both trucks into Minneapolis parking garages, where they were found empty and abandoned and no sign of the driver. The trucks were unregistered, and obviously they were delivering something illicit to the building or playing with us. Thermal imaging of the building gave us an idea of a dozen beings inside, and based on the anomalous readings, they were likely vampires. There were no telephone landlines to tap, no cell signals or router traffic to capture. After two days, we were all bored to death yet tired, a poor combination. I asked Henry what he was feeling, and he reported there was an increase in negative energy nearby, but since none of our shifters were changing shapes or interacting with the environment, it was still manageable. He thought the building itself felt even more wrong than I did. After a consult, Elias decided we would go in the next night.

I sent Jo, along with Seth and Simon, back to Iowa to set up a communications center. She was steamed, but I was adamant about not having her on the front line of a likely trap set up by a superior force. Elias kept a smile, and his distance, as that conversation played out. I thanked him later for helping. He just grinned and told me he was smart enough to stay away from a live grenade after I had pulled the pin. I guess he had a point. The other two went with her for other reasons. Seth was a brilliant tactician, and Simon had worked extensively with everyone and knew their strengths and had a good head about operations. His personal combat skills were unmatched, but I had a premonition that if he was that close to the action in this operation he might not survive.

Henry and Nan were commanding our group, four three-person teams set up behind Elias' teams. My goal for them was observation first, and support for when Elias' people needed cover for their retreat. I wasn't cynical, I told myself, I was just realistic. My gut continued telling me this operation was trouble.

We were all outfitted with the best available radios and tiny latest-generation webcams. Jo and her team had real-time input coming in from all the radios and video feeds. She could, with Seth and Simon's help as needed, coordinate the information and suggest responses and action plans. I had a tendency in the past to forego that type of preparation and planning, but no longer. I would be handling our teams, with Jo's assistance, while Elias was handling his direct reports, and could expand communications with the reserve force he had ready at the fallback position. He had heeded my gut feeling and lined up the reserves.

The next evening, everyone was in place and ready. My instincts that this was about to go bad were buzzing so loud I couldn't think. As I crouched with Elias, just over a hundred yards from the front of the building. "Elias, I think we have a baseball analogy here. A powerful-looking hitter up to bat, with unknown stats, sitting on a 3-0 count, bases loaded."

"What do you do?"

"Knuckleball."

"Know anybody that can throw one?"

"I just met somebody recently, actually." I smiled at my cleverness, as I called my favorite fairy and asked for a favor. She was confused, but I knew she would figure it out quickly.

"What was that about?" Elias asked.

"I just placed a bounty contract on myself."

"Isn't that somewhat self-defeating?"

"Not when the hit I just ordered comes with the information that I am in that building over there."

"Ah, the knuckleball."

"One set of baddies shooting up another set up baddies is a positive thing. The enemy of my enemy is the best way to get rid of both."

A large group of walking catfish soon arrived; with some guy I didn't recognize. Obviously, he was the ringleader from fae-land, and I guess Oggie was sitting this one out. As they moved toward the building, the defenses showed up. Three auto-turrets popped up that I could see, one in front of the building, two on the roof, and I could hear another out back. The bullets affected the fish but were not knocking them down quickly. Then laser fire started from the turrets.

"Damn, Elias, ever seen that before?"

"No, that's new, and not likely of local manufacture, or any manufacture on this world."

"I'd say the Sky Lords have invested in this facility. More proof they are working with master vampires."

Small arms fire also started from the building, then they started using hand-held lasers. The lasers were not knocking the fish down either, but the burning seemed to hurt them more than bullets, and they stopped their advance. Their human leader stayed far back and out of the way. Things took a bad turn for the building when two massive jellyfish-type things, each the size of a house, dropped out of the sky. One landed on the front lawn and squashed the turret there. The other landed on the building and took out one turret as it crashed partly through the roof. The other roof turret concentrated on the front lawn jellyfish and was turning it into Swiss cheese. But its tentacles were more like prehensile ropes, and in its agony, it reached out and punched through the building's windows, grabbing everyone it could find and squeezing them in half. Watching that, I realized those in the building were vampires, same look as the ones I had run into in Prague. The anomalous thermal images were right. The top half of the vampires could still fire their weapons, as it took them a while to realize they were dead.

The other jellyfish reached out and destroyed the other roof turret. It was taking a lot of small fire from within the building, so tentacles reached down inside and also started slicing the vampires in half. All the remaining catfish went out back and ganged up on the last turret, and it finally went silent. By then, it looked like most of the defenders were dead, as well as the catfish and one jellyfish. A few vampires were still engaging the last jellyfish, but I estimated over ninety percent of both defenders and attackers were dead.

"Hey Elias, I think we need to clear out of here."

"Why? Looks like everyone is down, and we can easily mop up what is left."

"I'm going to order my people to clear out, then I'll tell you what I'm thinking. Henry, Nan, get your people clear, and do it now," I said into the radio. "Immediate evacuation once you account for everyone, to the initial fallback site. No stragglers, get moving." My orders moved my people away from this area and they should be gone in the next two minutes.

"You're serious. You guys are bugging out?"

"Yep, and you must as well. We just hit a well-defended building, mostly empty and with no value. What we just saw wasn't the trap. It has yet to show up."

"Damn, you might be right. I'll move my people back and send in drones to see if there is anything in there."

"Good idea. And alert them there could be a counterattack coming soon."

"Will do." Elias issued orders to fall back, and to assemble in defensive positions. His surveil team was to send three drones into the building.

Nan and Henry radioed in that they were all accounted for and on the way to the fallback position. It was several miles south, in an unpopulated area to minimize collateral damage. I acknowledged and told them I'd be moving their direction within ten minutes. Elias' teams would also fall back there depending on what happened the next few minutes.

"Elias, we need to get the reserves ready as well. Have them at the initial fallback point."

"What do you think is coming?"

"No idea, but if they will expend that much on a pre-trap, the actual trap might be a lot worse."

"OK." Elias messaged out and had his people move back another quarter mile, and ready to move towards the fallback point. Elias and I had just started moving when the drones entered the building. I saw from a distance that the guy wrangling the catfish do a double take when he saw the drones go in, then he disappeared. A second later, I felt an immediate, dull sickness.

"Elias, you feel that?"

"Yeah, my guts are turning inside out."

"I think that's a deep subsonic wave. Most likely from some bad crystals, meaning the trap is active. We need to get out of here right now."

We started running away from the building at full speed. The subsonic pulses got worse, and Elias slowed. I threw him on my back in a fireman's carry and sped up. I heard odd explosions behind us as the drones exploded. Creatures started rising from the ground around the perimeter of the building, most of them popping up from under the asphalt. Luckily, we had already cleared the area. Elias' surveillance team, slow to move back after the last order, opened fire on the things nearest them. Even though they were some distance from the creatures, it was a fatal mistake. The things ran at them with no effect from the gunfire and swarmed and overwhelmed them. I kept running at my full speed, while also trying to see what was going on and what might gain on me. There were many man-sized things, plus a number of tall, gaunt, and ugly creatures. I also smelled something worse than the laser-cooked catfish. I continued to put distance between us and those things, while also trying to see what was happening.

"What the hell are those things?" Elias asked.

"I think I'm seeing the largest gang of Uya I've ever seen, plus the tall things I'm unfamiliar with. Regardless, I'm going to keep moving away from them at full speed."

I heard Elias tell his people to keep retreating in order and not engage. After the surveil teams' mistake, everyone else was moving away quickly. The effects of the subsonic pulse were less this far out, so I set Elias down as we kept running. It wasn't cowardice, it was self-preservation, as the two of us against that mob of Uya and whatever else was with them would be quick suicide. I heard Elias calling in backup from somewhere, requesting air support and ammunition with the binder coating. That was the best chance of corralling the Uya and their buddies.

Henry came on my radio and reported they had accounted for everyone, evacuated and were moving south at speed to the fallback site. I was glad we had stashed vehicles around for just this eventuality. If things went terribly wrong at our fallback site, we'd retreat all the way back to Des Moines, Iowa, where Jo was. When Henry had described the implications of operating in unfriendly Minnesota, we decided we'd need good retreat routes and sites to be out of that situation as fast as possible. We also needed to be away from the Great Lakes and the strong influence of the crystals if things went catastrophic, so Iowa was the best bet. Then Henry said he was coming towards me since everyone else was safe. I told him I didn't need help, but he disagreed.

"Boss, no time to be stupid. I'm smelling Uya and something worse. I'm tracking you now cause you're going to need the help shortly."

"OK, come on, but Elias and I are still moving away, going due south to the initial fallback."

"Yep, see you soon."

Elias had kept in touch with his team and all we moving as fast as possible away from the original target. They were ahead of us and moving quickly but he gave them permission to confiscate any available vehicles if needed. It was a nice way of giving them a license to steal parked cars or carjack moving ones. Of course, the carjacking would probably end up saving the life of the car driver. Elias was down to twenty people across the five remaining teams, so running was the best option. They should make it to the fallback site before us. Everyone reported that they were still being followed if at a distance. With foresight, we had chosen a state park well south of Minneapolis, vacant tonight since there was not a campground, as or fallback and rally location. We would make a stand at the park while reinforcements arrived. Then Iowa if we were overrun, but I hoped it would not devolve into that.

"Hey Elias, can you hot-wire a car? We need to get mobile before we get eaten."

"I don't. It appears we are now looking to carjack someone."

"Yeah, let's grab the car sitting at the gas station over there."

"Good catch. After you."

We ran up, threw the driver in the back seat, and took off south. I radioed Henry and told him we were driving and would soon be at the park. He acknowledged and would meet us on the way. He also said the tall things were Wendigoes, and between them and the Uya they would follow us until they killed and ate us. Maybe not so good for us, but good for all the other people around. I told the guy in the backseat we were in the middle of a terrorist operation, and that I would release him and his vehicle in less than thirty minutes. I pulled a hundred-dollar bill out of my wallet that I kept for emergencies and handed it back to him. Elias also told him he would get reimbursed further for his trouble if he submitted a request via the email link that he would send him if he provided an email address. I don't think he believed us, but he was smart enough not to argue with two armed men.

Chapter Sixteen

We were close to the park when a heavy pickup showed up coming the opposite direction. Watt and Sam were in the cab, while Henry was in the bed manning a Gatling gun mounted on a swivel stand. It looked impressive. As they went past us, they spun around to follow us, with Henry covering anything behind them with the gun. The Uya and Wendigoes were still following but were yet to close on our position.

The road to the park was straight, passing through a grove of trees, then went into a large open area of pasture. The road ahead was blocked by a truck, with others off to both sides, in a line across the open pasture on both sides. We passed the truck, Elias and I got out, gave the car back to its owner, and told him to keep driving south and fast. He took our advice. Elias' teams and all of my people formed up on the truck line.

Henry jumped out the truck as Sam drive it to the line, so I asked him what was coming.

"I'm guessing you saw the Uya. Those other things are Wendigoes and bad news, tougher than the Uya," Henry said. "Won't go down without lots of those special bullets since they don't have much mass or circulatory system. And they won't stop for nothing, now that they are on our trail."

"Well, how about that? We got us whole crates of those bullets on the way. Plus, we have brought them right into our killing field."

Henry smiled. "I believe those ancient scarecrows are about to get a lesson in firepower and gravity."

"You mean 'shot and fall' rather than 'shock and awe' or something, right?"

"You need to stick to your strengths. You might think that's funny, but it ain't."

"I'm hurt. Now let's load up and shoot those damn things," I said, as three helicopters came in fast, and the two smaller ones landed.

"Damn Elias, I didn't know you had this much backup."

"Yeah, we hoped not to need it, but after you told me your concerns, Michael insisted we at least have this on hand as a last resort."

The two helicopters on the ground disgorged several strike teams and several large and small crates. Teams opened the big crates as the sides fell off, revealing more Gatling guns. The small crates were full of machine rifles and multiple boxes of binder ammo. We grabbed rifles and ammo and got set up and ready for the monster squad. The two helicopters rose and assumed positions off to either side, holding each flank. That should keep us from being overrun. The big one went behind us some distance and hovered.

The menagerie appeared in the darkness, loping down the road. At forty yards out, we unleashed our trap. Both side helicopters cranked up blinding lights that illuminated the pleasant evening with several million candlepower. The big copter behind us went screaming overhead with lights, plus two Gatling guns blazing. Those rotating-barrel guns chewed up the things running down the road, and the road itself. Those were regular bullets, but they were so many that it slowed them down considerably. Then we land dwellers unleashed the binder-coated bullets. It seemed every bullet hit something, and we massacred the forty Uya on the spot. The Wendigoes kept coming but much slower. It took a lot of bullets in each to knock them down, but we had lots of guns and lots of special bullets, thanks to Michael's special project at the Center. Within a few minutes the shooting was over.

Cleanup was by teams. First person approached a prone form, shot it several more times, and two other team members put on smart ties. It took a lot longer to do that properly and safely than it had to mow them down. Other teams stacked them on the backs of the trucks. They were being sent to a massive municipal incinerator for summary cremation. There would be no survivors from this encounter.

I saw Zena in the field and was glad to know she had made it. I did not know the four soldiers that Elias had lost. Elias was holding up OK, but I could tell it bothered him. I knew from my Roman days how hard it was to lose your soldiers.

After a rest, our people were heading south to North Carolina. The long drive gave me a chance to ask Henry about the things that chased us.

"Henry, you called those tall things Wendigoes. I am confused over the Wendigo name, or Wendigoes."

"Those things are an abomination of the original Wendigos, of which I am a member. It is a long story, but they are ancient and evil, and fortunately, few are left. Some of those things bred back to one version of humans and spawned the Uya. Or at least that is one story, of which there are a few versions."

"Seemed to be a lot of them, and a lot of Uya."

"I did not think there were that many Uya left in the Americas. It would not surprise me if half of them were from South America. Wendigoes are a harder to count, as a lot of them drop in the ground and can hibernate long periods. Come up when they smell something appetizing, like a young family on a picnic. Disturbing to see so many of them in one spot, usually they don't ever group up."

"I think it is odd as well. Somebody was really gunning for us. OK, so you are an original Wendigo, and based on what you told me a while back, you must be considerably older than me."

"Yes, to both thoughts. Somebody is after us, and I been around longer than most. I am a shifter from the old school."

"Not sure what that means regarding old school."

"Let's just say very old school. After what I'm seeing lately, I need you to take a few days off and come with me. I know you been learning from Kal, but I need to train you a new way. Might keep you alive a lot longer."

"I'm good with that. Less dying is a positive thing."

"Yep. Let me think where this will best be done. I'd rather do it in Siberia, but that is getting harder to get to. Maybe out past Alberta, Canada would work."

"I'll leave that to you. Give me a day's notice and we'll head out."

"Yeah boss."

"What the hell you keep calling me that for? All the things I might be, I know one of them ain't your boss."

Henry just laughed. "You kids, always trying to not be what you are."

"If you want a boss, I'll sick Nan or Jo on your ass. Then you'll know about the boss."

"Yep, but that's a whole different kind of boss."

Back at the Farm, we took a break and did another spa day. I took the lull in action to go find another old guy as I had an idea. We did our dance of getting into contact, and this time he found me at the Farm. I must score higher on his calendar than previously.

"Odin, I had an idea about inviting your group to our Farm for a party, or whatever you want to call it. Just a few hours of food, drink, and music for our folks and yours."

"If we do it on your site, I can pull another group into defensive positions, so you will still be covered. But woe to whoever attacks with that many einherjar around and ruins their party. I don't foresee an incursion, but better to be thorough." Odin thought for a moment. "So yes, that is a good idea. But on condition of two rules. Everyone wears their rune amulets the entire time. At there must be at least two kegs of mead. I will also attend to keep them in line, as the warriors get rowdy after a while."

"They eat, don't they?"

"Of course. What the hell is good about being dead this long if you can't enjoy it?" He was looking at me like I was crazy.

"What do they prefer to eat? Planning to have a load of meat from the grill."

He looked at me like I was crazy, again. "After the mead, they don't care. Which is why you must wear your amulets."

I didn't know if he was kidding. But we would check amulets before the party.

The first keg was gone before the slabs of meat came off the grill. Three different species of meat were represented, since I didn't know exactly who I was feeding. I also had several chickens and guinea fowl roasting, but one of those guineas had my name on it. I turned over the grill duties to Jimmy, Ned, and John Henry, to mingle in the crowd.

For the first time, I got a good look at the men. Normally, I was too busy dodging getting sliced up to see or talk to them. They were considerably more diverse than I realized. They also did not dress in their "costumes of their day" which made it even more difficult to figure out who they really were. Some looked Viking, some Asian, African, and a dozen other combinations. I saw one that appeared Scythian. Odin introduced me to one who spoke passable English with a strong burr.

"Senecus, this is Dougald MacDonald."

"Hi Sen, just call me Duggers. Appreciate the get-together, mighty obliging of you."

"No problem. Glad to have all of you here. Not going by Mac?"

"Already a half dozen of them in the bunch."

"Is that Scottish Highlands or Irish?"

"Yes," he answered. "Lived in both, fought in both, married and had kids in both, but died in Ireland."

"Interesting resume. Who else is here?"

"Want it by culture, by language, or by country which is problematic since most of them don't exist anymore?"

"Whichever is easy, and I don't mind mixed categories."

"Well, let me see. Going around the crowd that way is Scythian, Japanese, Russian, three Vikings, Zulu, Egyptian, Lusitanian, and that unique fellow is Maori. The woman over there is Greek, and gods, she is a terror, and that other woman is Finnish. The third one is from Gaul. Some others that didn't make it today, cause they're on another assignment, are a scattering of Assyrian, Mongolian, Roman, one crazy Sardinian, two Frenchies, Moroccan, and a big fellow from the Congo."

"That is a hell of a diverse group."

"You don't know the half of it. Probably a thousand different groups, at least back in the main hall. For our group here, there are no limitations or requirements on anything. This is the only place I know that is truly based on equal opportunity, with competence the only criteria."

"No Native Americans?"

"We lobbied for them, but they have their own union. Wonderful group of people, and they have the best drugs. Their parties start off crazy, then get quiet after the peyote and shrooms come out. We do an event with them every decade that is a blast. We just remember little afterwards."

"Is that like a dead soldier's Olympics?"

"A bit but add violence and subtract the bureaucracy and corruption."

"Also, I don't see anybody 'newer' from the past few wars."

"There's a guideline about being on this side of the veil at least two hundred years after the personal demise. We also need to be careful about who we let into this elite group, plus there are just so damn many these past couple of centuries. They are being sent up by the millions. Can you imagine the job HR has to do now?"

"I got it. A probation system, and too many at once, so no new guys or girls."

"Right. Have to go through processing. Afterlife still has its queue."

I wandered back over to Odin. He was talking to Jo and Nan, of course.

"This is an interesting group you have. How long do they stay in your realm, or is this it for them?"

"This isn't heaven, although most of them think it is. It's more of a purgatory. Eventually, they tire of this and need to move on. That's a realm beyond mine. You'd have to ask someone else that has that jurisdiction for more information."

"No, just didn't know the system."

"You might get to. The best warriors come here."

I was not sure what to say to that. I nodded and kept wandering. It was about time to bring out my surprise. It wasn't anything grand, but I thought it might be a nice touch. The van pulled up and spilled out a bunch of older men that looked a little disheveled. They opened the back and started pulling out their equipment. One walked over to me and asked where to set up. I pointed back toward the party and told him anywhere near the fire, then handed him rune amulets and said they had to wear them. He squinted at the group behind me, grunted, and went back to get stuff. A moment later, a bagpipe cranked up, and the musicians trudged over to the fire. After that, the fiddle and banjo started up, as the guitar and bass player were still tuning.

The string divas were late to get tuned, as always. Before long everyone was dancing except Odin and I.

"Delightful party. Tame for this group, but they seem to enjoy it," Odin said.

"Can't always be killing and carousing, I guess. Coming here and dancing with a live pretty girl or guy isn't all bad."

"No, it is not, and thank you for reminding me of that. Why aren't you dancing?"

"Ingrown toenail or something."

"You idiot. She won't wait forever. Even pregnant, she's a real dancer." We watched Jo dancing with Duggers.

"Noticed that, did you? Life is full of surprises."

"You have no idea yet, but you will. You will be a good father to her."

"I'll try."

"You will do better than that. She is more yours than you think. And she is more important than anyone yet realizes. Everyone here may need to give their life for her."

"Damn Odin, you know how to put a damper on a party!"

"That is not a damper. That is the highest honor for any of us. The girl is the key to your race. Remember that always, and act accordingly. I already know you will, of course, but expectations are such that I must pronounce god-like bullshit regularly."

We grabbed a mead and sat by the fire to talk about swords versus spears in single combat. Two minutes later, he moved his hands and teleported me in front of Jo. We were both a bit surprised, then we laughed and started dancing. I looked over, but Odin was gone; there was just an eerie outline of a smile made of floating smoke where he had been.

The next morning there were some bleary faces walking around the Farm. Since I neither got drunk nor had hangovers, I somewhat enjoyed pestering those feeling the ill effects. Before long, my phone rang.

"Good morning, Michael."

"Good afternoon, Sen. We have credible evidence that your Minnesota master vampire, or in this case, a pair of vampires, arrived back in Russia," Michael said.

"Russia? What the hell were they doing in Minnesota?"

"Living there, part time."

"How does that happen?"

"They are a pair of incredibly wealthy arms dealers. America is a premier country for moving weapons and for money laundering. All the Russian oligarchs spend time in America, as London is old news."

"I thought that had ended after the recent troubles."

"Money that big knows no boundaries."

"So, what is the plan?"

"Nothing, for now. It's too dangerous to move a large enough force to deal with them in Russia, especially after seeing the resources they had in Minnesota. But we know where they are, and we will eventually get them."

"Good, that encounter was entirely too close. And it seems they are getting a little too cute trying to bait us."

"It may take some time, but we will show them the error of their ways."

CHAPTER SEVENTEEN

Henry drove us away from the Great Falls, Montana, in the general direction of Canada. We made a couple of mysterious stops on the way in very rural places. We loaded the truck up with supplies at several stores when we finally got to Edmonton. Then we went west and into the foothills of the Rockies, to a nowhere filled with endless valleys but fairly dry land. And no humans within miles. The roads turned to gravel, then dirt, until we were in an old wash that had probably never had tires on it. When it leveled out, high up, we were in a high valley with good views. We unloaded and set up two tents. This was our practice area supposedly, but I knew Henry would not have brought me here if there wasn't something more going on. We could have practiced in places closer to home.

"Hey Henry, what are we doing here?"

"Some things you have never done and never thought about doing. I'm going to train you to shapeshift to any form you can imagine. And to help with that, I need to call up some of the old ones of my people."

"And who are the old ones?"

"Ghosts of the First Peoples, mostly, and a few others. But just the friendly ones. Dinner first, then we start."

After we ate around the fire, he methodically set out the things we had picked up on the way. He had brought some boughs of white cedar, bundles of different sages, uncut tobacco leaves, a few boxes of other herbs and barks I didn't know, and yaupon holly, which he had brought shipped from North Carolina. Also, one of the oldest pipes I had ever seen. He laid several ancient leather pouches beside the pipe.

"I assume those are some potent concoctions."

"Any single one of them will get you twenty years in prison. Of course, half of them is unknown to your people. These are necessary because most drugs do not easily affect folks like us. But these will affect you."

"Weren't you afraid of getting them through border customs?"

"Nope, used an old Indian trick. You noticed they just waved us through. I gave them the notion that we were Canadian. Besides, your name is on the rental, so this is your contraband."

"Thanks."

"Tonight, we will use the pipe, but only lightly with a couple of herbs. Just enough to heighten your memories. Not your regular memories, but those down deep in your DNA, that are really your ancestor's memories. Later you will find your future memories, the important things that are yet to happen, but most likely will. Gets confusing, but you will figure it out. All of those things will swirl up as I talk about my memories. Might feel overwhelming at first.

"Tomorrow we will start on major shape shifting practice. Then, tomorrow night and each night after, you get a heavy pipe as I call in the spirits for consultation. That's when you will see lots of interesting things." He handed me the pipe and lit it. "Just a couple of light puffs to start, then a few more through the evening."

I did as he said, and within a minute, I could feel my mind changing. Nothing like my old days in the Legion when drinking. This was my brain walking into a larger room.

"Now I am going to go through history, mostly of my people, as I know it. There is a lot to tell, and I'll need to tie it back to what is happening today so most of the old stuff will get left out. I'm also going to show you some things that just aren't done, because it's too dangerous, or because the knowledge has passed out of this world.

"I was taught by my grandparents, from what they learned from their grandparents, that the world has gone through cycles of destruction and rebirth. The last big one was pretty bad. After that, the Makers, who were not human, came to start things over again. Several batches of different peoples were created, well before humans existed. These were the First Peoples, and each group had their own unique adaptations and survival techniques. Some of these or their descendants you have met. Many of those groups have not survived. Again, not all were human or even human-like. Their adaptations for the world back then were not always sufficient to guarantee survival; or the side effects of the adaptations were too severe, leading to extinction. All that was trial and error based on the best guesses of the Makers as even they did not know the long-term consequences of their creations. All that was done to eventually get to the true humans we have today, the oldest of which we call the Original Tribes.

"My people were one group of several First Peoples created for the new epoch on this planet. We were the original Wendigos, generated with the ability to shapeshift. It was a strategic advantage, as we could transform into other forms to survive hardships, whether resistance to drowning or frigid weather, or ability to fly to better hunting grounds, or being able to hunt almost anything. Shapeshifting is not a fun or cute way to deal with a temporary problem. For us, it was a way of life, of survival.

"But the long-term cost was severe, as the ability to turn into any other form eventually turns us insane. I am one of the very few left that did not turn insane. I been around long enough to remember spending lots of hunting time on the glaciers as we traveled back and forth between here and Siberia. Lot of hardships, like severe weather and hunger, get solved when you can shift into any animal form. But that forced us into shapeshifting a lot, which doomed us faster.

"Over a very long time when all that was going, a few of the Makers and some of the First Peoples were mucking things up. Interfering with the entire process, whether helping one tribe against another, or mating with some of the tribes. Those offspring were highly unpredictable, and once again, most of those did not survive long term. A lot of those situations got messy and had to be cleaned up.

"Some of us were called to defend against the evil creatures created by those messy situations I mentioned earlier, by Makers and First People misbehaving. But we also had to hunt our own, as Wendigos went insane, turning into Wendigoes. I and others became something akin to wardens, employed at different times and places to control those problems.

"Our territory stretched from these Rocky Mountains to nearly the Ural Mountains. A vast area to roam and to patrol. We would also sometimes head south, down into China on that side, or Central America over on this side. But we tried to be respectful of other people's areas, so we limited those trips to those only necessary to deal with the worst creatures." As Henry spoke, in my mind I could see figures moving on immense plains or across unending glaciers. Sometimes they were in human form, sometimes as animals.

"We are here in these hills and mountains as this is where my people's spirits are strongest, other than Siberia. The spirits know things never known to us, or no longer known, and they can help guide us in the practice of the old ways. How to survive, thrive, and return to human. We are doing this so you will have a better idea of who your family is and what you are becoming. Might just save your life as well."

"If you've been around that long, then you must know Kal's people, since they were another of the First Tribes."

"Yes, we knew of each other, but we did not socialize. They were a younger people, and mostly kept to the West coast of North America, and we left each other alone. They were becoming ascendant in their power as we were dwindling. Kal's people were not shifters at first. With only their one body, they had no insanity issues. Over time, they looked inward and made discoveries, including slant and shapeshifting. They shift, but only when needed, a much safer approach to shifting. They were nonviolent to begin with and became more so. Now they are experts at defense and deflection, and they basically cannot be killed or captured. They are masters at telepathy, teleportation, shapeshifting, and time travel. Yet they use none of their advantages to harm others or take offensive action. That is why they will ascend off earth and gain acceptance as a higher form in the galaxy. Only the second race to do so from this planet if it happens. But most planets don't produce any ascensions. Something kills them off, or they kill themselves off. There are some signs that a third group could ascend from here. But some entities will try to prevent that from happening. That is what we are in the middle of right now.

"For instance, the Sky Lords tried a few cute moves over the years. They have a ship out there somewhere. It pushes small comets or asteroids toward us for a glancing blow to knock out any troubling groups. Centuries back, some tribes in America had gotten back to slant and were making progress. For their efforts, they got a comet blast, nearly wiped out what you people call the Hopewell culture. Sky Lords don't play nice when there is a threat. Gives me concern about the Farm, although I doubt we are big enough to get their attention yet. But when we do, it will get ugly."

"I hope we have enough of the right allies to deflect something like that."

"I think we do now, or we will soon. So, any questions so far? Even the history summary has many layers, so it might take time to think through."

"Just one, about shifting. If I learn to shift, and end up staying alive, will that increase my chances of insanity? Or Jo, or Isabel, if they learn it? Or for the rest of my family, if they end up taking the turn and living for two thousand years instead of two hundred?"

"Don't know for sure, but I kind of doubt it. Shifters taking the turn, or you folks already turned that then learn to shift, is a completely different mechanism than how it was integrated into my people. I think the sheer age we live to, with the constant shifting, must trigger something in us that was a glitch to begin with. The worst case for us is that the oldest of us, once crazy, turn into the Wendigoes like we saw in Minnesota.

"Those bad ones, the Wendigoes, occasionally breed with humans, at least when they take a break from eating them for dinner. That union produces offspring that are Uya. Of course, Uya can also interbreed. Those are crazy because they are basically born crazy, not because they shift. So, us Wendigos have been around forever, at least in human history. Then we go crazy and become Wendigoes; some breed with others and make Uya, which are born crazy."

"Any chance of that craziness showing up in the Nunehi? Will my family turn into that?"

"They were one of the very last Maker creations. I believe they are based on the Wendigo, but with much shorter lives, can only shift to one animal form, and have more beneficial powers. They were created to counter the Uya, who were proliferating and causing problems all over. I believe the Nunehi are immune to insanity as they are not in the Wendigo chain at all."

"Good, that makes me feel better."

"OK, Sen, time to turn in, or at least take a break and take in the stars. It's a nice clear night."

I lay watching the stars, while my ancient ancestor's memories kept parading through my head. The next morning, it was practice time. Henry taught me a lot quickly, but the learning was the simple part. Doing it was much more difficult. Like anything, it was about having the right mindset, which took practice.

As we ate lunch, I asked Henry, "Why did Odin call you Wol?"

"That was what I was called most of life. I was the warden, or protector, for a time, of the vast area my people called home."

"What happened to your people, the ones that did not go insane?"

"Don't think any of mine are still on this continent. Not that many of us are left. Most went insane and needed to be put down when they were found. Some were just tired of life and jumped into volcanoes. That is a good way to end us, compared to most methods. I doubt there are more than a dozen of us left."

After that bleak statement, I went back to practicing, which was mostly me trying to get out of my own way, mentally. But I was getting frustrated.

"Sen let's try something a little different. Move slightly into slant and stay there while concentrating on the shifting steps. Then restart again, after going deeper into slant. Next, go real deep before trying to shift. Maybe the key is getting out of your head."

I went through the process and made progress. There was a sweet spot in the level of slant I needed to be in before trying to shift. Finally, I was having success.

It was time for dinner before breaking out the pipe and the night's weirdness. I wondered how Henry had gotten hooked up with the Cherokee. "Henry, how did you get from where you were as a Wendigo to where you are now, with our group?"

"As you know, I am one of the old ones. Had to make a choice during the middle of the last Ice Age. Was supposed to pick a side on some stuff going on back then. But I did not, I'd had enough. Ten thousand years as a warden had burned me out. By choice, I became the omega wolf, the one that needs no pack. Can join up with others when I want to, but never for long. Traveled a lot and was getting bored when the latest batch of Europeans showed up. But unlike the earlier small groups of Europeans and Asians that came to this continent, this batch was more determined and stuck.

"I was asked again about choosing sides, but again, I did not. Sometimes I wonder if I should have and helped to stop the invasion. Over the past five hundred years, the Europeans did more harm than good to this place. But an inner voice kept telling me to stay out of it. I talked to others, some First Peoples, some ghosts, and they all said the same thing. I don't know what it all means, but I was smart enough to know there was, and is, something bigger going on than fighting colonization.

"Anyhow, I heard about Hia, how she'd found a mate, a strange creature with medicine from the Old World. Came by and watched you guys over in the Brasstown. Real strange you looked. If you'd come over a couple hundred years earlier and traveled south, you'd have been called Quetzalcoatl, with that silvery shine. You left and I waited around, then joined up with the western Cherokee a hundred years back. Decided I needed to see where all this was going and keep a closer eye on you. You spent long decades away, but I kept patient. People like you always come back to family, eventually."

"I did not know you were watching, of course."

"Had to be careful. Hia nearly caught me once."

"She never mentioned anything like that, although a few times I saw her get nervous. Just assumed she was worried about Uya."

"I think she got my scent, which would have made her nervous, not knowing if I was an Uya or a devolved Wendigo. She was a good woman."

"Yes, she was. We did not have nearly enough time together."

"You had exactly the time fate gave you. Say, this far north the northern lights show up. Ever taken Jo to see them?"

"No, I have not, but I would like to. Why?"

"There's magic in them lights for people like us. Don't know the reason, but they give you the ability to see inside each other. You might try it one night."

"I will. We'll make a trip of it. When you mentioned before about being a warden, what was that?"

"Being a warden for me usually meant going after something bad. Trying to keep the peace and make the world better. It's a siren song that draws you in, all that doing of good. But here's something you need to know. No matter how much you dedicate your life to that, you never get all the bad. You be careful not to obsess over that, otherwise your life passes by without you noticing the good. And even the good you do can sometimes turn bad, as situations change. Not a good choice for a life."

"I think I'm figuring that out now. I will chase the bad ones and protect my people as much as I can. Then I plan to stay in place and enjoy what I can, as long as I can."

"Good. Folks like us spend too much time being wardens rather than living life. Some, like Odin, have devoted themselves to it at the expense of their own happiness. Others, like Kal, take a different approach and protect themselves and others by excluding the bad. Then they live good lives in that exclusion zone. They must know something, because they seem happier than us warden types."

It was pipe time after that. My mind was expanding again, but then things got hazy, and things began moving in the night. They came in fearsome. Henry had not told me that most were in some state of metamorphosis between human and some animal. Men and women mixed with buffalo, mountain lion, wolf, mammoth, what had to be a sabretooth cat, a bear, snake, and a dozen other concoctions. Some were showing multiple animal forms, including one with wings that looked like a New World griffin. Of the menagerie, only three men and one woman appeared in fully human form. The shapes drifted in at Henry's invitation, then drifted on or disappeared.

They told tales of the old days, ancient enemies, victories, lost lovers, glaciers and plains that no longer existed, disasters beyond imagining, and animals that no longer walked the earth. Henry would sprinkle in questions and get answers with multiple meanings. I was sensing more of what they were saying more than hearing it. I suppose the drugs allowed for the meaning to come through, since I didn't know the various languages they were speaking. Even so, I understood little of what they said, but Henry did. He gave me the highlights the next morning after coffee, after each of the previous evening's episode.

I practiced with Henry each day. I started turning into a deer or small rodent, either squirrel or chipmunk, relatively easily. That was OK if I wanted to get away from something, but I really needed to go to wolf or mountain lion form. Henry told me I was thinking too defensively, that I needed to think more offensively.

Then each night it was back to the spirits; spirit training is what we ended up calling it. Henry would put portions of the things he had brought with him into the fire, and we'd let the smoke coat us. Then he would pack the pipe up with a blend from the pouches, and we'd proceed to getting blitzed. Henry had a set of words he'd repeat for some time while drawing symbols in the dirt with a stick. I don't know which part or parts did the trick, but within a half hour they would come. Beyond hearing the histories they told, Henry related tactics about shifting that could be helpful to me. He gave me their ideas on which forms to use in particular situations, and which combination to use in order. It was almost like kata in martial arts. Which I guess it was, since the shifting was meant for battle.

Interestingly, on the last night, the three men and one woman came by themselves and sat by the fire. A possibly ominous sign. I understood what they said to Henry with no problem.

"You must make this one ready," one said. "The next ascension portal depends on his success in readying and protecting his people. After, his journey will be long and arduous as he passes out of this time and place. But his sacrifice will ensure that the One will succeed. She is the only hope." They said their goodbyes to Henry and left, so it was a brief night. We didn't need to discuss anything because it was obvious what they meant.

Early the last day I asked Henry, "Got any more advice or tricks I need to know about?"

"Some. You been getting along pretty well on your own, now picking up this training right along. Let me think. OK, here is something you can try. Worked for me a few times, and it's real sneaky, so you should like it."

He gave me a scenario where he had walked into a grizzly one day while not paying attention. Without thinking, he had changed into a wolverine. Not very unusual for him, but for two things. When he turned into the wolverine, he found himself on the other side of the bear, and was shocked to see his body still there, with his shoulder in the bear's mouth. Meanwhile, in his new form, he sliced off the bear's gonads, bit through the tendons in both back legs, then went after the major arteries. The bear was still trying to chew his human form while he was killing it from behind in wolverine form. After finishing off the bear, he thought about what had happened. He had inadvertently tapped into a new way to shapeshift and translocate a short distance at the same time. With a lot of trial and error, he had figured out how to do it at will.

He initially tried to reform his body, as the bear had made a mess of his old self. But he realized it wasn't necessary, the old body was no longer needed. But in his new form, it took longer to change back to human due to all the energy spent for the first change and translocation, and the lost mass. He later tweaked the process to make it faster and easier to change forms, then change back to human within a couple of hours. The trick was, for the first transformation, to change into something smaller than the human form, and not go back to human for a few hours.

He showed me the same trick and told me how to practice it. He also told me that as far as he knew, nobody else could do it. It was something I was definitely going to use someday.

He also gave me instructions to keep an image or two of something in my conscious at all times so I could turn quickly if need be. After some time, I could conjure up just about any form to deal with whatever the situation was, without even thinking about it. But that would likely be some years away.

"Henry, what about turning into inanimate objects like a tree, similar to what Kal's people do?"

"That, in some ways, is easier than turning into other animal forms," Henry said. "However, the trick is getting back out of that form and into yours. You will need supervised practice for that, which we will address once you get your offensive animal forms right."

"Is it possible to turn into any form, whether a train or a car?"

"It is theoretically possible. However, the more complex form you try outside the animal realm, the more likely you will have errors. I would not even try the car transformation. The amount of energy you would need, and the ability to control it at a fine level, would likely be too great to handle without errors. I would predict a massive boom. Maybe that is your doomsday failsafe device instead, if you need to take out a county-sized patch of land full of enemies."

"I believe I'll save that lesson for another century or two."

"Probably best."

"But overall, is it the same principle, whether going into something enormous or tiny? Say something like a sequoia tree or a flea?"

"Yes, but the wider the difference between your body and the form you are trying to achieve, the more careful you need to be about proper energy transfer to balance out the difference in mass."

"That's when I assume the whole 'boom' thing gets problematic."

"Yeah, for you and anyone within rifle range."

We loaded up and went back to Edmonton, then made it to Asheville. It had been a most illuminating few days. Once I mastered shifting, I should be a lot more dangerous, and I would be better able to protect Jo and Isabel. Not that I'd ever say that out loud to Jo.

CHAPTER EIGHTEEN

K al sent me into the links, and I popped out alone on a cliff above a rocky shoreline with pounding surf at night. I could be in Ireland, Portugal, or northern California, I really did not know. From the darkness, a darker shape appeared and moved toward me. I was a little nervous thinking about a similar situation I was in nearly two thousand years ago. The shape moved to a few feet from my left side. It looked like a roughly human size and shape black shadow. No facial features or eyes that I could tell.

"Greetings Senecus," I felt more than heard.

"Hello there. I was planning on calling you Smokey unless you had some other name you would have me use."

"That is acceptable. Thank you for coming."

"I appreciate the invitation. Kal and Odin recommended a meeting, and I do have a few questions."

"I'll answer what I can. Later, I also have something to show you."

"The demon I saw on tape in Bangkok, and at the Center in Italy, resembles your form. No offense, but is there a relation?"

"I wish it was not so, but it is better for you to know what you face."

Smokey went on to give me a summary of the past 65 million years in five minutes. It was quite a data dump. Smokey's distant ancestors were from Mars, arriving on earth when the Martian atmosphere and surface environment collapsed due to war some two billion years ago. They were a water species so had little choice to leave. Earth was still an unwelcoming environment and most of them died. Eventually a small group of survivors progressed enough to re-engineer their species for dwelling on land, as the water was too limiting to develop technology. The land was full of dinosaurs, so the compromise was a floating city in the general area of the Gulf of Mexico. They developed rapidly, explored space, and soon changed forms again, in anticipation of ascending into the galaxy.

A malevolent being sent the asteroid to Earth, but Smokey's people had escaped to a base on the moon. They then left for the galaxy, coming back millions of years later to repopulate earth with sentient life. They became known as the Makers.

But a few had stayed on Earth, and over eons some coalesced into one form composed of several beings but went insane. Those were the smoke demons, and they were not normally dangerous, unless other beings prodded them into action.

"Danu was one of you, a Maker, wasn't she?" I asked.

"Yes."

"So through her, I am partially one of you?"

"Partially, yes, but what you would call an older model, as she had reverted to our earlier water-based form."

"What happened to Danu? Other than her name, almost nothing survives of her history."

"She was one of best and most successful scientists we ever produced. But ultimately, perhaps, not the most stable one. She created most of the advanced sentient races on this planet, some of which you don't know about. Danu grew too close to her creations. Things were done to favor some and powers or technology given against our principles. She was not the only Maker to do so, as some chose other people or groups for their own purposes.

But that power came at a cost, as those recipients are bound to this planet and cannot ascend. Realizing that, some of them turned to evil purposes or went insane. Your mythologies are full of the problems associated with that group, recounted from Gilgamesh to Olympus, and a dozen other examples. Sometimes good, but mostly bad, came from those gods.

"Once we realized what Danu had been doing, she knew that her punishment would be severe. She escaped to the planet's waters and reverted to her older form and became a god in her own way. Over time, whether by her design, or by natural causes, her form dispersed into multiple life forms, including the one you encountered, and we thought she was gone forever. Then you showed up, carrying some version of her with you. Knowing her, that could have been some version of her plan all along. I knew her well, and she was the longest-range thinker, and the most creative, among us.

"The fae are another of her indirect creations. We had four bases for research, and Danu gave the fae technology from those. Other beings that were created during that time escaped notice. Some of those stayed hidden long enough to pass as human, then move into the future. There they manipulated and schemed, turned against the Earth of their past for gain. Wealth at the expense of slave labor and food."

"And now they are called the Sky Lords."

"Yes. The humans of your time have been manipulated and we don't think you will survive and pass through to a higher plane of existence."

"That is what you are here for, isn't it? You are watching us. What happens if we fail and try to exterminate ourselves and the planet's surface? You will intervene, wipe us out, and leave it to the planet to recover?"

"Basically, yes. Humans as a people are too aggressive. It is possible you would already have been cleansed from the Earth, but for the knowledge that your aggression is not entirely your fault, because of the virus introduced from the future. Since the Sky Lords unbalanced development, we could, under tight restrictions, attempt to right the wrongs. But you have had ample time to progress, even with that handicap. You have been 'quarantined' while those watching are waiting for you to overcome the virus. I believe that the further discovery of the virus feature which amplifies propaganda may buy your species another thousand years, but after that, most in the galaxy will be done waiting. Humans, if they don't progress rapidly, will be swept from the surface."

"Do we have a chance to turn that around?"

"A slight chance."

"Based on the combination of influences and genetics from Danu, the Nunehi shapeshifters, and your own better human tendencies, we think with enough time to develop, your group will have a reasonable chance to ascend. Coaching from the Tsul Kalu has hastened the process for some of you, and that is a promising development."

"You mean with the slant?"

"Yes. If you continue, you have an excellent chance to move forward within a thousand years."

"My daughter, Isabel, could ascend?"

"Yes, likely. Your group is the best chance for any humans to make that ascension. Now you know why it is so important that you travel to the future and end the menace of the Sky Lords. Your people don't need you with them to ascend, but they will not progress to that point if Sky Lord interference continues."

"The Sky Lords sense that, don't they? They won't ascend, so they are trying to prevent us from doing so."

"Yes. But that is only one reason for their interference. Another reason is economic, as they steal resources from your time. Their agents here are always on the lookout for ways to obtain precious metals for their fusion generators. They have become too lazy and incurious to find and mine the asteroids where those elements are abundant. It's just easier to have that little transport portal to feed small amounts to them. They have developed into a strange, and dangerous, race."

"What are your plans to deal with them?"

"You."

"You what?"

"You are what we are going to do about them. Through a most unusual series of events, too odd to be coincidence, you are the most likely solution to this problem."

"How long have you been watching me?"

"About three hundred years. There were anomalous ripples long before that, but we did not know that you were the cause until much later. A small network of mostly what is left of the First People tries to keep a lookout for anomalies, mainly to thwart the Sky Lords and similar threats. Once we recognized your potential, we nudged things so you would come to Michael's attention. On a rare occurrence, something shows up unexpectedly, and you are one of those. And for various reasons, some of which you don't know yet, but will, you are the most likely weapon to move against them. They will not expect you, as only a few of them even realize you exist. You have kept such a low profile over the years, plus many of the entities you encountered were wiped out. Your kill ratio is very efficient. If you continue with a low profile, and changing your appearance if engaging in larger battles, then other than Caius, I don't think you will be noticed by them.

"But know this. Our assessment is that you will not return from the future. You must wreck their ability to interfere in the past without exterminating them. After all, they, just like you, are entitled to their future. But in no instance do we see a way in which you can return after destroying their paths to the past. If you survive, you will be trapped in that future. We understand that will be a great sacrifice."

"I will do it. But considering what I have here now, I am coming back."

"We hope you can find a way. But logic tells us that is likely impossible. However, this is not an imminent trip. This will require long-term planning, and we still have to determine both the where and when of sending you there to be most effective."

"I will still take the fight to them. I'd do it willingly to protect my people."

"Unlikely, but perhaps you could somehow. Odin will not tell you, but the old voices that echo in the links have spoken of you. They cannot always be believed, but the message, while piecemeal, speaks that you have three tasks; one is done, one will always continue, and the third is yet to come."

"That's about the dumbest thing I've ever heard. It could mean anything."

"That is the way of fortune and fate foretold. They always mean almost anything. That is why the oracles are drugged, insane, or both."

"I know you are forbidden to help us on Earth, but is there anything you can do to protect my people, especially if I'm not around?"

"I know that Kal and Odin have set up a secure location on your planet. But I can offer you a failsafe retreat location if that has remained secret for quite a few million years. It may require some effort to recondition and upgrade to meet your needs. It is what I wanted to show you."

"That is good, but if that old, how could it still be habitable?"

"It has self-maintenance and self-replication system for essential components built in. The same technology we currently use, so I am confident it will fit your needs. Only strikes from massive meteorites can damage it."

"So where is it, if it has the potential to be exposed to vacuum?"

"On the body you call the moon. We built it as a shelter facility during our time on earth, when we were under threat. It was where we hid after the asteroid strike."

"OK, but how can I evacuate my people there? It's a bit far away to drive to."

"We can easily fashion a portal to the site. I will take you there to examine it."

"Thanks. Will it be large enough for our group?"

"The series of caverns and modifications are quite large. I estimate it could comfortably house a few hundred thousand humans indefinitely. Food, water, oxygen, and temperature regulation are all part of the system."

"There is a ship in the area, but it won't be a problem regarding portal setup or transferring your people."

"What kind of ship?"

"It is from your future, courtesy of the Sky Lords, which is much too pretentious a title for that lot."

"I might have to do something about that ship. I think they have already tried to kill me."

"At the moment, it may better serve you to ignore them, at least until you have a way to combat them. However, I suspect they have been looking for ancient bases on the moon and Mars, so it would be best if you could come up with a solution."

Smokey reached over to touch my arm, then I felt like I was falling into a kaleidoscope. A second later, I was standing in an enormous cavern. It was dimly lit, cool, and the air was metallic, yet musty.

"I would suggest you bring a group of your people up to go through the facility and set it up to provide your people with the environment they prefer, such as the foods, day length, and temperature range. I will immediately set up the portal. I assume you want it secured in your current camp?"

"Maybe, but better yet in the place that Kal has set up for us as a fallback location. His place should be more secure."

"It will be safe and completely outside of the regular linkage system, to prevent its discovery. It allows travel to and from Earth, just for you and your people."

"Thanks. From what I can tell so far, it looks good as is, especially as an escape option."

"I agree. Oxygen is good and will recycle basically forever, and the lights are automatic. I'll show you the food replicators, waste recycling facilities, and the replicators so you can produce anything you need, from medical supplies to beds. Then you can decide whether to bring others to modify further."

An hour later we were back on Earth, in a pleasant mountain meadow. We were a short walk from the Farm. We said farewell and I walked home after a surprise visit to the moon. Quite a day.

CHAPTER NINETEEN

The alarms sounded, but there was no einherjar attack scheduled, and we no longer had unannounced drills. The defenses were ready within a few seconds, a testament to all the preparations we had made. Even in the middle of the night, everyone was acting on quick reflexes. Gunfire began from outside and was immediately returned from the barn and house. Less than five seconds later, the outside gunfire changed tenor, heavier and on rapid fire. The einherjar defenders had arrived and were chopping up our visitors. Then a different alarm went off. Damn. I yelled for evacuation to get everyone to the portals, although they already knew what to do. Out in the opening between the barns, I could see two shapes, so dark they stood out against the night. Since we had a portal in the barn and the house, everyone had access to one. A few last shots of cover fire, and then silence from our people. I could still hear battle with that looked like regular vampires with the einherjar. Any second now, the additional wave of einherjar would arrive, and that should be the end of the vampires. The problem was the two smoke bomb demons. I needed everyone gone so I could try out our new toy.

Within seconds, everyone was gone but me and I ran for the barn. One shape floated toward the barn, the other for the house. The welcome gift was in the barn, so I needed to turn it on, then bail and turn off the last portal. Nan was designated as the last to go through the house portal and that should have shut it down. As I dashed into the barn, I was surprised by two friendly shapes, Henry and Elias.

"Just making sure you got here safe as a kitten," Henry said. "Never know when you might need cover fire."

"Yeah, thanks. Is our gadget ready to go?"

"Yep, soon as one of our friends shows up we'll juice it. Then time for us to go. Sounds like the einherjar got everything else handled."

The wall near the door turned a darker shade of black. It pushed on through and began floating closer to us. I could feel a malevolent presence and a strange vibration that I realized was coming from my body, somehow reacting to the demon. Henry aimed the large contraption rigged with multiple nozzles, then pulled the lever, dousing the thing with our concoction of copper and silver ions. The charged particles hovered in the air, then quickly attached to our unwelcome guest. We had a metal grid in the floor and ceiling, and when Henry hit the next lever, our smoke buddy with his new coating completed the energized circuit. An electric arc lit up the barn and the smell of ozone hit us. The thing stopped, then began slowly spinning in place. We didn't have long to observe as Thing Two showed up. All three of us jumped through the portal as I turned it off by stepping through.

We stepped into the rest of our group in a valley on a dirt road. I quickly scanned our people and saw they were all present, although I looked for Jo first. The road was flat, and the sides were clear except for tall grass that ran from the road to a tree line at the base of ridges on both sides of the valley. I got a shiver when I realized it resembled the setting in the famous movie where Native Americans ambushed a British column after the surrender of Fort William Henry, in colonial America. I probably should not have thought about that. Kal and friends were here to greet us, as the system alerted them when the Farm sensors triggered. I saw him suddenly tense up. I also felt that something was wrong with the air.

"That has not happened in a while," Kal said. "The Sky Lords, or rather their minions, have come for a visit. They must have triangulated the most likely escape paths and sent out teams."

Kal motioned with his hands and told everyone to pull in tight, close to him. He was putting up some type of invisible shielding, as best I could tell. Then he pulled up a fog bank to cover us as he stood still in concentration. A translucent layer of something that appeared to be woven out of the fog surrounded us. Kal finished his thought creation.

"That should protect us long enough to remove ourselves."

"What is that?" I asked.

"I whipped up an alternative form of chitin shell. Stronger and more elastic than what earth creatures make it. I find it very effective against the projectiles your kind favor. Stones, arrows, spears, bullets. They all bounce off. Then, when not needed, the chitin readily dissolves back to the earth. However, it does not work as well for larger explosives. Now let's move everyone to a safer location before they try anything like that."

Kal's other five people each took several of our people with them and blinked out. Soon, it was just the three of us from the barn, and Kal.

"Hey, before we leave, I have a thought to confuse these guys and keep them from following us. Can you do this?" I explained my idea.

"Yes, I can do that in a minute or two. You really think that will cause these attackers to pause and throw off any pursuit?"

"I believe they will find it irresistible. They will spend lots of time investigating, trying to understand where we went. Same concept of throwing a squirrel in front of a dog."

"Why would one do that? Oh, I see, a distraction that they cannot ignore."

"Exactly. Except dogs might be smarter than these vampires."

That strange rumbling that passed for laughter came up from Kal's throat.

Kal concentrated, and a tunnel formed under our chitin shield. It went down at an angle and ended at thirty feet. He opened up a small, flat-bottomed chamber at the bottom. It had a smaller hole, about the size of a small door, on the far end, which led nowhere. I gave him a radio, and he embedded it into the solid rock on one wall of the chamber. Absolute nonsense, but it would give the other side some inane project to investigate, thinking we had escaped through it. Then Kal moved closer to the three of us, and all four of us appeared some quarter mile further down the valley, but just high enough on the hill on the edge of the trees, to see back to where we had been. Kal shaped the air in front of us into a magnifier three feet in diameter, allowing us to see clearly. After more small arms fire, two missiles hit the chitin membrane, tearing it open. Two dozen vampires rushed down to finish us off. They milled around, then another group flashed into existence, and all went down the tunnel. After five minutes they were still investigating, and Kal blinked us to the next destination.

We were now back with the group and in a large valley. Meadows interspersed with woods and streams, steep mountains all around, with a waterfall on the narrow end that fed a large creek running through the valley. Downstream at the far end of the valley was a narrow cut that appeared to be the only easy way out of the valley.

"This is the most protected spot on the continent," Kal said. "You will be safe for as long as you wish to stay. We can turn it into a permanent site with some modern construction. It will take us about four days to put in proper accommodations for this group. Until then, it will be temporary housing. Is this adequate?"

"Thanks, and this will be fine," I said. "We should probably stay here a few days to see how things are going in the world, and if they compromised all of our locations."

"Very good. Along with protection, this site has portals leading to various locations, and we can also set some for other places you may wish to travel to. If you have a list, we can put those in the system."

"Great. I imagine Elias will need one back to his base, Jo to the Cottage, and I'm not sure where others need to go, possibly to Oklahoma now that North Carolina is compromised. And my new friend Smokey has a special portal we need to arrange. Kal, I assume you can contact him for that?"

"Yes, we can set one up for wherever you want."

"OK, Kal, how about those temporary accommodations? I assume ladies first, not because I'm sexist, but because Jo is pregnant and probably needs rest."

She hit me in the shoulder, hard. "Just because you say you aren't a pig does not mean that you aren't one. And whether I need it, and I do, does not mean you won't go unpunished."

"Yeah, Kal, what she said."

A structure that looked like a tent sprang up from the ground. The walls were an inch thick and flexible. Cots sprang up in the same way inside. A rock fireplace grew out of the ground. Most of the materials appeared to be chitin similar to what Kal had produced during the attack. I remembered chitin was present in fungi and abundant in the ground. The first tent was a demo, and several of us went inside with Kal to discuss other specific needs for the tents. Each tent would be customized for the occupants; interior walls went in for privacy; and each received one privy hole with a one-way valve. A hollow vine grew in each tent to bring in fresh water. We had everything but hot water, as Kal had food sent in. Each of Kal's people went out and set the rest of the tents up. We would have permanent buildings in a few days, with a heavier and more traditional construction look. Those were also customizable since each building was built resource-free and immediately recyclable back to the earth if not needed. Everyone sorted out their new living arrangements with no issues.

Kal reoriented a hot spring into the Valley, so we now had hot water piped to each structure. The houses had real bathrooms with showers and toilets and a heat sink for refrigeration. For now, we decided on a community food hall with a kitchen to centralize the cooking and eating. Each day, Kal or another would pull up a small slug of magma to a stone oven for cooking. Kal's people brought in food from the forest, so there was not much cooking, but sometimes I just had to sauté those wonderful mushrooms.

Elias and his team spent the first week with us, then they left to continue their duties. We really did not need them as a guard force in this protected location. The teenagers were going out to scout for colleges and business opportunities. They were also going home to North Carolina or Oklahoma to begin recruiting friends and family about coming for training next year. Normally an adult went with them to visit college campuses, and usually was Nan or I, but anyone could go depending on who was available. Travel in or out was only via the portal linkages. I did not mind at all, as I thought it beat the hell out of airplane travel. No one else complained either.

Jo went with us occasionally, but as she grew larger, she traveled less and grew pensive. She wanted to go back to Den Haag for the last month and to give birth at the Church facility. I agreed with her she was safer there with a full medical team. She talked to Michael, and he said there had been no sightings of the smoke demons, nor obvious activity from any master vampire. I escorted her back to Den Haag, then told her I would be back in a couple of weeks. Back in the Valley, I chanced upon Kal while walking along the stream. Not that I ever thought that I just 'chanced upon' Kal.

"I trust you find this place acceptable?" Kal asked.

"Very much so. I will miss North Carolina, but I appreciate the safety provided for these people. I know we have been incredibly lucky so far, and I cannot imagine losing any of them."

"You are growing in a good way. Your appreciation for defense, protecting people, and avoiding altercations will prove beneficial in the coming years." He said that with special earnestness, which I guessed hinted at Smokey's comment about Kal's people and their ascension.

"I suppose so. Oh yeah, travel around here is a lot better than using airplanes."

"You should be able to begin minor trips of your own soon. Your training appears to be going well."

"Not sure about trying that yet. But I look forward to it."

"To help with defense wherever you might need it, we have discovered a method to neutralize those you call smoke demons. We produce a type of glass to encase them rapidly, and we alter the silicon atoms so that the smoke demons cannot interact with the glass, either physically or through resonance. This glass is incredibly strong, but someone on the outside can break it, releasing the creature. Our intention is to encase the creature, then move it before anyone can aid its escape. We will drop them into an active volcano."

"That is harsh, but I like it."

"It's not what you think. The glass dissolves and releases the creature unharmed. But they seem to like volcanoes and wander inside them for weeks or longer before leaving."

"That is an elegant and nonlethal solution."

"We think so as well, and it fits within our philosophy of defense and nonlethal action. If you use the electrostatic metallic mist to confuse them and contact us, we can arrive quickly and begin encasing them within seconds."

"We definitely will do that if any show up. Any chance we can set up a sensor system where Jo is at?"

"That should not be a problem, but we will need to change it to work within an urban environment and housing. Also, it will only work when she is at home, not when she is outside the sensors."

"I understand, but it is better than nothing. But I wonder how Den Haag will react to having a few Bigfeet working in the neighborhood?"

"They won't see us, of course. Who should be alerted if there is an incursion?"

"Jo, Michael, and me, I guess. I'll be over there soon, so I could react quickly. I assume you will know first."

"Yes, and in this case, we will react to set up any defense needed, as well as an escape option. If anything happens, we will bring her here."

"Great, that makes me feel better about Jo being there."

"It is our pleasure to offer her protection."

"Thanks again. After our Minnesota trip, I think we need to always consider the unexpected."

"Yes, and that reminds me of something. Do you have time to take a brief trip with me?"

"Sure, I can go now."

We appeared in a cavern, but I did not know where. Kal noticed my thought and said, "We are not that far from the Valley. You know the Pacific coast is still a volcanic region, and we are in a cave near an active volcano, although there has been no major activity for twenty-thousand years. As your eyes adjust to the dark, tell me what you sense."

"I sense a faint light coming from somewhere. There is also something like a very faint pulse I can feel in my body."

"A group of sentient crystals abides here. They are aware of my presence and have put out a faint glow."

"Are you talking with them?"

"Not exactly. They don't think or communicate as we do. They sense my presence, but a brief conversation may take years. But after your experience in Minnesota, I wanted you to know that sentient crystals are not necessarily evil; they are a product of their environment and experience, as are all thinking creatures."

We walked further into the cavern, and now I could tell we were moving toward the faint light. I could detect faint subsonic pulses, mostly in my abdomen. There was a cluster of crystals sprouting from the floor of the cave, perhaps twenty crystals in all. The largest was about the size of my body, and the smallest was about the size of a water bottle. They were rhombohedral, similar to massive quartz crystals.

"They sense you, but do they sense me or other humans?"

"Normally no, but mining operations or underground nuclear tests have alerted them to humans. Some are triggered by other entities for their own purposes, such as the ones around the Great Lakes. But likely you won't have any interaction with them. These do not sense you directly yet, and likely won't unless you could send out signals they could understand."

"But they can react, as I've heard the story about the asteroid sent from Mars sixty-five million years ago."

"Yes, they will protect the planet once aware of a threat, although the response can take millions of years. Unfortunate that communication is so difficult, as some crystals have a billion years of knowledge stored. I believe it is time to proceed to the next location."

We winked away and then we were in a redwood forest, so I knew we were still in the same region as the Valley. Kal stood by a tree for a few seconds, then motioned me over. "Concentrate on emptying your mind, then listen for the tree."

I did as he said, and in a moment, I heard something like wind blowing in branches. I looked up but there was no wind, as I slowly realized a presence occupied the tree, somewhat cold, but I could also sense life within the tree itself. Kal asked me what I was experiencing, and I told him.

"You are sensing the tree's life, then. It may take further effort to have much communication. They are not as slow to converse as the crystals, but they still have a very different perspective than we do, which affects communication. Concentrate again and try to feel the forest."

I did as he asked, and gradually realized that I could sense the surrounding area, including below the ground. "How does that work? Are the trees connected?"

"Everything underground is connected unless the area has been recently disturbed. The older the area, the more connections. The tree roots connect with each other, all other roots present, fungi, nematodes, and everything else that lives together underground. Sometimes in the deep woods you can experience a hundred miles of forest connections, but sensory overload is a problem. You can learn how to do this with ease, and make sense of what you feel, if you use your slant."

"This is the basis of how you set up the sensors at the Farm, isn't it?"

"Yes, we used the existing connections from that site, added new fungi and roots where needed, then connected those to us. It's an elegant way to conduct surveillance of an area without disrupting it."

"With that knowledge, nothing can surprise you unless something comes in via air. That's why Odin uses crows and suggested owls at night."

"Correct. But there is another way to perceive the air. It's a much harder discipline to learn. You are aware the air is alive with microbes?"

"Yes, it is full of bacteria, fungi, spores, pollen, and other things. Some are free floating; some are on dust or water aerosols."

"The air changes quickly, but eventually you can learn to read it. The constant movements of the medium and the life within it makes reading it difficult. A warm, foggy night with no wind is the easiest time to practice air reading, as all the components are there and static, at least close to the ground. But it is difficult, and even some of my people cannot do it consistently."

"OK, then, that only leaves someone moving through the links to surprise you."

"Our ancestors, as they learned of the links, and both the advantages and dangers inherent in the system, learned to expect threats from it. That discipline is a unique type of perception compared to what we use on earth. But sentient creatures have a sense of time and the future, that they sometimes glimpse through incidents of déjà vu or visions. Through slant, you can learn that perception, recognizing patterns in the links and make you aware of what is happening in your vicinity."

"That is how you knew something was happening in that first valley, during our escape from North Carolina."

"Yes, I knew something was coming before its appearance. Once they touched the ground, I knew what they were, how many, and where they were."

"That is a significant advantage."

"Yes, my people have been using that knowledge for hundreds of thousands of years. It is what has allowed us to be a peaceful people during that time, as we do not fear unknown attacks. We can prevent them or leave the area before they occur."

"I think we need as a group to work on all those types of awareness. Will the trees be the easiest place for us to start?"

"Yes, that is the easiest for those who have knowledge and practice of slant. The shifters within your group already have an innate understanding of the tree awareness. Reading the air and link perceptions may be beyond most of your people until they become more proficient. I doubt most of you will ever need to converse with the crystals. However, I think you will soon have one that can master all those disciplines easily enough."

"How's that? Or rather, who is that?"

"I can already sense that the child Jo carries has an instinct for what we have discussed today. That surprised me, as she is the first human in many centuries to possess any innate ability. Even unborn, I sense she is more powerful in that respect than any human we have ever encountered. We will offer her our full protection. If it can be done, I would advise you to persuade Jo to return here. There will not be any place safer for them on this planet."

"I definitely will try. I know she has her own life and ideas, but maybe she can base her life here, and travel for her needs and career. And then she would know the child is in the safest place possible."

"I know you cannot and should not coerce another individual, and that is a main tenet of our principles and beliefs. At some point, I would advise you to suggest it to her and let her decide for herself."

"I will do that. And I know from experience to not even try coercion with her. Otherwise, I'll need your protection from her."

"Wise choice. We have accomplished today what I wanted. I believe that you and Henry can begin training your people on the tree and forest awareness. If Jo's child lives here, she will teach all of you that and more."

"I look forward to that day. Thanks for letting me know in advance."

"Knowing that you will keep her safe is my thanks. Time to return to the Valley."

CHAPTER TWENTY

Caius

I was in a bad mood; I might even say apoplectic. Such an arrogant word for rage, but that is what I felt. My servants, the few who remained, had never seen me in this state. That was usually bad for them, as I felt the need to kill one every few days for stress relief. Centuries of plotting and building my way of life were now over. No elegant homes or successful businesses. My years of good deeds helping all those young humans now wasted. Even worse was the loss of my personal human deli.

Puzzling that my latest success had led to my downfall. My efforts to persuade the Sky Lords that Senecus was their primary threat worked beautifully. Those smug, measly bastards from the future had given me the assignment and unlimited funds to end the prick. Lured to Prague, he was easy to trap there in the attractive park that covered the ruins of the ancient fortress. I had explored the area several times over the years and liked it so much I had a small bunker rebuilt there. It worked out well for an ambush site, and he fell into it.

My servants began cutting and shooting him apart to disable him for the dissection. The Sky Lords wanted just enough torso to contain his intestines and his head attached. Then the disaster struck. Those damned Church commandos, including Michael's new pet bitch, showed up and ruined everything. They killed most of my servants and were within minutes of finding me. They rescued Senecus, and he has now recovered. It quite disappointed the Sky Lords they were not getting a new microbiome to play with. That was only the beginning of my problems, however, as Michael's people tracked down almost all my assets and tried to ruin me. My shell companies, charitable organizations, multiple mansions, bank accounts, and nearly everything else. But they missed some things, plus I still have access to my contacts from the future. Meanwhile, I'm hiding in this disgusting industrial site near Arnhem as the next stage of this operation begins.

I have convinced the Sky Lords to help finish some of that old business and take care of the new threats. I expect to finish those old enemies, deal a blow to the Church, get my life back, and placate those dimwits from the future. But that is just the beginning of my real ambitions. In the short term, I will rebuild my loyal army of servants, use the two demons on loan to pursue the Sky Lord's goals, and plot with my colleagues how we will rule this world. And I already have plans set in motion to kill all my colleagues afterward. No reason to think small when all the world will soon be disrupted and the bold, which only includes me, can take all that is left. Who needed boring and slow climate change when sea levels could rise in weeks rather than centuries?

The two twin demons I now had control of would take me a long way to overcome my current enemies and then my colleagues. They now spent most of their time under the glaciers and ice caps doing their best to expedite the melting and cracking of the ice. The resulting disaster should reduce humanity by twenty-five percent and send the rest into chaos and decline. Perfect conditions for us master vampires. I already have locations ready in the mountains for when they finish their business and sea levels rise. In fact, I already had the blueprints prepared to build my palace in the Alps for when and the remains of the world are mine.

Although the Sky Lords had lent them to me, controlling those two was sometimes a problem. Mostly, I just gave them a list of places to go, things to steal or destroy, or people to kill. My demon blobs already had success in Bangkok on a simple task. They had been less effective at the fae realm and the Church Center, where my orders were more complex. Looking for important items, whether technology or powerful artifacts, and killing specific people. Their next orders were simple - kill Senecus when he appeared.

And he would appear, I will make sure of it. I am going to steal one of his darlings, and that will bring him back to me. Since his little favorite is pregnant, afterwards I'll have the additional pleasure of tasting her and the baby. The woman is quite attractive, and I was not sure whether to keep her and eat her before or after she gives birth. There were positives to either course. I had considered eating her in front of him, just before killing him, but the timing would be tricky. I do not expect there will be much left of him once my two big demons chew him up. Simple was better in this case. Trap and kill him, then later take my time eating her and the baby, or the fetus, depending on how long I could deny my urges. I will have plenty of time to consider my options without concern for Senecus or the Church interfering, since the demons from the Old Times have never been defeated. I can get even more credit from the Sky Lords for killing him, since two of my rivals recently botched assassinating Senecus and his Church friends in America. But my new plan I feel sure will work.

I once again thought about the details. The woman should be an easy grab and go for my men. Execution of it only awaited my order. I texted the team the order to move ahead. They will follow her and then kidnap her when the opportunity arises. The new facility is now finished, so no reason to wait. It was not far, and that was why I was here in this dreadful place. The Sky Lords had put significant efforts in the facility, an old air base, and intended it to be the operations center for northern Europe, thus its location in central Netherlands. And soon it would be on the new coastline. It will be nearly impregnable and that's where I'll set the trap to end Senecus and all his Church friends.

What once had been a problem for me was now a blessing. Somehow, he had gotten into the Church's good graces. Lucky for me, he will bring them with him, so I can ambush them all at once. Curious, all the time I had been aware of him, I assumed he was a vampire like me. Yet his actions and allies belied that. I did not know how a vampire could have allied with the Church, as none of the rest of us will ever get an invitation. I just could not think of anything else he might be, however. But now those allies and resources, which had been causing difficulties in my quest to kill him, would all end on the same day with him. I shall ask him what he is as I have the demons kill him.

That brought me to another issue as I thought back to Michael's new pet. Sources told me she was a research librarian for the Church, but now she was a commando, with enhanced physical capabilities. That was unlikely but intriguing. She even moved like a vampire, too, which was very odd. She needed to be dealt with and deserved an ending that was both insidious and degrading. She had been a problem for a while, evading my admittedly weak contract hitters twice before. But I will not make that mistake again. Hmm, a new plan formed, but I needed to improve it and then forward it to the Sky Lords. Maybe I will tell them Michael has a new way to create super soldiers and I can provide an example. That will get their attention, but I might not get to eat her if the Sky Lords wanted her instead.

I noticed I was salivating while thinking of eating people. It must be near dinnertime again. Tonight, was my weekly feast. I normally waited two weeks or more between feedings, but all this stress and the wretched living conditions were contributing to nervous eating. The young meal, wild caught nearby, was now tied up and awaiting my presence. I had to be careful with not scaring the meals too much before I ate them, as fear could give an off flavor to the muscle. A little sedation was the solution, which also made it easier to tie them up and hang them. Having them hung vertically, with legs exposed and both feet fastened to the floor, allowed me the freedom to move around my dinner. That way I could eat the hamstrings first, then move to the front for the quadriceps. Hmm, once again, thoughts of dinner were distracting me.

Senecus and the Church will both fall into my trap. Possibly even the fae would show up, as intelligence sources indicated Senecus was allying with them. Even if they were involved, it did not matter. The Sky Lords have no use for them and will be happy with their deaths. Anyway, they are a non-issue after hundreds of centuries of squabbling and murder within their realm have weakened them to the point, they are no threat. Their political turmoil reminded me of a few years I had spent in Constantinople centuries back. Byzantine was the word that best described the fae's needlessly complex politics. Of course, anywhere power and wealth concentrated, attracting the unfettered greed of royalty, religion, or both, humans became a mass of shifting alliances and evil intentions. Not that we minded, as it was a perfect feeding ground for my kind. But the pettiness grew old after a few centuries.

The Sky Lords reminded me of them, with better technology, of course. But they often acted the same and most of them were only puny humans and nothing special. Other than their advanced technology, I thought they were weaker than current humans. I would kill all of them I could once I ran this world, right after I had my colleagues killed. There was one from the future, however, that was not weak, but terrifying. A master vampire, but much older than me, and I sensed nothing but true evil. I doubted I will easily overcome such a monster, so I must ensure that this world was cut off once it was mine. The two demons might be an advantage, but I knew better than to count on such simple and insane creatures.

My list was long but achievable. Kidnap the woman, kill Senecus and Michael's forces, then have a snack. Let the demons finish their destruction and send the human world into turmoil from natural disasters as my colleagues and I take over. Kill all my colleagues, as many Sky Lords as possible, then shut them out. Rule the world forever. It was going to be a hectic couple of years, but well worth it to have everything I deserved. Now it was time to quit planning and get undressed for dinner; I hated getting blood on my suit or shoes.

Chapter Twenty-One

I was still bleary after traveling again. For some stupid reason I had flown over rather than getting Kal to send me through a link. I stopped off at the Amsterdam house to check on everything. After reading the mail, I went down and got in the car and drove to Woerden. I checked the place over, but everything was fine. I read the mail there, then grabbed a cider and sat in the living room to vegetate. I was too wound up, however, so I went out and started walking. It was another beautiful May in The Netherlands, full of exploding greenery and flowers, new dairy calves, and humans hogging the sun at every opportunity. I walked the town three times, then went to the market to get food for a week.

This was the week that Jo would likely deliver the first child born without a father's "input" for two thousand years. I decided I should be here and waiting, rather than hanging around the Valley. My memories told me that Hia had easy births because of her constitution, which might translate to Jo having an easier time than many first mothers would. Which meant the baby could come very fast. Plus, I was an excited father although nothing was happening. So here I was, walking miles a day, keeping my phone on at all times, and patiently waiting. I refrained from constant texting, and just sent one each morning to Jo to check in. After three days of that nonsense, I got in the car and drove to Den Haag.

Jo answered her door as I'd texted her that I was coming over. She looked just the same, except for the bean bag she was now wearing where her waist used to be.

"Hi Sen, what brings you over? Here to view the fatted calf?"

I thought about a dozen fat jokes but decided quickly that anything along those lines was taboo. "Hi Jo. Actually, you look pretty damn good, even with the big bump. I just came over to see you and ask if you wanted to go out for a walk, coffee, or a roller coaster ride over at Scheveningen?"

"A walk sounds nice, if we can hit up the bakery on the way back. If I thought the roller coaster would speed things up, I would be up for it. But I better desist and let nature wend its slow way instead."

"OK, your choice. How is work going, getting anything done these days?"

"Not much, just desk work. I have the joy this week of looking at next year's departmental budgets. If boredom were to dislodge babies from mothers, I should have disgorged by now. But no luck."

"Well, let's go walk and enjoy the day."

"Sure, I need to put my shoes on. That should not take me more than twenty minutes. And I can pee both before and after putting them on, which should get me through a fifteen-minute walk."

"Wow, you are quite a date." That earned me a death stare.

We strolled the neighborhood, over to a nearby park, then turned and went up the street to a local bakery. Dutch pastries could be hit or miss, but I had figured out which ones were consistently good. We picked out several to take, then we sat outside at a table for a cappuccino.

"Have you definitely decided on a name yet, or still waiting on the father's input?"

"That would be a no, on any of the father's choices. I've gone through a lot of possibilities, but my favorite has always been Isabel, as you know. I am going to stick with it."

"As the 'not the father,' nor someone that expects the mother to be swayed by his opinion, I'll be honest and say that is a beautiful name and a superb choice. I liked it since the first time I heard you say it."

"Despite all the qualifiers you just mouthed, thanks."

"Isabel, Isabel York, that is a good name."

"I think so. You aren't disappointed that I didn't take your name?" She was smirking while she said that.

"Not disappointed, just totally devastated is all." I faked a swoon, then Jo leaned toward me to hit me on the arm.

"Hey, don't be hitting the baby daddy proxy."

"You are still weird. Are you planning on being around for the delivery?"

"Yes, that is why I am here. I suspect that despite this being a first baby, the labor may be much shorter than normal."

"Well, that would be a welcome prophecy. I hope you are right. I assume you base that on experience?"

"Hia's labors were in the two to four-hour range. Of course, that was with no doctor present. Are you delivering here at the Church facility?"

"Yes, it is close, private, and Michael has arranged a small team of doctors and nurses to be on call. Helicopter is on standby for the hospital is something goes seriously wrong."

"Good, sounds like you will be in excellent hands."

"How long are you staying afterwards?"

"As long as you need me to be around. I expect you will be up and healed in a couple of days, but then the real fun begins. Sleep deprivation won't be such an issue for you, but the wear of the constant day and night attention that Isa will need can be overwhelming. Especially since this is your first one."

"Isa, you say? Already got that nickname picked. I kind of like it too. But you are probably right. I remember the first child born of both my sister's.

There was always a six-week ordeal of insanity, followed by a few months of simmering nerves."

"Sounds about right, but you are uniquely adapted to get through this better than they were."

"That is good to know. I will keep you at my beck and call to change diapers and for night feedings, at least for a few months, then."

"At your service, my dear."

We walked back, and I left her at her house. She was too miserable to want much company. That night I was in Woerden and dozing in my chair when Jo called.

"I hope you were in bed and that I woke you up."

"Right on both counts, my dear. What can I do for you, other than brighten your evening since now you know you disturbed me?"

"I was trying to sleep but couldn't, and now I'm having contractions. I'm walking over to the clinic to see if this is the real thing or not."

"Thanks for letting me know. I'll see you in thirty minutes."

"No reason to yet, as this could be false labor."

"Yeah, no, I don't believe your new body works that way. I know it sounds like mansplaining, and it is because you woke me and gloated about it. I'll see you soon." I hung up before she could reply.

I got to the Church clinic in Den Haag and the guards waved me in with a cursory security check, as they had seen me before, both as a visitor and patient. Jo was in a bed with two nurses and a doctor in the room. They had all seen me before, too.

I sat in the room and watched as they got all the wires attached and the machines running. Jo went into a contraction and the nurse checked her, then I heard her telling the doctor that things were moving faster than expected. He moved over to Jo and told her to relax between contractions, and work on her breathing during the peak of the contraction. Then he told her it would be hours before much happened and asked if she needed anything for the pain before he went home.

I got up to intervene. "Hey doc, if she has been in contractions for an hour, she should deliver in less than two hours."

"I doubt she will proceed that quickly. I appreciate your concern, but we will continue monitoring through the night and keep her comfortable."

"Uh, no, I don't think so. This is my eleventh time through this, and I've never seen one get to four hours yet."

Right on cue, Jo went into another contraction. The doctor looked like he wanted to argue, but the fast contraction convinced him to check for dilation instead. "Oh, yes, I see now. She is at seventy percent, and it's been... thirty minutes. OK, everyone, we should prepare for delivery."

The nurses just looked at each and smirked as they already knew it. I knew they were both competent and wondered if I should have just let the doctor go home. The nurses picked up the pace and started moving things around while the doctor was doing nothing but acting busy. I knew he was good, but he probably had not been in this situation since residency, and of course, had never attended a pregnant woman quite like Jo.

I stood by her and grabbed her hand. "Ok, this is going to hurt like a bitch the next hour. Then it will be over. I'll be standing here if you need something to squeeze on or beat to a pulp. Just not the face, OK?"

"No promises," she said and laughed, then went into another contraction. I might have guessed long on that hour. Sure enough, twenty minutes later, a baby girl arrived. Two hours total for the labor and delivery, but the effort was worth it. She was tiny and adorable as the nurses snipped the cord, wiped her down, and did the first round of checks. The baby was making noises but not crying. Then they handed her to Jo, as they pushed down her gown, so the little human I was already calling Isabel could lie on Jo's bare chest. The doctor had already checked Jo and seemed surprised there were no issues, as the placenta easily passed, and she needed no stitches. I doubted he ever attended a birth as easy as this one.

"Hey, decide for sure on that name?" I asked Jo.

"Isabel it is. A beautiful name that fits a beautiful little girl."

"Yes, I second that. How are you doing?"

"It was rough for a couple of hours but based on what I heard from my sisters and others, I had it easy."

"You did well. And your payoff is that little bundle lying on you."

"It was definitely worth it. Do you want to hold her?"

"Of course."

I had Isabel for a few minutes, then the nurses came to start their rounds with Jo and check Isabel again. They talked to Jo about breastfeeding and other topics out of my jurisdiction, so I tuned out. I regained awareness once they had left and told Jo that I was staying for the night. She nodded and then seemed to doze off, now holding Isabel.

I closed my eyes, reached out with my other sight, and saw two bright comets. All was good in the world. Then one comet seemed to move closer to me - that was new. I reached out in my mind and felt a warm, curious presence. After I sent out feelings of comfort and love, the comet grew brighter and then went back to the other comet. I guess I had just had a conversation with my sort-of daughter. That was something I would keep to myself until I could talk to Kal.

I never really went to sleep, just light napping as I kept expecting Isabel to wake up and howl. But she never did. I think she wanted her mother to rest first. A few hours later, still dark, Michael came in. I waved, saying nothing as he stood over Jo's bed, admiring Isabel. After a few moments, he made to leave, and I went with him.

"I heard everything went well."

"Yes, it did. Jo had much less trouble than most, thankfully. And Isabel is already an exceptional baby."

"I would expect nothing less. But what do you mean by exceptional?"

"Oh, I think people should find that out for themselves."

He looked at me with the look that I suppose most saw just before he killed them. But I just smiled cryptically.

"Are you inferring that she is already special?" he asked.

"That I am. But that is all I'm saying for now. Other than she needs the best care and security within the Church's purview. Possibly higher than that, if you can convince others."

"If I understand your implications, then this is a special life."

"Yep. But you know better than me how dangerous that is."

"Yes, I do, unfortunately. But I will handle this myself."

"Good. You are coming back later when Jo is awake?"

"Assuredly so. I want to spend time with them both."

"I'll stay with them until you get back. Goodnight."

He gave me a wave and walked out. I think I had accomplished my goal of alerting Michael, without others that could have been listening, that he needed to bring in his best people. I went back to the chair and resumed my watch. Isabel looked over at me, which should be impossible at her age. I closed my eyes, and we traded ethereal hugs again.

Isabel had slept most of the night, as had Jo. Both were now wide awake, and Jo was ready to get up. Another day and she would heal completely. Hurrah for enhancements. I walked with Jo out to the garden as she carried Isabel. Michael came over, and I said my goodbyes and left him to get acquainted with Isabel.

I got the call earlier than most people should be alive, while sitting in my Woerden study, wondering about all the recent changes. I was annoyed by the call, as I thought that what cell phones had become - a supreme annoyance.

If this was another robocall about car warranties in America, I was going to track them down and rip out their liver. I envisioned that sight when I picked up the phone. It was Thomas instead.

"What the hell, Thomas? It is five am. You are never up this early."

"I'm here with Kate."

"What?"

"Anna is missing."

"What?"

"Are you still asleep? Anna is missing, gone. We think she's been taken."

Dammit was the least of the curses I unleashed in the following seconds. "OK. Are you at Kate's right now? Stay there while I drive over. Meanwhile, tell me everything you know so far. I need to know everything, any detail that Kate can think of."

"I'll put the phone on speaker."

Kate began talking while I jogged down to the car. I switched my liver removal scenario from the robocaller to someone else. I was worried I knew that identity, however, and that Caius was back on the game board. Kate met me at her door and hugged me as I came in.

"Thanks for coming. Do you think you can help find her?"

"Yes, Kate, I will find and bring her back." And I was thinking about how I would destroy whoever took her at the same time.

"Oh god, Sen, I'm so worried. Who would take a pregnant woman?"

"I'm not sure, Kate, but I will get her back, I promise."

"Can you really do this?"

"Definitely. If you have any doubts, ask Thomas to fill you in, if he has not already. I've been doing this for hundreds of years, and now I have one of the world's largest organizations to help. And a few more of the world's oldest beings as allies."

"You sound so sure. It makes me feel better just hearing you say it. Wait - hundreds of years?"

"Yes. Kate, my job is to find things and to make things better. Thomas can give you more details, as I can't stay long. Now that you told me what you know, I need to start some things in motion. I'll explain the rest after you talk to Thomas. I am the guy to get Anna back."

"Oh, thank god, Sen. Please get her back. Thomas... can tell me the rest?"

"Yes, he can. Kate, I do this for real, and you can trust me to get Anna back. Trust Thomas, trust me, and this will be over soon."

I left, made one call, then I called Michael, and started for the Cottage.

Another call came in a few minutes later as I was on the road. I answered and heard an old acquaintance. "Oh, Senecus," Caius cackled. "She is so lovely, and quite plump with child. I can hardly wait to taste her. You really should come out and play. Maybe I'll have a BBQ, and you can come over to help eat her. Hello, are you there? Senecus? Senecus, don't make me lose my temper. I might just have to start early. Be a dear and bring the buns, would you? I think I have everything else here that I need."

"You sure that's what you want to have for your last meal?" I hung up after I checked the call timer.

Monk texted me back a few seconds later. I had alerted him I'd need a trace. The call was from near the old Deelen airbase north of Arnhem. I turned around and went back to Kate and Anna's house.

Thomas answered the door, with Kate behind him.

"Hi Sen, did you forget something?" Thomas asked as I came in.

"No, but I wanted to tell you I know who took her, and I know where she is. As soon as I leave here, I'll be meeting with a group of allies to get her back. But it may be tomorrow before we can do it."

They both stood looking at me like I was speaking a foreign language. Then they both hugged me.

"I can't believe you found out that fast. What is happening? Why would they take her?" Kate asked.

"This is part of a much bigger piece of history, where groups have been at each other for thousands of years. Anna has nothing to do with it, except that they probably saw her with me. I think they took her to get to me, as they need to kill me. I'm so sorry, Kate, that I'm the reason they took Anna."

Her face told me she was mad at what I had just said. She also had been looking at me tentatively since I had come back.

"Thomas, have you told Kate about me?"

"Yes, just the highlights, not the details. But even the highlights are difficult to explain."

"Yeah, I know. Kate, I'll explain as much as you want, but after I get Anna back tomorrow. Kate, look at me. I'm the same guy you have always known. That hasn't changed. What has changed is that you are finding out that I have a much deeper past than most, and lately, a much more exciting group of friends. But all that comes together now and is a plus to get Anna back. OK, are you good?"

She nodded a yes. "But aren't they going to kill you when you show up?"

"The joke's on them. They can't kill me." Kate and Thomas looked at me like I was crazy, then I took off.

I was on the phone again, setting up logistics for multiple people and scenarios. Michael and his people were a tremendous help, and I appreciated it, because he also had to get his people and plans in order. I requested he put Jo and Isa into whatever version of Fort Knox they had around here, but he was already on it. I was going to end things, and whether I had help or not, I would fix this and keep my people safe. Michael had given me a safe address, and I called Thomas to take Kate and Willem there. Now I could concentrate on killing Caius.

We all met at the Cottage later that day. Michael was hosting; Henry and Nan represented the American contingent, with Elias, Zena, and several I did not know from the American Church. Simon was there as well. I just wasn't sure who he was representing since he worked with everyone. Altogether, that must have been one expensive jet trip. Morrigan sat on the sofa apart from everyone, and looking bored, sexy, and attentive all at the same time. I don't know how that worked, but she had been practicing it for a few thousand years.

Everyone settled in as they spread out several large maps, showing the expansive, mostly abandoned, airbase. I broke character by speaking first. "To start this gig tomorrow, I'm going in solo, and take all this open middle area under my control. While I'm doing that, I need everyone else to get into position on the periphery and stay covered for five minutes once the action starts. That will give me time to destroy all the defenses."

"How the hell you gonna do that, Sen? Not only can't you do it, you can't survive it." Elias was blunt, as usual.

"Can and will. I'm bringing party favors from some an old ally. Those first five minutes I'm going to destroy everything on the surface and it's going to be mostly indiscriminate. That's why I need that section clear of our people. Then you guys seal up the periphery, of which there is a lot, as the map shows. I need the shifter team in the air, on the ground, and underground out there and relaying me and central communications anything that is seen that could affect the mission. I'll stay up for a while and put on a show that will keep occupied any ground forces I miss. They'll be too distracted from that to be shooting at you all. After that, I go underground for the genuine show. When I clear most of that, you guys need to move in and come down for cleanup. So, that's the basic plan. I'm not going into specifics but trust me when I say I can and will do what I just outlined."

Everyone looked as I thought they would after that rant. It ranged from "he's crazy" to "oh, hell no". But they didn't challenge me, much.

Michael went through the detailed maps of the base. He had to explain a little about its history to get everyone to understand what they were facing. Even though I was handling ninety percent of the enemy forces, the other ten percent scattered in that large of a periphery, that included some massive bunkers and tunnels, could be a problem.

"We should begin the operation tomorrow night," Michael said.

"Tomorrow about noon should be good, if we have everybody in place," I said.

"Uh, we have a better chance of success with at least some element of surprise, and darkness is in our favor in this case," Elias said.

"At any other time, I would agree with you. But I need daylight for this. I'm going to give them 'shock and awe' the likes of which would make the Americans and Russians piss their pants. I intend to disorient the enemy by making myself the focal point, destroy their central forces and armaments, while our teams will probably be unnoticed, especially at first."

"That type of display is short-lived for the displayer," Michael said.

"Not in this case. You are just going to have to trust me. Everyone will be watching me, especially while I'm smiting the hell out of them."

"Smiting has a certain connotation not usually associated with mortals," Michael responded.

"Exactly right. Smite is the word. Now let's plan out the rest." Everyone was looking speculatively at me. I was being generous with that. Most were still looking at me like I was batshit crazy. Which I was, right now.

Surprisingly, Morrigan spoke up. "We must trust in Sen's stupidity, as it is what he does best. Whether he succeeds or fails, this will be a grand gesture worthy of remembrance and possibly song."

"Thanks, I think," I responded.

"Sen, just one question."

"Go ahead, Michael."

"You can do all this?"

"Yes."

"Good. I'm convinced, so let's plan all the periphery action to support Sen." Michael knew I was planning something big, and between the fae, Kal, Odin, and Smokey, he figured I had it covered. The only other confident looks were from Henry and Morrigan.

The Deelen Air Base was mostly closed down except for a few trainings. It was a substantial WWII airfield built by Germans. Hangars and bunkers were built to look like barns and farmhouses. It was isolated, built on one edge of the Hooge Veluwe National Park, the same place I had conducted a number of secret meetings. There was just enough traffic around to cover for Caius' activities. And a great place for me to do something epically grand and stupid, kind of like what Morrigan had said.

There were quite a few buildings around the far periphery. The old airfield itself was wide open, with landing strips and grass fields, making it difficult to approach easily. We set up teams on foot to sweep the individual buildings. The shifter team was under Henry's control and would do as I had already mentioned, then support Michael's veteran units. Morrigan was bringing a contingent of hers. She told me it was time to try out her new toys, indicating her team were fae that had taken the injections and turned. I was grateful for all the help we could get on the ground.

We knew the enemy was in the existing hardened bunkers, and in a new large underground facility built right under one of the concrete runways. So that meant tunnels as well. Not the easiest nut to crack, but I was bringing a massive nutcracker to the party. I excused myself from the planning, as I had somewhere to be. Michael caught me before I left.

"I know you don't want to hear this right now, but when you find Caius, we would appreciate having him alive. Taking down his remaining network would be easier if he were alive for interrogation."

"Sorry, I can't promise that."

"I thought so. Here, take this dagger, and if you run into something unexpected, use it. You know it has immense power and will conquer any enemy you face."

"Thanks, I always appreciate extra help." I put it on my belt and left. I sent out a mental message to Kal for help as well. I knew he could not actively participate, but I asked him if he could tap into the "ground network" of all the underground biota at the base and give me information as to who was where. Thankfully he agreed.

Chapter Twenty-Two

I found him where and how I always found him - I put myself in a likely place and let him find me. Another graveyard at night, full of military dead, this time in the Netherlands. The door of light appeared, then I tossed him the bottle of mead, and strolled through.

"It's a good night to die. But an even better one to live, don't you think?" Odin asked.

"I haven't died yet, so I can't comment on that. But living tonight, and having a swig of mead, sounds preferable."

Two horns appeared in his hand, and he poured us each a draught. I had gone the extra mile to get the good stuff. He handed me a horn, and we touched them together, then drained them.

He looked at me. Then he looked through me with that one crazy kaleidoscope eye and that other crystal one. After a moment, he turned around to the table behind him. He handed me both Thor and Loki, the hammer and the stone, with a sigh. "It is the only way to accomplish what you need to do, in the time that you have to do it. But you already knew that. To do otherwise means that she and most of the others you care for will be dead by nightfall. They will only be the first of millions. But you know the cost. Are you sure?"

"Damn right. It's a trade I'm willing to make."

"If you really knew everything that follows after using these gifts, you might not make that decision."

"If I knew everything, I would be a god, and I'd get somebody else to do it. But I'm not, so this decision is mine. Sorry to cut this short but got to go. I need to practice some things before lunch tomorrow."

"Well, you have the right attitude for a god. If I may, I'll open a portal to a secluded place to where you can practice unobserved."

"Thanks, that should save me some time. Or I'll be driving my car around the countryside like some ordinary pedestrian god."

"Since the same person has never before wielded Thor and Loki together, there may be pitfalls, or there may be synergies. Either way, they will super-charge you enough to kick a god's ass. Skoal."

"Skoal," I said as I stepped through the opening he carved out of air.

I felt like I had once again fallen into the world's strangest elevator shaft. Then I was standing in a field of dunes in the middle of nowhere. Of course, it wasn't nowhere but the wild lands between Haarlem and the North Sea, north of Zandvoort. Less than five miles away, I could catch the train back to Amsterdam. Or I could flap my wings or snap my fingers to get back.

I hefted Thor in my right hand and felt the incredible raw power it fed into my body. My left hand held Loki, and I felt the power and weirdness it fed into my head. Drugs never had tempted me, as they had little effect on me, but what I was feeling now must have been like mainlining a cocktail of all the major substances. I freaked out a little as the hammer and stone melded into the flesh of my arms. With a thought, they dropped back out and into my hands. That would be handy if I needed to answer my phone, hold a beer, or urinate during the fight.

I reabsorbed them, then began exercises into slant and shapeshifting. I immediately felt the power of the Loki stone. Shifting was effortless, not just into animals, but into anything I could imagine. It gave me the ability to see all the linkages around me and highlighted the ones I might need as I thought through them. My strategic and tactical abilities were now off the chart, and a whole new level of sneakiness overtook my consciousness. Then I realized I was also accessing memories bound in ancestral DNA.

The hammer gave me the unlimited power to change into whatever I wanted, regardless of the size or amount of energy needed. I could also stomp on any nearby god and crush them like a roach. Damn, this was going to be the best ride of my life. Of course, I was trading some twenty-four hours in exchange for early onset dementia and centuries of life. Might as well enjoy this time.

Both objects in me were thrumming with energy. Somehow, they must be linked with another dimension and constantly pulled on that energy. I was not even competent enough to postulate how physics like that might work. But it was awesome for me. I worked through the list of things I had thought I might need to be for the battle tomorrow. The Loki stone completely changed my plans. Amazing things were about to happen as this god stuff could be addicting. Which was probably why the associated costs were high, preventing mortals from surviving long enough to act like, well, gods. Time to work on my plans and make sure I could turn all my strange thoughts into practice.

Hours later, as I fell from my own conjured door and into the sky, I changed to a Cherokee Thunderbird, as big as a commercial jet. Not that I really knew what such a creature looked like other than vague ancestral memories. I was just making it up as I went. I was above the Deelen Air Base and looking for my targets when I saw the likely turret and missile locations and started my run. My T-bird spat down a massive, concentrated ring of force meters in diameter, with a bolt of lightning in the center that swept buildings away. Thunder roared after each emanation. Defenses popped up, including turrets that looked familiar to the ones from Minnesota. They were the first to go as I realized how much fun I was having.

Coming from the other direction was a huge, armored attack helicopter. The defenders thought it wasn't showing on their radar screen because of stealth technology. The real reason they didn't pick it up was because it didn't exist, which I suppose was quite stealthy. But they spent gunfire and missiles against it, which obviously had no effect. The few installations left gave away their locations, so I finished them on a second pass.

Then I turned around resorted to the old tried and true giant dragon form. I didn't know which color was baddest for a dragon, so I went bantam rooster, with multiple iridescent colors. I was big, bright, breathing fire, and having fun. I concentrated and turned the scales on my underside into titanium to deal with any scattered fire coming up. My fifty-meter wingspan sped my journey. Flying was hard at first compared to the T-bird, but I quickly realized how much fun it was. There were two other dragons flying in formation with me, and they were fake as the helicopter. I flew over any installations that were left and brought fire to each ruined building and defensive troop positions. The damage was impressive, but I knew the real defenses would be underground. But there were no surface defenses left to impede Michael's teams.

My fake helicopter then landed and disgorged scores of giant furry spider creatures the size of dogs. I assigned one each to all the enemy ground combatants left. The spider illusions were also impervious to bullets and kept hounding each soldier as they wildly spent ammunition while trying to run away. I then created a second layer of goodness as drone-sized stinging dragonflies and sent one after each soldier just for fun. After a bit, they realized those things were not real. Then I thought up some leopard-sized cats covered in porcupine quills. They thought those were fake too and didn't bother wasting ammo on those. But they were just corporeal enough to claw the enemy to death or fill the soldiers with poison spines. I needed to whisk those away before Michael's teams moved in from the periphery. I was using the advantages granted by the Loki crystal. The only cost was your brain afterward.

Meanwhile, I was cloaking Henry, Jen and Seth as they flew in from the north. Henry dropped and turned into a triceratops crossed with a sabre-tooth tiger, and cleaned up all the troops above, mostly along the periphery, or those re-emerging from underground. They were so disoriented they didn't know what was real and what wasn't. Not likely their bullets could penetrate Henry's armor, anyway. Jen and Seth were busy checking each building and recording and transmitting real-time data to send to Michael's forces, which were inbound in three minutes. Morrigan's group of enhanced fae looked almost like werewolves, and completely cleared their area with no prisoners taken. Very effective yet brutal, as they had no love for vampires because of previous encounters.

It was time to change tactics, as all the toys had disappeared on the surface. I dropped to the ground and changed forms. I was now a huge green biped hulk figure, but I didn't like the green, so I changed to blue and put on scales, per my Danu nature. I thought up and detonated an EMP-like device underground to fry any portals out of the place to eliminate escape routes. Then I went into a partially standing hangar building with an oversize elevator. I took a second to think all my porcupine-kitties out of existence, then I ripped off the doors and surrounding frame, and dropped below to go kick some ass. I fell several stories and landed on top of the elevator car, crushing it like a grape, then I clawed through the wreckage and into the facility. Sporadic gunfire hit me, but I was impervious to anything up to and including a depleted uranium round from a tank. I had learned my lessons from past mistakes. Go big or go dead.

The few soldiers in front of me quickly broke and ran, and I pounded down the hallway. I entered a huge open area that I suppose was the common space for the new underground portion of the compound. I saw the running soldiers stop, then try to move sideways to get away from what was in front of them and that which was coming from behind. Running through them like they were not there, I ran right up to the bouncers for this joint. The two things were large and disturbingly disgusting, looking bigger than the night I had last seen them. These were the demons, here to set the trap Caius had planned. Oh yes, things were about to get fun, at least for me; not so much for these guests. They did not register on my senses, other than maybe blobs of black ice. They did not show any fear as they advanced toward me. I would rectify that.

The first one morphed into something roughly my size and shape, with lots of horns and teeth and spikes everywhere. Very amateurish. The other did the only smart thing I had observed so far, stepping back to watch the initial conflict.

The first thing swung a ponderous arm with spikes toward my head. Before it reached me, I extended a long sharp spine from my chest, under its arm and deep into the center of that demon. That spine also held Michael's dagger near the tip, as I saw no reason to play fair. A weird whistling sound immediately erupted from the creature as the dagger completely sucked the black smoke into it. It was over in less than a second. The dagger felt heavy for a fraction of a second, then back to normal weight. There was a clinking noise once the smoke critter disappeared, as a pearl the size of a basketball dropped to the floor. Well, that answered the mystery of the missing pearl from Bangkok. I needed to tag it so Michael could get it back to Thailand. But first I had another issue to deal with.

The second creature spun around to flee. I turned a shade of red, added some more amphibian features, then I materialized in front of it and put twenty spines throughout it. Metallic spines charged with electricity, but not the dagger this time. It was my time to play, and I needed to practice my Loki skills. It screamed and morphed into a series of monster forms. This thing was stupid, or at least limited in its thinking. It only tried organic forms of monsters I supposed it thought would scare me or overwhelm my organic form. I had no intention of playing fair or staying in the box.

I turned into an F-6 tornado, stronger than any ever seen on the Oklahoma plains. Only forty feet tall but with 400 km per hour wind speed. The base of the vortex was a much higher rotational speed than that. I also materialized thousands of razor blades, pieces of broken glass, and a roll of barbed wire in the funnel. As I had figured, the demon goon never thought out of the box, but was rather a one-trick pony that only morphed into other biological beings. If it turned into a titanium ball bearing, then I couldn't hurt it in this form, but then I would turn into a hydraulic press and crush it, regardless.

The thing never had a chance. I blenderized each form it tried until it was a reddish grey lump about a fourth of its original size. It then tried to escape by turning into smoke, but I quickly contained it and concentrated it back to the ground. It then changed back to the lump, mewling like something alive. I changed back to bipedal, then smiled as I leaned down to the lump and slid the blade into the middle of it. Same result as the first one, as the knife instantly hoovered the lump into the blade. Again, a heaviness, then back to normal weight. I sent a mental message to all my allies that the heavyweight defenses were neutralized. More gunfire sounded as Michael's forces swept into the underground.

Not one to gloat too much, I morphed back into something close to my size and shape, then into just plain old Senecus. The pissed off version, now strong as a god. That was a terrible combination for my enemies.

I found a vending machine and felt the need for a snack, so I ripped off the front of the machine to grab two bags of chips. I spent a second eating, then sprinted off for where I sensed Anna was via Kal's network. A wide hallway led away from the common area, with several metal doors along its length. I got to one and ripped it off the frame, then slid it down the hallway. Anna stood there with her hands on her hips, looking coolly at me.

"Well, it is great to see you, Senecus."

"And you as well, Anna. Hungry?" I held up a bag of chips.

"Hah, you know I like pretzels," she said as she came and hugged me.

"Good to see you, my dear. I have one quick piece of business to deal with, then we are out of here. Are you OK?"

"I'm good, now. Is your business finding Caius? If so, I'm going with you."

"You sure? It's going to be gory."

"I can handle it, since I deal weekly with childbirth and sometimes get to rummage in people's guts and other delicates. I want to watch."

"OK. Just don't hold what you are about to see against me."

"I won't. I just want to see that vermin exterminated."

"One dead whiny bitch coming up. This will be good for both of us."

I felt Caius' presence one level down, so I sent my thoughts out and I found a stairwell that ended after one flight, with a short hallway closed off with an armored door. I took Anna downstairs with me, then kept her behind me as I morphed to another hulk form and kicked the metal door down. Caius looked both quite surprised and worried. There was a small open portal on the other end of the large concrete room, but I was between he and it. He was fiddling with something that looked suspiciously like a bomb, possibly nuclear. He began to speak, but I did not give him the chance. Today I wasn't into banter, just killing, and he was going to be the last. A spike from my body pierced his chest and slung him fifty meters across the room. I didn't want him to finish playing with the device. I turned back into Senecus as I blinked across the room beside the groaning body of Caius, as I picked him up to face me.

Just for fun, I thought about the knife that the Uya had thrown at me in Arizona, now floating with the asteroids. I located it and brought it screaming back into existence, right into the base of Caius' spine. It was just a couple of degrees above absolute zero and it did not go well with a master vampire's flesh. I reached around to grab it as I encased my hand in a glove and swirled the knife around his intestines to be sure and introduce his little beasties to the null temperature steel. He screamed as I moved the blade around inside him. I yanked it out, then beat him completely senseless onto the floor. I picked his mostly limp body up and slammed him on his stomach. With both my knees on the back of his neck, I grabbed his head with both hands, and twisted and pulled as hard as I could.

His head popped off with a memorable sound. I stood up and drop kicked the head as hard as possible into the far concrete wall. It partially popped open with a sickening crunch. It was a few centuries late, but now it was done. Just to be safe, I trotted over to the head and stuck Michael's dagger in it.

To Anna's credit, she looked quite satisfied as she waited for me on the far side of the room. I wondered if my actions might have been a little over the top for her. She just gave me a grim smile and a positive nod. I put my arm around her and walked her out of the room and into the hallway. I sent a priority message to Michael that I need his presence immediately. Three minutes later, he was there.

"Hi Senecus, and you must be Anna. Dreadfully sorry you had to be put in this position. Please let me know if you need anything, now or in the future."

"OK Michael, turn off the gentleman charm, and come in the room to talk me out of doing something stupid."

We went in and he looked a little pale when he saw the device.

"I don't know if he had time to activate it, but if he did, I have a plan," I said. "Which is tossing it through that portal over there, the one that I imagine he was going to use for an escape after leaving us this bomb. Not sure where the portal goes since my device should have shut all of them down a few minutes ago. So, talk me out of it."

"Hmm. The portal could lead to somewhere else on Earth, so a nuclear bomb would not be good idea, especially if local. If it led to the Sky Lords, then it could be useful, but again likely to wipe out innocents as well."

"Very well, I am talked out of it. Could I at least get a bag of explosives to toss in there?"

"Sure, just a moment." He radioed in his request as he walked to the portal. He stuck his head in for a second, then pulled it back out. I had never seen that before. I heard footsteps as his person came in with a bag, which he handed to Michael. He reached in, turned on a detonator, and flung it through the portal. I had expected that, so I had retrieved the armored door, which I now held against the portal. We heard a muffled explosion, then the portal disappeared.

Michael's people were everywhere now, as they had come down to secure the bomb. I wondered where that would end up as I walked Anna upstairs, then to a functional elevator. At the top, we were greeted by sunlight, as most of the surrounding building was gone, courtesy of my earlier dragon form. Two of Michael's people were guarding the area.

I saw some of our group, and I left Anna and hurried toward Henry's figure as he was leaning over Jen and Seth. Before I got there, I saw an old man materialize for less than a second behind Henry, touch Seth, then disappear. When I arrived beside Henry, I could tell both Jen and Seth had been shot, and Seth was seriously wounded. My first thought was that Odin had claimed a mortally wounded Seth. Jen was OK, and suddenly Seth was looking much better. Henry had an odd look on his face.

"Did you just see or feel anything odd? I thought Seth here was about to pass. Now he's looking much better."

"Henry, I think we just got a mulligan from an old friend. I'm pretty sure I saw Odin for just a second. He can be a healer, rather than a reaper of warriors. I'd say that Seth just entered a new reality. Odin must have something special planned for him, rather than taking him to Valhalla today. Anyway, let's get these two over to the ambulances before Odin changes his mind." We picked Seth and Jen up, and I asked Anna to come over and go with us. No reason she needed to be here any longer. All three went into the oversized medical van, and I told Anna I would see her soon. I also grabbed a phone so she could call Kate.

Michael was near a truck bristling with guns and antennas. "I'm guessing that Caius was that mess of a torso downstairs and no longer among the living?"

"Correct. I felt the need to play a little old-style Mayan soccer."

"With his head?"

"Most definitely."

"I see. That would hamper any interrogation efforts. Did you get your friend Anna taken care of?"

"Yes, got her a phone and then over to the med van, just in case."

"You seem whole, but are you OK?"

"I'm pretty damn wonderful right now. Probably won't be able to say the same for tomorrow or next year, though, once the glamour wears off. I need to get back to an old friend and drop off some party favors. You guys got all this handled for cleanup?"

"Yes, all the resistance is now killed or captured, so our cleanup teams will finish moving out any bodies and munitions, then disappear. Rumor has it you took care of a couple of other major entities?"

"Oh yes, that reminds me, here is your dagger back. Splendid piece of swag as it sucked Nasty and Black Lung right out of existence. They were the two great big dark things that seemed more demonic than organic."

"I see we may need a debriefing when you get back. I assume that your old friend keeps company with ravens?"

"Oh yes. Those damn birds can eat. Probably strip a water buffalo in two minutes. But I digress. Michael, things may go bad for me soon. We need to chat so I can get things in order."

"We definitely will. If you have done what I think you have, then sooner is better. From what we have seen remaining of the compound, all this could not have been done by you alone. And we have a video of some odd airborne objects."

"That was me, of course. I had a couple of presents from that wily old one-eyed coot."

He looked stricken. "Oh no, not that. You used both weapons?"

"Yep, only way to get it done right."

"You don't do things halfway, do you?"

"Things worth doing don't deserve half an effort. Caius and his group needed ending."

"We agree on that. But what was the cost?"

"I'll let you know when I know. Gotta go now."

I blinked out and landed back in the war cemetery. Odin opened the door and motioned me in. I morphed Thor and Loki out of my body and into my hands. A table was just inside, already set with food.

"My son, you did not start this war, but you may have just set those fools back by millennia. Good show, I have not seen such a display of smite in many a year. Not only did you get that sniveling vampire, but you also took out two top lieutenants."

"Uh, thanks? I'm always happy to take out the trash."

"Here, drink this mead and take this bread with honey. It will replenish you in the near term. Nothing will help long term, but it will honor me to escort your soul when it's your time."

I handed the hammer and crystal back to Odin, then picked up the mead and bread. He hefted both weapons, then grunted. He looked closely at me. "Damned appropriate. Never seen this before, but damned appropriate. Welcome to the club, boy. Hope you survive it. I see your eye is already turning color."

I just smiled. The hammer and crystal had felt slightly lighter now than when I had first gained them. Somehow, I had just picked up another little piece of a god.

"Enjoy it while you can. Those tiny splinters will help, but you don't have very long, even with them. After your demise, those portions will migrate back to the source."

"Thanks for the notice. And thanks for the save on Seth. Meanwhile, I'll keep these splinters a little longer. I believe I have some more business to take care of, although hopefully not the martial type."

"Yes, you have some more business. Your surprises aren't over yet. On the positive side, your traveling will soon be easier with that eye." He laughed, grabbed my shoulder in a fatherly manner, then the bastard stepped back and kicked me in the chest again. I fell backward and landed on my sofa in the Amsterdam house. He was getting entirely too much enjoyment from his habit of kicking me out of his realm.

I got off the sofa and went to the mirror in the hallway. The outer half of the iris of my right eye was no longer a bright green with a dark ring, but a solid silver. There was no dimming of my vision, just an idea that I could see certain new things. Over the next week, the entire iris went silver. It was going to cause some issues with people, I knew, but with that also came new abilities. But one I had to harness before my greatly shortened life ended.

CHAPTER TWENTY-THREE

The following day, I did little other than call Jo, but there was no answer or callback. She was probably busy with Isabel. I called Michael to find out if there was any further debriefing or discussion needed about the prior day's events, but there was not. I asked him if he had talked to Jo, but he gave me a vague answer about her not being around. So far, I had noticed no odd effects from the battle weapons I had wielded, but I expected something to happen. I just wasn't sure what or when. The first weird thing to happen had nothing to do with the battle, however.

I was standing on my balcony in Amsterdam with a nice cup of tea. I damn near spilled it when Asif, or at least his image, flickered into existence three feet away. It was definitely Asif, although his clothes were nothing like I had ever seen him wear.

"Hi, old friend. I have only thirty seconds to do my greetings and explanations before this message is traced back to me. Currently, I am with those you call Sky Lords, since they took me off the island after my near death. I soon realized their evil intentions for our world and joined a small group to undermine and betray them. Your recent experience with a jinn, following behind an old enemy to alert you to certain events, was one of our experiments. But now, my colleagues have taken one of yours and changed her. She has been here for a week, but only a few hours of your time. Beware, as she will betray and then capture you, although it is not her fault. They will then bring you here for a similar reprogramming and send you back as an assassin. Goodbye, from the future. We will meet someday."

The image and sound disappeared. Holy shit. I sat down and recovered my senses. Asif was alive, living in the future, and sending me warnings. Oh shit, and 'she' could only be Jo.

I furiously began going over what he said, and how to plan for the warning. My instinct was to call Michael, but I stopped myself, because I needed finesse, and that included catching Jo and stopping her without harming her. Perhaps best if I did that alone and without a strike team. Otherwise, mistakes could get her or someone else killed. I needed to deal with her on my own and bring her back to us.

I also needed to talk to Kal about what I had just seen. How could that message be sent, and could we trace it back to find Asif? I didn't want to go to the future, but if they could take Jo, play with time, change her and send her back, then they were too dangerous to leave alone. If Kal's people could not eliminate their paths to us, and they continued to come here, then I could go there and play offense, much as Smokey had said. I knew Kal's people would not take part in that conflict, but maybe they could help get me there.

OK, no Michael yet, but I needed Kal. I concentrated and sent my message. A few moments later, he appeared in my house. Luckily, I had high ceilings framed with the massive old oak beams. He still made my living area look small. I offered him the sofa, but he looked at and shrugged.

"It looks like a nice sofa. It won't be once I sit down and break it."

"Oh well, let's stand. Any refreshments?"

"If you have any fruit or unfiltered cider, that would be lovely."

I had fresh apples and pears and passed him the bowl, while I poured two ciders. He held five apples in his palm, and a mug of cider in the other. He made it look more like an oversized shot glass.

"Kal, I just had a visit via hologram from someone I knew and buried a thousand years ago. But that isn't the strange part. He was revived from his tomb and taken by the Sky Lords, where he's now acting as a resistance fighter against them. He warned me they have taken Jo and reprogrammed her and are sending her back to capture me. They plan to do the same to me, where I will return as an assassin working for them."

"That they are still operating outside of our prohibitions is disturbing, but even more so that they have abducted and somehow changed Jo is reprehensible. We must get her back, of course. At least your friend is there and working against them, which could be useful with a proper strategy."

"Agreed, and I am confident I can get Jo back. I'll trust Michael's group to treat her and return her to normal. As you said, I think that with my friend Asif there, I or a group could go there and take the fight to them."

"It is possible. But we would need to study the links and try to ensure that anyone sent would end up in the right place and time. This will go to my group for study and planning."

"I have a last question for you. I have been training with Henry on animal forms and can transform easily enough into several things. But I need a little more advice on other forms."

"What did you have in mind? If I know your purpose, I can help."

I told him what I had in mind and my purpose. He suggested one of three different forms. Once I told him I needed to do it today, he understood, gave me the key advice, and we practiced for half an hour. It would have to do. We said our goodbyes, and he disappeared. I went to my vault to get weapons. I was in a hurry because I realized I needed to get to Isabel if Jo was gone.

As I turned and walk into the living room, a crossbow bolt punctured my shoulder, then another bloomed from my chest, and a third appeared in my upper arm. I immediately went numb, and a second later I felt the first brush of a hallucination. It was similar to my salamander experience, so I suspected

I was being treated to my binder potion. That all went through my mind as I toppled backward onto the floor. I saw Jo standing above me with a tri-bolt crossbow. An effective weapon when the binder potion was added. I'd have to try that someday, after I escaped.

"Well now, the troublesome lads on the floor, ready to wet himself, I suppose."

I had a smartass reply, but already my face was not working, so speaking was not possible.

"Cat got your tongue, I suppose. I never enjoyed talking to you anyhow." The only thing after that was the vision of her foot moving quickly towards my temple.

Sometime later, I awoke. They had strapped me to a gurney with what appeared to be smart ties. If I tried to shift to something larger to escape, they would cut through my flesh like butter, or if I shifted smaller, they would follow me down to ant-size. Since all I could move were my eyes, I did not worry too much about doing anything, anyway. Plus, I was not carrying either of Odin's gifts, which could have helped.

The vehicle I was in stopped, and the back double doors opened to reveal that I was in the back of a large delivery van. Jo was present, along with two armed guards, and I heard two more talking up front. The two I could see were vampires based on their movements. Jo did not even look at me or address me. I was just a bag of glop they assigned her to deliver. She told the guards to get me out and take me below.

The two vampires rolled me out and over to a concrete building that had nothing inside but three elevator doors. The bad guys really needed to learn how to decorate their dens. We all went into an elevator car and the doors closed.

I thought back to what I had learned from my time with Kal, and all the hints I picked up from Odin and Henry. If I was ever going to do something hugely stupid and dramatic, this was the time and place. I slanted my thoughts to a familiar place and pushed energy into that place. I pulled the mental trigger I had built, fueled by a larger dose of energy than I had used previously.

The gurney collapsed at the same time the straps popped off with a sound as loud as a gunshot. Funny how a massive tree trunk materializing in place of the comatose victim can do that to a gurney and straps, even smart straps. They could hold ten thousand pounds of pressure, but instantly turning into a giant redwood trunk overpowered them a bit. The two ends of the tree trunk also pushed out into both sides of the elevator, crushing its sides against the interior of the shaft and stopping our descent immediately. When changing, I had directed two massive branches from the trunk to impale and instantly kill both vampires. Messy but effective.

Jo was incredibly fast and immediately tried to stab me with her blade to inject more potion. But the tree bark was too tough to penetrate as I had fortified it with titanium. I spun along my trunk toward her, and a massive branch struck her across her chest and neck, slamming her into an unconscious heap on the elevator floor. She was not going anywhere soon.

I carefully focused my thoughts and began dissipating the energy I had taken in. Some went into the concrete and earth, more into the heavy electrical lines in the elevator shaft. I overloaded and then burned them out just before the last of the energy disappeared. Oh well, the people at the bottom of the complex would now have to climb twenty stories up a ladder to get out. I imagine the power was out for the entire complex, not just the elevators, but I did not feel too bad.

I slowly turned back into myself, then rose off the remnants of the gurney now crushed into the floor. The remnants of the binder were still in my system, but I concentrated and oozed it out through my skin and dripped it onto the elevator floor. That was another tip I had just picked up from Kal. I picked up Jo's knife and jabbed it into her leg to make sure she did not wake up and cause me any trouble. I had bruised her face, along with a possible broken or dislocated shoulder, and some nasty scrapes from the bark. She should heal herself in a day or two.

I jumped up and popped open the emergency door on the top of the elevator car. Then I picked Jo up and put her over my shoulder and jumped up hard to get us both through the opening and land on top of the car. We were only about three stories from the top. I started climbing up the ladder that was on the side of the shaft.

At the top, I sat Jo down, peaked out the door to see the two other vampires still near the van. I took Jo's knife and sprinted outside to finish them. No quarter, just brutal and quick. I went back to pick up Jo and dropped her in the back of the van. I found a phone in her pocket and used it to call Michael.

"Hey old one, got another facility that the master vampires and Sky Lords left for us. It's mostly wrapped up if you guys want to come over and dismantle it."

"We surely will. Where are you?"

"No idea. You need to track this phone. Also need a med van for Jo, as I had to get a little rough with her. You also will need a big enough team to get twenty stories below ground, at least that's how many numbers were on the elevator buttons. Unfortunately, I blew out the elevators and all the electricity in the place. It will be a slog to get down there and tie things up."

"Ah, so you have found Jo. I take it she had changed sides, probably against her will, when you subdued her."

"Yep, and she will need you guys to patch her back up to the old Jo. I had been expecting it since I got the warning from the future."

There was silence on the line. "I know you well enough to know that was not a joke. Of course, we'll take care of Jo. We have your location and will be there in twenty minutes, since you are near Venlo. An explanation would be welcome."

"I'll give you what little I know when you get here. But it's a little crazy."

"I expect nothing less."

Two helicopters flew in shortly, then four trucks came in later. I guess there were still forces nearby after the recent battle. One helicopter landed and two guys pulled a gurney out as Michael jumped down. Another bout of déjà vu from the tulip field. They loaded Jo up and were gone in three minutes. The other helicopter circled while teams of commandos from the trucks went down the elevator shafts. A couple of other cars pulled up with what looked like IT people, a fancy designation for geeks. I guess they were here for the computers, which had been a gold mine for information from those recovered at the air force base.

Michael nodded as he walked up, and we traded salutations. "Michael, looks like you got this."

"We do. Thanks for the call. Is this a good time for explanations?"

"Nah, I am going to steal one of those cars and drive back to see Isabel, since Jo won't be seeing her tonight. Tomorrow work for you?"

"Tomorrow is fine. The helicopter just completed its sweep and found no other entrances to this location. To save you the long drive, they can get you back to Den Haag."

"Thanks. I'll see you at the Cottage or the med facility. Was Jo being taken to the Den Haag facility?"

"No, she is going directly to the large medical facility at the Center. They will have better treatment options there. Let's do the Cottage in the morning. Keep Isabel safe."

I was off to see Isabel. A two-hour drive became only twenty minutes in the helicopter. But I still did not like being in one.

Isabel was with a nurse, and I got her after the feeding. She burped and decided not to cry, which was fine with me. I walked around with her and extended my feelings of love and comfort. In my other sight, I could see her doing the same. She fell asleep on me as I dozed and worried about Jo. I woke and handed Isabel off to the morning staff nurse, then drove to the Cottage. Michael and I had coffee in the study.

"We had some unusual reports back from that elevator car. A tree had exploded inside it somehow, but there was no trace of it remaining," Michael said.

"Strange, huh?"

"Very. I don't suppose there will be any logical explanations forthcoming?"

"What would be the fun of explaining everything and leaving nothing to the imagination?"

"I see. There is also the mystery of you escaping that gurney and those straps that no entity has ever broken. At least not to our knowledge."

"Yes, obviously another mystery."

He waited, but I would not tell him anything else. He sighed and continued.

"We caught all the staff, as they had so many stories to climb up the ladder in the shaft. They had physically destroyed most of the information in the rooms at the bottom level. But a lot of the digital information should be recoverable, since you cut the power, even the backup systems, and they couldn't delete much. But with what we have so far, it should finish most of the master vampire network in Europe. This was a major communication and operations center, with massive servers full of data."

"Good news, for once, and hopefully another bad day for the bad guys."

"It is and was. Now tell me about your tip."

"As I mentioned, I knew this was going to happen."

"How?"

"It is even stranger than normal, as I had a hologram visitor. He was from the future, a guerrilla fighter of sorts, working against the Sky Lords. Apparently, he is the one that sent the jinn, to give a warning about Caius and his group."

"That is strange but could also be very helpful."

"Wait, that isn't even the strange part. You know him."

"The person sending the hologram?"

"It was Asif."

Michael blinked but said nothing for a moment. "Senecus, I know you are not joking with me, but could this be real?"

"I think it is real. He said the Sky Lords took him off the island after his burial, and he's been working against them. I wish I could tell you more, but he only had a few seconds to talk. I am hopeful we can work this against the Sky Lords and get Asif back."

"That would be... a tremendous relief for me and aid our cause. Do you have a plan yet?"

"Not really. I told Kal to get his people working on it, and I hope you can get a team together as well. Smokey has already told me I was likely taking a trip to the future, so I might as well consider it. I just don't know how much time I have left."

"I'll start putting a team together. If we need to coordinate with the other groups, I hope you can facilitate that."

"I can and will." I was feeling pretty good about everything.

Michael looked at me darkly for a moment. Crap.

"And now for the bad news. For a few minutes after waking, Jo was uncooperative. No talking, other than screaming obscenities. Then she went quiet and unresponsive. The doctors have diagnosed a form a catatonia."

"What the hell, Michael?" I yelled. "I expected her to be hostile, but why would she collapse into catatonia?"

"We are not sure. There must have been a failsafe switch put in her to keep us from recovering her. We believe there is some amount of psychic damage she has suffered from the kidnapping and brainwashing. Plus, there are physical issues from a new virus they introduced, which has completely changed her microbiome. We suspect that they also loaded the virus with a kill switch that was timed to go off after some length of time or was triggered after we captured her. Either way, the doctors and specialists believe she will never recover. The virus attempted to kill the host and the microbiome. We were lucky enough to prevent Jo's death, but the microbiome is mostly gone as is the virus. It will make it more difficult to study in order to prepare a treatment for Jo."

I could not believe it. I was sure if I captured her then she'd be restored. The damned Sky Lords went to great lengths to capture her, change her, and then discard her if they lost control. Those future humans were real scum. "This just sucks. After all she has already gone through, I just can't believe it. What happens to her now?"

"We will keep her secure and alive. Then wait to see what happens while running tests and planning treatment options. I really don't know where to go after that."

"That is not what I was expecting."

"I know, and I feel much the same way. I just hope we can treat her and get her back to normal. My anger has been building since I've had longer than you to mull this over."

"What happens to Isabel now?"

"You need to take her and care for her, as her father. When Jo recovers, you can bring her back. I think your new location is perhaps the safest place on the planet for her right now."

"God, Michael, none of this should be happening. Isabel really needs Jo, not me."

"I know, but that is really the best and only option."

"Of course, and I'll keep her and take care of her until Jo is back."

"Isabel will be at the Den Haag facility until you are ready to take her to America. We had set up a care room there in case Jo had to leave her for any reason. Jo dropped her there on her way to run an errand for an hour. When she didn't return, they notified me, and we set up twenty-four-hour care for Isabel and began searching for Jo. When you are ready, we'll send you over on our jet, and can send a nurse along as well."

"Thanks for the jet offer. The nurse can come with us, but then can return on the plane. I've got enough experience with babies to muddle through, and Isa will be swamped with attention at the Valley."

"Good. That is the best of an unpleasant situation. For now, we will keep Jo at the Center while we determine how to care for her. We will continue searching for treatments, and already have medical researchers and a group at the Center working on new ideas."

"Thanks Michael. I need to check on a few things before going to America. I'll pick up Isabel and be ready to go as soon as I can."

"Go with God. I'm so sorry this happened."

"I'll try the God thing, but I mostly feel like he's on an ill-timed vacation."

We boarded the plane and went south after a change of plan. I wanted to see Jo before I left. At the Center, the nurse stayed outside with Isabel because I did not want Isabel to get a sense of nothingness from Jo, or worse, a negative energy. Jo was in the hospital bed, hooked to all the official equipment. Physically, she looked fine other than the bruises and scratches I had given her in the elevator, although those were healing. Mentally, there was no measurable response, and even the machines showed that. I dropped into my other sight and found nothing. It was like she did not exist. I left quickly and took some time to recover before going out to Isabel. I'd say we both went to America heartbroken.

The Valley was a good place to be back to. Isabel responded well, especially to the shifters. They seemed to sense each other on several levels. There was a fierce competition among the group to take her whenever I had to leave to do something.

I called Morrigan and told her happened, to check if she knew any treatments that could help Jo. She did not know of anything to help as the gifts from the Old Ones and the things they had made since then covered many areas, but almost nothing in the medical field. I thanked her, and later thought about Odin. He did healings, but from what I knew, that was only on the battlefield. I figured Morrigan would tell him, and if he could help, he would let me know. For myself, I still worried about my coming downturn, but so far so good.

CHAPTER TWENTY-FOUR

I watched her play in the field. A beautiful blonde wisp running through the grass. Hair so blonde it might as well have been white. I saw her skin glowing very silver, with a burnish of blue, green, and gold. That color combination was unknown among all the special beings that could see it. Everyone that could see it told me I looked the same, without most of the gold. I once thought that somehow that came from her mother. I still was not sure, but perhaps that came from me somehow, and my new ability to shapeshift. All courtesy of slant. It made little sense though. How could a trait I developed after her birth be retroactive to her? But the past few years had changed just about everything I knew about anything.

I was going to continue to give her mother credit. Of course, Isabel was special enough that she might be born a shapeshifter. There were enough other odd things happening with her lately like that. Small things, like knowing people's thoughts and pulling her toys over to her with her mind. Watching her play, my mind inevitably went back two centuries to think about my children when they were small. So similar, yet so different. Watching her play made me happy. Then also sad, since her mother was not here to see her. It felt like a piece of my soul was missing.

I also felt the physical pain in my knee that had appeared a few weeks ago and not gone away. It was all I could do to hide the limp. I could see the gray hair that was not there before. Things were changing; things, like me, were moving on. All I knew anymore was that I was finally where I needed to be. And when I needed to be. Yes, things about me were changing, but I was home. I planned to spend the rest of my days doing just this. Now it seemed those days would be many fewer than I had once expected. But I had already had tens of thousands of days more than I should have had.

Perhaps being a good father to a child, and guardian for the other children, was all that I needed to be. No hero, or supervillain chaser, or Church enforcer, or monster slayer. Just a father. At least I knew which of those things was really important now.

Another young girl, about the same age, came down to play as well. She was a little dark-haired beauty, already showing flashes of Anna's features. Kate and Anna came to visit and stayed a while. Perhaps for a long while. Anna loved the quiet but close-knit community full of children. And that it was very safe. Between Kal's people and my people, and a few very scary friends, it would take more than a full army with air support, or even an asteroid, to get close to this place. The Valley was now our home, and a safe place for our people. I had not told Anna or Kate yet, but I occasionally saw Isabel teaching Rachel some "tricks" when they played. Apparently learning slant and other things were easier at their age, or maybe Isa was an excellent teacher. They now had butterflies coming to them and landing on their hands. I also saw them conjuring ice cream cones a few times. Once I had closed my eyes and reached out with my alternate sense. Isa was still a bright white comet, but with rainbow flecks, like snow falling in the sunshine when it reflects all the colors. Some of those flecks were migrating to Rachel, and she was glowing. Isa did that with the other young children as well. Life around here was going to get interesting. I wish I would be around to see it.

Kate was already accepted here, and the community was asking her to stay and lead the community. She was a natural, and I hoped she would stick around and be the mayor. I liked them being around. I was teaching them slant, as I thought we needed all the help we could get, plus they knew it was a great defense against the bad things in the world. Even better, the children played well together. We were trying to get Thomas to take a vacation and bring Willem over for a couple of weeks. Might be a little slow for them around here, but I would like to see Thomas again before I forgot who he was. Meanwhile, the sun felt nice while I watched the children play. I would like to take a nap, but then I probably could not walk afterward if I fell asleep on the ground. All good things end. At my age, I knew that more than most.

A few weeks later, I knew it was time to leave my idyllic life one last time. New aches and pains kept showing up, and I was moving slower. My falling-apart phase was speeding up by the month. My thoughts kept wandering to what I had left unfinished, and the time to fix it was fleeting. Unfortunately, more often, my thoughts just wandered randomly. I was also forgetting people's names that I had known for years. Despite plans for my life, life was having other ideas. There was something I had to do, and it must be soon.

Without saying goodbye to anyone, I dropped Isabel with Anna and Kate, then drove to the airport. I was dreading the flight and the destination. But I had no choice, as soon I could not function well enough to complete this task. Flying was excruciating but I did not trust I could travel the links and needed to conserve that for my last act. I must deal with some debts before I reached that stage.

Hours later, the plane landed, and I was driving again. At least I still remembered the way. I parked the car and went into the Cottage. It looked the same, but now it somehow felt lifeless. I went through the study and into the back, turned left down a hall and to a stainless-steel door. It opened for me. I was sure they knew I was coming. I knelt before the bed and the body that was within its covers. She looked very pale and thin. And unresponsive. That is what catatonia and coma look like. Years of it, now.

I kissed her forehead while putting my hands on her shoulders. I forced my tired mind into a different version of slant than I had tried before, as I focused and found the energy I needed to complete the task. Much more effort than I had tried before. It seemed like forever but was only a few seconds to find the right path. I pulled the trigger in my mind. We didn't move, but it felt like we dropped into a vortex without gravity, like a jolting roller coaster or falling elevator for a second.

Then we were lying on a thick bed of moss under massive trees. The sun was up, but the air was slightly chilly. I held Jo close to keep her warm. It amazed me I could pull that trick off. My last great journey. I knew my mind and body would have trouble trying that again. In fact, after this, I wasn't sure I could get us away from here if things didn't work.

A familiar voice vibrated through my body. "Hello hairless one. I see grasshopper has grown much." He laughed in his disconcerting way.

"Hi Kal, good to see you again. I guess it's been a while since last we met. But not sure I'm really growing much anymore. Or maybe the problem is that I'm growing too fast. I'm about used up."

He studied me for a moment. He also had that look in his eyes when he was accessing his database. Of course, his network was actually a few dozen incredibly intelligent Bigfoots somewhere far away. Humans had a long way to go to catch up. We just thought we were the smartest species on the planet, but we were really somewhere around the sixth smartest. His look turned sad, and his voice reflected his eyes.

"Ah, I see that not all has gone as expected. You are about used up. And who is this hairless one? Hmm, I remember her. She looks and feels different than she used to." He studied Jo for a moment. Then he knelt down closer to us. "Interesting. Two hairless linked but in ways that I have never seen, and both injured in unique ways. Ah, this is most troubling. They took her against her will to the future, infected her with new technology, then brought her back. Against the rules, it was. The same ones that baited you into a most unfortunate course."

"I guess so. But Kal, one of us needs to survive to take care of the child. I've brought Jo here to see if there is anything that you can do to bring her back. I don't expect to be around to raise the child myself."

"I am not sure we can help her. Let me grok this a while."

He became still and did not even blink for several minutes. He stood up and then he disappeared. I felt out for him with my mind to see if he was cloaked, but he was physically gone. I had seen Kal travel like that before, effortlessly appearing and disappearing. Beyond impressive, like watching an iceberg fly. I would miss not having the time to learn how to do that.

This was not going exactly as I expected, but I was glad Kal had been here. I had sent him the message, but my addled mind didn't sense a reply. But he had known that I was coming. I continued to sit beside Jo and hold her. She was so tiny I worried about her being too cold.

Kal reappeared, along with two others. "My friend, you have caused a great stirring. My people have conversed together, and we have reached out to other entities. Some of them you know well, and others you don't. It will take too long to describe the discussions that are taking place and that will continue. But you are now in the midst of larger movements of the gods and galaxies moving against each other. Yet you are failing physically, and unfortunately, your condition is beyond our healing. All of your body and brain cells are dying at an accelerated rate. Odin's tools are not of this world, so the damage they did is outside of our purview. The best we can do is make you comfortable for the next months. That said, we must address your companion, as debts owed must be paid. The other side took actions that caused an imbalance, and we must restore the balance. This may not be comfortable for her, but over some days of effort, we can restore her."

"Kal, that sounds great. I'm hoping you can get started with her right away."

"Yes, we will take her to our group of healers. Her treatment requires healing on multiple levels beyond the physical. We have the people to do this, but we must do it carefully and in the right stages."

"That is wonderful. Michael's people tried to help, but they were unsuccessful."

"We will be. You two will have some months together at the least. And I'm sure her daughter will be overjoyed."

"Thanks again, Kal. Say, can I catch a ride with you guys? I'm kind of on empty and don't see any taxis around."

"Certainly. I will take you back to the Valley while my colleagues transport Jo to the healers. In a few days, I'll come for you and take you to her, so you can be there when she awakens."

"Good, let's go."

Back at the Valley, Kal left me siting in the sun and watching the children again. I felt a new joy that Jo was coming home, and that Isa was about to get her mom back, a person she had never really known. I told Isa a surprise was coming. She stood and looked at me a moment, then brightened up and hugged me.

"You brought mommy back! When will she get here?"

Yeah, I was no longer surprised that such a young child could read my thoughts. "A few days at most. Kal's people need to work with her and fix her body first."

"Thanks dad. Let's have a party. I'm sure she would like that."

"Sure thing, and I'm sure you'll want some ice cream. Let's invite the whole Valley, and I'll get some of our old friends to come over as well."

"Bring the fairies, dad! They are so cool."

"OK, I'll call them and see if they can come. Now go play while the sun is out."

"Oh dad, you know the sun is always out here. Kal only lets it rain at night."

She skipped off with a big smile. Maybe this was going to work out after all. After spending the day outside, I tried to read that night. I no longer had either the eyesight or the concentration for that, so I listened to music instead. I dozed off, then when I woke up, I sensed a presence in the room.

"Hi Smokey, how are you doing?"

"I am always the same. But lately, after some centuries of concern, I am more relieved than expected. This planet has been reprieved, in some part, at least, thanks to you."

"That is good. What can I do for you?"

"I have one last problem, one which I cannot resolve by any direct action. Your solar system is still under threat, which also affects this sector of space. Although in my jurisdiction, I am restricted in what I can do in this case."

"I am not nearly as fast as I used to be, but is there a favor I can do for you?"

"Yes, there is, and I can return that favor with another." He told me what he needed.

"Smokey, I can do that, I think. I am concerned that I may not be in shape to complete that task, however."

"That won't be a problem. Let's take a trip. We will be gone at least a day."

"Sure, I'll get Nan to stay with Isabel. And I'll send a message to Kal, in case they revive Jo before I get back. Is this a long-distance trip?"

"You might say cosmic. We will leave as soon as you are ready. You also need to bring that special black bag of the Danu biologics. Not completely necessary, but it could help."

"OK, I might have some in the freezer." I struggled up and limped to the kitchen. I called Nan, sent a mental message to Kal that I'd be out for a day, and checked on Isabel. Once Nan arrived, I was ready to go. She looked concerned that I was leaving with Smokey but said nothing.

CHAPTER TWENTY-FIVE

Smokey moved closer, then I felt that falling sensation again. I found myself back at the moon base. It all looked the same as the last time I had been here.

"OK Smokey, what did you have in mind?"

"Let's walk over to that wall." We did, and then through the wall of rock. I wasn't sure whether it was a hologram or some sort of Smokey magic. The lights came on and illuminated a row of devices, approximately the same size as a compact car. We walked over to the nearest one.

"Still working perfectly, just as expected. I'll need the samples from your bag to calibrate the device." I handed the vials of Danu essence to him. Various hologram screens began popping up with colors and symbols I had never seen before. The vials disappeared and more holograms began flashing. "Good, it is ready. If you will climb in and lie down, it will begin. You will feel a light sedation, then not much else. In less than twenty-four hours, it will complete the process. You will not be aware of the passage of time."

"What does this thing do?"

"It will restore you to full functionality, physically and mentally, based on the operational level you had when those samples were taken. This is called a regenerator. We didn't give imaginative names to our equipment, obviously. After we ascended, we didn't need these anymore, but we kept them around to restore other physical specimens from earth. We recorded the baseline health of most species on these units, so placing an individual in one restores its health. In your case, due in some part to the samples you have, all your cellular DNA and mitochondria will be repaired, and your failing microbiome healed to its former state."

"Well, hell, that is a good deal. Guess I'll see you tomorrow." I climbed in, and a minute later, I woke up. I felt strange, with no cloudiness in my mind and no pain in my body. Everything was working perfectly. I needed to get one of these to put in our spa back at the Valley.

Smokey appeared beside me. "Twenty hours. That is quite a long time in one of these. I would suggest not borrowing any more of Odin's gadgets."

"Yeah, I believe I'll pass those up. Unless I absolutely need them again."

"So that you know, your first time through this device will yield the best results. Additional sessions will not be as successful."

"I understand. I'll try not to get hit by a garbage truck."

"Something else you need to know. The samples you provided no longer accurately match to your current body."

"OK, what does that mean?"

"Either the wielding of Odin's weapons, or your body's efforts in trying to fight the massive cell damage, resulted in significant mutations throughout your body. Scanning the differences, I see no fatal mutations. Most seem beneficial, but it will be difficult to know for a while. But over the next days and weeks, I suspect you shall discover you are different from you once were. Perhaps more enhanced."

"Great, maybe now I'll be smart enough to quit saying stupid shit."

"I did not say it was a miracle cure."

"Smokey, I believe that was your first joke. Congratulations."

"Perhaps and thank you."

"Do these regenerators run automatically?"

"Yes, they will detect any biological specimen from earth and effect repairs as needed. Oh, and looking at your enhancements, perhaps you should know that you are still linked to Odin's gifts, but they no longer drain you."

"Why am I still linked?"

"I am not sure, but it's not a problem for your health. In fact, you should be able to access their power without any ill effects."

"Glad to know that. I don't plan on using them again, however. Now, what's next?"

We moved to a different area and Smokey brought up some sort of advanced data screen. On it appeared everything in near space, between the orbit of Venus and Mars. Smokey showed me several ways to observe the data and how to access it remotely, including magnifying the area around the moon. I was studying up for a future project that would provide some payback to an old enemy and also get Smokey out of a jam.

Then Smokey sent me back on earth to my favorite Valley. I had lunch with Isabel as usual.

"Daddy, you got better. Did that happen on the moon? Can I go up there someday?"

"Yes, and yes."

"Now you and mommy are better. You will both be here forever."

"Maybe not forever, but close enough."

That afternoon, as I was sitting in the sun as I always did, Kal appeared. "Hello Sen, are you ready to take a trip and see Jo?"

"Damn skippy, Kal. I've been waiting a long time to see her healthy again. I'll let Isabel know I'm going to pick Jo up." As I stood up, I noticed Kal watching me. Then he started that strange rumbling laugh.

"Senecus, I should have known that you are more competent than most and are always full of surprises. I sense that once again you have somehow conquered that which should have ended you. I celebrate your survival."

"Yep, now let's go see Jo. Then I need to bring her back here and introduce her to her daughter."

We blinked into a forest of massive trees. In a clearing were several of Kal's people in a circle. Jo was in the middle of them, lying on a bed of moss. She looked normal for the first time in years. I admit I teared up looking at her.

"She is ready to awaken. We will do it slowly, and it would be best if you were by her side."

"I'd be happy to." I sat beside her and held her hand.

Kal nodded, and I felt a tension in the air, almost ticklish. Then it stopped as Jo opened her eyes.

"Sen, is that you? Where am I?"

"It is definitely me, and you are in Kal's forest. They have healed you of what the Sky Lords did to you."

She cried a moment. "Where is Isabel? Is she OK?"

"She is great and looking forward to seeing you. She is planning a party for you."

Jo looked oddly at me. Then I realized she did not know how long she had been out.

"Jo, you have been asleep for a long time, while they tried various treatments to heal you."

"Really? How long?"

"Three years." She cried again.

"I know it's been a long time, but things improved while you were out. Isabel is a wonderful little girl. I know it will take a while to sink in, but you and she are immortal now, so you have a couple of thousand years to catch up. You missed night feedings, diapers and potty training, though."

"Let's go. I need to see her."

"Sure."

"Do you need transport?" Kal asked.

"I think I got it, Kal. Thanks for everything." He laughed again.

I grabbed Jo and blinked us to the Valley.

Jo looked at me, surprised. "You can do that now? And what happened to your eye?"

"I just started the link travel the past few days. And this eye is courtesy of Odin, and that bashing of Caius and the demons. Both are long stories. But we have plenty of time to talk about all those things."

"What is this place? It looks like... the Valley, but there is more here than I remember."

"Yes, this is the Valley, but it has grown a bit since you last saw it. Most of the old gang is here, at least most of the time, and we have new people. Some are faeries. And that blonde comet coming at us is Isa. Oh, before she gets here, I need to tell you she is special."

Jo couldn't take her eyes off her. "Oh, how beautiful she is. But how is she special?"

"Well, she is telepathic and psychokinetic, and probably other things. I think she is just getting started and will probably be link traveling soon."

"What? My god, there is so much I've missed."

"Yeah, she is quite a kid. And she's teaching the other kids the same tricks. Won't be long until they're well past us. But don't worry, you'll catch up in a week."

Isa never slowed down, she just leaped onto Jo, and they both fell down, as Isa laughed. Jo was laughing and crying at the same time. It was a good day, and they didn't let go of each other for the next hour. I had to get the party details sorted out, so I reached out in my mind and told Isa I was leaving, and she mentally nodded. I heard Jo ask her what she was thinking, as she had stopped talking to Jo and was concentrating.

"I was just talking to daddy. He's going to organize your party."

Jo looked sharply at me. I just nodded, grinned, and kept walking. They needed time to get to know each other and it should happen pretty fast. As I went through our little settlement, I told everyone that Jo was back and spending time with Isa. Everybody was happy to hear it, and they would wait until the party to greet her. People were going to give her time to be with her daughter. After that, she wouldn't have a free moment for a year as they talked her to death. But Jo would enjoy getting to know everyone's new life here.

Later, all the Valley came for the party. Including Kal's people, along with Morrigan and a few of her less dangerous court. I swore I saw an old man and a smoke monster standing away from the fire, but nobody else noticed them but Isa. On a hunch, I grabbed her hand and walked over to them. Kal joined the other two beings as we arrived.

The three of them stood still as we approached. Isa had no fear of them, but she was unusually quiet. Then, with one of my new senses, I realized she was talking to them. For the first time in my life, I had a multi-party conversation entirely telepathically.

"Thank you for making my mom and dad better," Isabel said.

Kal and Smokey traded glances, but said nothing, while Odin looked on with interest.

"You are welcome," said both Kal and Smokey. "How is your mother doing?" Kal asked.

"She is great. It has been a lot for her, but she really likes it here, and all the people. Well, almost everyone. She doesn't seem to like Auntie Morri much."

I burst out laughing, and everyone looked at me. "I can't wait to tell both Jo and Morrigan about 'Auntie Morri,' I'm not sure which one will be more amused," I told them in my mind. As I looked at Odin, I said, "I guess that makes you -" before he cut me off.

"Don't say it," Odin said to me.

"Oh, it's not a bad thing, being called granddad," Isa said.

"You are right, beautiful Isabel. But you are the only one allowed to say it," Odin said. He looked warningly at the rest of us. I could not tell about Kal and Smokey, but I was smiling.

Odin addressed me, as I had not seen him since the smiting of Caius. "You are looking better than ever. Have not seen colors like that before. And I like that eye you got there. Nobody ever took both, nobody ever survived just one. You have now moved up to a unique status. Might even rate as god status soon enough."

"Nah, too much responsibility and not enough pay. I'll just hang with the mortals."

"Good move. Enjoy yourself, at least a little longer." I guess he was trying to tell me something, and I was pretty sure I knew what it was.

Isa and I said goodbye and went back to the fire as Morrigan sidled up to me. I saw Jo give her a look. Guess she never truly got over that incident in Ireland.

It was my second telepathic conversation tonight.

"Hi, Miss Morrigan," Isabel said.

"Hello tot, how are you this evening?"

"Very well, thank you. I am making daddy take me to visit you soon."

"That would be wonderful, Miss Isabel. We live in a most interesting place."

Now Jo had daggers out from across the yard. I was expendable, and could be thrown to Morrigan, but I guess Jo figured Isa was too close to Morr for comfort.

"Isa, go see mom for a moment."

"Sure daddy. You and Miss Morrigan can finish talking, and mommy won't be mad anymore."

"She continues to surprise, doesn't she?" Morrigan asked me, as Isa ran over and jumped on Jo's leg.

"You have no idea. She is already past most of the 'special' adults I know. Oh, and now she's calling you Auntie Morri."

She frowned a moment, then smiled slightly. "It is acceptable."

"I'll make sure she is the only one to call you that, and only in private."

"You also continue to surprise me. I thought I had seen almost everything, but then you came along. Can I entice you to come stay in my realm? I could promise you a leadership role."

"Morr, I'd love to come to see the realm. And Isa has been pestering me about taking her for a visit. But I don't want to rule anywhere. I've got more journeys ahead, as my war is just starting."

"I thought most of earth was now safe from current threats."

"At this time and place, yes. But there are threats in other times that I must deal with."

"Ah, I see now. Then come see us before that. You can even bring your warrior bride. I sense she feels a certain desire to decapitate me. Oh my, and she might now be strong enough to do so. What have they been feeding you two?"

"The 'food' we have gotten from the ancients I suspect is not exactly legitimate. But I worry that what they gave us is not because of what we have been through, but because of what they expect of us next."

"A wise suspicion. Gifts from the gods don't come without debts."

I took my leave as a surprise guest showed up. I had invited him but was unsure if he would make the trip. Right now, I was wondering how the hell he had gotten here, as his presence was impossible given regular travel methods. But I knew Michael had hidden talents as a Guardian. He nodded to the three outside the fire, nodded to me, and then picked up Isa and talked with Jo.

I wandered back over to the fearsome threesome. A massive biped, a smoke figure, and an old man. They were quite an assembly, but apparently, they were keeping some sort of cloak up, and only visible to some of us. Kal, Odin, and Smokey; I owed each of them my life in different ways.

"Things are right with this world at the moment," Smokey said.

"I think so. But I'm guessing there is more to this, isn't there?"

"I cannot tell you what happens next, but I believe your lives will become most interesting," Kal said. "And Isabel is now key to the future of your race. And Senecus, you won't be retiring soon. You and Jo have a child to raise, although now most of that will fall to Jo. You have a different destiny to fulfill, and probably sooner than you would like."

"Thanks Kal, now I won't get to sleep tonight."

"We will be around to assist and advise as much as possible. But eventually you will have to do what the three of us cannot."

"Oh yeah? What is that?"

They told me, and I realized I needed to spend as much time with Jo and Isa as possible, while I could. Damn. Things just kept getting weirder. After that sobering moment, I left those guys and went over to spend time with Jo and Michael, as Isa had already joined the other children to go play games.

Chapter Twenty-Six

Weird was not an adequate word to describe the past year since Jo's welcome home party. But it was the best kind of weird. I was happy for the first time in centuries. I woke up each morning free of physical pain and with an intact memory. But that was not what made me happy. I had resigned myself to that fate and so I knew to appreciate the time restored, putting off imminent dementia and death to a distant future. But the real reason for happiness lay beside when I woke up each morning. Jo stretched and looked at me with still sleepy eyes.

"What are you looking at, sir?" Jo asked.

"Same thing I do every morning now. My joy."

"Flattery like that may get you somewhere."

We took a long time getting out of bed, like most mornings. We were now careful enough not to break any furniture most of the time. Jo had been here since the night of the big party and showed no sign of leaving. She and Isa could stay anywhere in the Valley, but she seemed happy here, which made me ecstatic. I enjoyed every moment as I knew my time here was limited.

Jo had gone through a relatively painful healing process with Kal's people. They completely replaced her microbiome, tuned the new one, repaired and reprogrammed her DNA. Back in the Valley, she had needed another couple of weeks to return to full strength. Then when she came there were the two weeks of flushing tens of thousands of calories a day through her system, along with intense physical rehab. Mostly because they had to heal her from extreme injuries, but also because they had added a few enhancements.

Jo probably had it worse than me in regaining her health because of her poor physical condition after years in a coma. My healing in the regeneration chamber was comparatively easy. The result of all that was that she was now back and above normal levels.

A major benefit from all that was that my and Jo's microbiomes were no longer closely related. We had not been apart since we discovered that other than to take time to play with Isabel and the other children. An hour or two of lovemaking in the morning, followed by breakfast with Isabel, then we went to teach class and play with the kids. Afternoon hikes or travel with Jo and Isa, then home for dinner, usually with friends. I don't think anyone has a better life than I do. Sharing that with Jo just made it better.

Meanwhile I was learning some new physical and mental aspects of my new body. I wondered whether Smokey might have misled me about his machine. Did he tell me about my mutations because they were real and responsible for new skills, or had he surreptitiously programmed the Maker regenerator to give me some First People enhancements? Either way, I was learning to do things that I once thought unlikely or impossible.

We had one trip to make together as a family that I had promised Isa. She was more excited than I had ever seen her, but Jo was much more subdued. We were going to Ireland for a family vacation, to visit Auntie Morri and the fae cousins.

On the appointed day, Morrigan came to our house and knocked on the door. Isabel was so excited that when I opened the door, she ran to Morrigan and hugged her tightly. Auntie Morri showed remarkable restraint, and then beamed a genuine smile as she looked down at Isa and hugged her back. Isa just grinned and finally let go so Morr could come in. Jo looked worried at first, then relaxed when she saw Morr smiling. We traded hellos and then Morrigan opened the portal door, and the four of us stepped through and into her house. Jo was still holding Isa's hand, almost like she didn't trust Morrigan. Smart girl, but I thought in this case Morrigan would behave herself.

The room we were in was full of expensive but elegant furnishings. Morr obviously had excellent taste. "Welcome to my home and the realm of the fae. On your visit, we accord you full guest rights at all times. Isabel, what that means is everyone you meet will be nice to you, that you are safe here, and anything that is given to you, whether food, drink, or a present, is free with no obligation. All in this realm have agreed upon this."

Isa looked at Jo and me, and we nodded back in agreement. This was something I had previously discussed with Morr, as I did not want any complications on this visit. I already felt better about this trip.

"Now let us go wander around and find my special ice cream parlor."

We left Morr's house, really more of a small palace, to see the wonders of the Irish fairyland. It was all underground but made to be more enticing than the land above. We looked up into an incredible blue "sky" complete with moving clouds.

"The entire area above us is coated in blue diamonds that we make," Morr said. "They were sprayed up there, along with a network of tendrils, similar to your optic fibers that carry white light. It diffuses through the diamonds and gives us a brilliant blue sky. We simulate the clouds as well with optics. Some of the ground and walls, where there are not real plants, we decorate the same way with green diamonds, or clear diamonds and colored light."

"I would say there is a fortune here, but if you create them in that quantity, I guess not," I said.

"No, all we need is sand or carbon, depending on what type of gemstone we need. We can produce tons at a time, a byproduct of one gift given by the ancestors. There are other benefits from those gifts, but they are not as obvious."

We continued walking through town, and Isa was in awe of everything. I was too but hid it better. They made houses of everything from gems to sheets of every type of rock and metal imaginable. Many varieties of giant mushrooms were used as landscaping, along with some real plants. Waterfall features appeared out of thin air to give many homes a white noise. We saw quite a few people moving about, but few children. I would wait for a later time to ask Morr whether the kids were elsewhere, such as school, or if there was something else going on.

"Everything looks normal and sedate here, like a pleasant town just about anywhere," I said.

"Looks can be deceiving. We mostly stay like this, but there is always plotting and chicanery happening all over. But by now, most of the hotheads in society have been taken care of, or they have taken care of themselves. Now it is the quiet, smart, patient ones that cause the most trouble. Bane of our long life."

"Do all the fae live here?" Jo asked.

"We live here, but often travel up top, as we call it. We are just as comfortable at night as in the day, which is why most humans don't notice us. Not that they would, as most of us pass for human easily, since genetically we are closely human."

Jo and Isa were holding hands and not saying much, looking at everything around them. We continued to a shop lit up with neon diamonds.

"Isabel, this is a special ice cream, sorbet and gelato shop that can make any flavor you can think of," Morrigan said. "Or you can order one of the four hundred listed flavors. If you want to make up a flavor, it will come as a small spoonful, so you taste it before ordering a full cone. What do you think?"

"I like that. Mom, can we get one of these stores in the Valley?"

"I don't know," Jo answered.

"Isa, I'll ask the woman in charge if there are any franchise opportunities for these shops," I said, smiling at Morrigan. I'd be happy to have one of these in the Valley, but there would likely be strings attached back to the fae realm.

Jo picked up Isa as they stood at the counter and watched as the flavor list appeared in the air. If you saw something interesting and reached out to it, the aroma of that flavor would waft into your nose. It was quite a sales gimmick. The list even dropped lower for shorter customers.

Morr and I stood back and watched the precocious child and her mom delve into the flavors of fairyland. Just this one shop was worth the visit.

"Thanks, Morrigan, for the invite and bringing us here."

"It is my pleasure. And as with everything I do, I have additional motives. I hope to hook Isabel into visiting us more often, or even moving here someday as an adult."

"You got my attention, especially if that pistachio gelato is as good as I think it will be."

"I want you here as well. Maybe for more reasons than you would be comfortable knowing. I see that you and Jo are good together, so I would have difficulty breaking that bond. Just know that if you ever decide to try a different life, I will be here."

"I do appreciate the offer, but I am not interested in moving here, or perhaps the other unstated interests. I would also offer that you come to the Valley, to visit or live, if you need or want to."

She looked at me strangely. "In my life, no one has ever offered that to me. I can't leave here, for many reasons, but I want you to know it means a great deal to me, for you to have offered me a place with you and yours."

"I mean it, Morr. If things go bad here or you need a change, please consider it."

"I know you meant it. That makes it so much more powerful. As you said, right now my interests are elsewhere. But thank you."

Isabel finally decided on two flavors. One was the house list of fresh strawberries, the other was one she made up of s'mores, tiramisu, and Hawaiian fruit sprinkles. I just smiled at her ingenuity. Jo went with a fruit sorbet, I did the pistachio gelato, and Morr ordered the ice princess special. Isa heard that and looked curious, and it surprised me when Morr offered her a bite, which Isa took. It instantly became her new favorite flavor. I would have to get the recipe from Morr to concoct it at home.

After the cones disappeared, we moved on through the town. We arrived at a series of shops, and they entranced Isa, looking in all the windows. I admit it amazed me at all the things for sale that I never knew existed, right beside mundane things like hats, plates, and hardware. There were examples of all the things you read about in books about fairies, everything from unicorn essence to fairy dust and gnomestools.

I pulled Morr to the side. "Is any of this stuff dangerous for Isabel?" I asked.

"Possibly, so I would suggest adult supervision of her purchases."

"Would you or one of your trusted aides be able to assist with that?"

"Surely, what do you have in mind?"

I gestured to Jo to come over and join us. "Jo, Morrigan just told me that some of these items could be a problem, but we can get help with knowing what to stay away from. What do you think about bringing Isa back here for a Christmas shopping trip?"

Jo looked at me and Morrigan, then took a second and decided. "I think she would love it, and if it is safe, I'd be on board with bringing her back for shopping."

"Fantastic," Morrigan said. "We will plan a weekend shopping trip for December. Same rules as this trip, to include an overnight stay at my house?"

"Yes, please. Now let's tell Isa so she can pester us for months," I said.

We arrived back at the Valley, and it felt nice to be back in the sunlight full-time. I realized how much we had grown as a town when we walked through the length of it. When we started this, it would have taken only a few minutes. Although we were in no hurry, it now took a couple of hours, including many conversations along the way.

Kate and Anna were now permanent members of the community. They had also both taken the turn. But by request we gave them two different versions of the microbiome and alt-engineered virus that Michael's scientists had provided, so there would be no compatibility issues. They were smart women. Michael's scientists, with help from Kal's people, and possibly a few words of advice from Smokey, had provided several breakthroughs in that technology. Not only were different microbiome versions now available, but there was also a new version for treating human diseases. Their daughter, Rachel, was about to get a sibling. We didn't know yet if it was a boy or girl, as Anna didn't want to know and spoil the surprise. The only one that knew was Isabel, or course, and she would not tell even me. I was hoping for a boy and had already suggested the name of Tolkien. They were not amused.

Thomas and Willem had finally visited when they heard Jo had recovered and was living in the Valley. We had held another party after that first one, a few weeks later to celebrate and invite people from outside the Valley. Willem had immediately fallen in love with the community and volunteered to stay and help with all the food and agricultural aspects of our society. The place befuddled Thomas, but he quickly came around. He's now the logistics guy for those of us still traveling the old-fashioned way. He also found he had a gift and a love for martial arts and gardening. Simon teaches him and others, while he grows the Valley's best tomatoes in his spare time.

The most surprising pairing was still in the courting process. Every time I walked past them when they were close together and talking, I just smiled. I never saw it coming, nor would I have ever predicted it. Impossibly, Nan had taken a liking to Monk, and he adored her.

He had come, somewhat reluctantly, being drawn to my description of Kal's "organic computer network" without hardware. He did not believe me at first, but he came for a daylong visit and still had not left. The first evening he was incredibly excited, spouting off all kinds of geek jargon about organic quantum underlays and other terms that meant nothing to me. Over the weeks, he became convinced that he was onto the holy grail of putting together a quantum network with no hardware, destined to be the next breakthrough in computing. I certainly did not know what he was working on, but after hours of conversation with Kal, he was understanding their system and was sure he could put together something far more advanced than what the supercomputers did at present. Kal also got him interested in slant and was giving Monk lessons. I really didn't know where that was going to go.

One day, during all the excitement, as Monk was animatedly drawing on whiteboards and gesticulating with his marker while in a lesson with Kal, I noticed Nan watching Monk. The next day, she was beside him, and it seemed they had always been together. I don't think he ever saw it coming, and yet now that it was here, I don't think he could imagine existence any other way. Yep, the universe was absolutely strange.

Henry came and went often. I knew had a secret life or two that he attended to. He did not say much about it, but I sensed there was something brewing back in Siberia that concerned him. But I knew if it was serious, he would bring it up. The older guys, Watt, John, and Samuel, split time between here and their families in Oklahoma and Arkansas. They would likely move here full time with their families once their logistics allowed it.

The former Farm teenagers, now in their twenties, rotated in and out of here between college and their other interests. They also helped recruit new people, as we continued training sessions to keep our group growing and prepare enough people to not only survive the crazy world, but to thrive and improve it.

Funny how the complete lack of the need for anything, whether food or shelter or money, turns people good. Everyone now works for the community, which means we work for ourselves and each other. Money is not an issue when Kal can think up ten kilos of gold every few seconds by pulling it up from the earth. Damn wonderful trick. Screw the 'prosperity gospels' and all that greedy nonsense. We weren't communists or capitalists or any of those outdated terms, because our small group of very special people had transcended those categories. It was home.

Of course, paradise is not truly free. This wonderful life still has a purpose. We spent at least some time each day in discussion with the group mind, going over strategy and preparing for the next eventual battle. Interesting that the type of life we had made had also made us want to protect it, fiercely and at any cost. Yet, we deferred to Kal's ways of thinking, anticipating and preparing defenses rather than aggression. Slowly, we were learning.

I wandered out to what we called the training meadow. Simon was sparring with Henry. The 20,000-year-old Wendigo had his hands full, as Simon had also taken the turn. As had Jen. She was the first shapeshifter to take the turn, and it had worked out remarkably well. Now she and Simon could tax anyone at combat. Their son watched from a distance, occasionally yelling for his mom to kick some butt. Jen was out there actively spectating, while pregnant with their second child. I had a very slight pang thinking of Hia. But Jo was beside me, so the pang gently turned into a nice memory instead.

I was enjoying the moments we had, reminding myself every day how lucky I was to have Jo. Mainly because I knew it would not last. I sometimes had dark moments thinking that the chances of us lasting several hundred years together were essentially nil. Other than Michael and his wife, I was not aware of any other long-term marriage. Of course, by long-term, I was thinking in terms of a thousand years or more. We had to face too many centuries. Or, even more sobering, we still had many enemies to face. No, as much as I wanted to think differently, the chances of happily ever after likely would not hold up for centuries. I wanted to believe it could. Jo was back, seemed happy, and I wanted that to last as long as possible.

But I had a secret I had told no one, where I had seen flashes of my most probable future on my journey bringing Jo to America through the linkages. That second in non-time had shown me a future path most disturbing, but I knew it was my destiny. The night of Jo's party, my three mentors had confirmed what I had already seen. The past few days I had spent with Kal to work out a few things in response to that vision as the time was near. Jo was going to need everyone's support in the future, because I would not be around. In fact, that time was rapidly approaching, I thought as I walked in the sunlight toward Jo and Isabel. Right about now -

Chapter Twenty-Seven

Jo

My life ended when I stepped out the door in Den Haag to go the bakery, leaving Isabel with the nurse. I remember a sharp pain then falling to the sidewalk by a dark van. Then flashes of pain and agony strapped to bed, in a place I didn't know. Fighting, needing to get back to Isabel, but I could not get free. I wasn't sure how long I was there, but I must have been heavily drugged. Men in white coats around me, until suddenly I woke up by myself.

Then the real torture began. IVs and injections, with something clamped to my head, alternately shocking me and filling my brain with confusing images. A voice that kept saying I was abandoned, a nobody, but I could get revenge. I needed to capture a man then I would be rewarded with whatever I wanted. The man's image looked familiar, but before I could remember the electric shocks and pain slammed me again.

Again, I woke up alone. Then a man walked in and told me my assignment. Go to a building, apprehend a criminal, then return for a new assignment. It sounded easy and I was ready to go. I felt bad, and could not get rid of a headache, but I needed to leave this place and do something. Although whenever my mind wandered anywhere other than catching the criminal, the headache turned into a flashing migraine. I walked with the man to an oddly flashing grey door that he called a portal. He handed me a crossbow and told me not to touch the bolts. Somehow, I knew how to use it. He continued that I was being sent to an apartment where the criminal lived, I should shoot him three times, then carry him downstairs to a waiting cargo van. Nothing else, don't talk to him, don't do anything else, or think anything else. I agreed and he pushed me into the portal.

I found myself in a nice apartment that looked familiar. But then the pain started. A man began to walk into the room, and he was my target. I shot him three times, said something snarky, and kicked him in the face. Then downstairs to the van, where four things were waiting. I thought they must be vampires but then the pain came. No more thinking.

Two hours later we parked and put the criminal into an elevator, which somehow exploded into a tree. And that's all I could remember until I woke up beside Sen, laying in the forest and surrounded by Kal's people. He looked so concerned, then told me Isabel was fine, but I had been away a long time.

He took me back to the Valley where I met Isabel, the girl, whom I'd last seen as a newborn. It was wonderful to be with her, but I kept crying every time I realized how much time I'd missed with her. I did it away from her and Sen so they wouldn't feel bad. Meanwhile one of Kal's people was torturing me with massive amounts of food and extreme physical training the next two weeks. I crawled into bed with Sen and Isabel each night, too tired even think about anything but being near them. But I rapidly grew stronger, then surpassed even my old form. I attended two parties in my honor and got to renew all the friendships and acquaintances in the Valley. It had grown a lot and gotten more interesting with the new people. Sen told me everything that had happened when Isa was away playing. He held me whenever I got weepy, and I never felt uncomfortable being around him. Then one morning, everything changed.

I woke up and Isa had already left to play with Rachel. Sen was holding me and still dozing. I felt... very affectionate now that things were going so well.

But I was afraid of reliving that awful time in Finland, where microbiomes rebelled and made me so sick.

Sen woke up and smiled at me. I rapidly discovered he was feeling the same way.

"Sen, I want you, but I know it's not a good idea. We'll both be sick for hours if we do anything."

"Uh, well, that's not true anymore."

"What do you mean?"

"Part of your treatment required your microbiome to be replaced. Michael's medical team, with Kal's help, have re-engineered several different microbiomes. Yours is now different than mine, so we don't have any compatibility issues."

"Then what the hell are we waiting for," I said loudly, as I pounced on him. We broke the bed, a nightstand and lamp, and cracked one wall of the bedroom. It was really nice.

We practiced a lot more after that and started breaking less furniture. Without even thinking about what I was doing, we became a family. It just felt so right and seamless. I talked to my family in the UK, and we made plans to visit there. Michael had already told them about my miraculous recovery from the coma. Otherwise, we fell into a rhythm of enjoying each other, playing with the children and teaching classes for all the new people coming in for training.

That was my perfect life for a year. Of course, it had to be ruined. I noticed lately that Sen had been less engaged, and he spent the past few days watching me or Isabel or staring into the distance. I knew well that something major was bothering him and he was about to do something stupid. The kind of grand gestures that would get him killed. When Kal showed up and started plotting with him, I decided to confront him.

Yes, he was going to do something stupid, he confirmed, sort of. Honorable, but stupid. The Sky Lords were going to assassinate him here in the Valley, and he was going to let them. He and Kal had it all planned out, to put on a show, then strike back at them. And it was happening in the next couple of days. It sounded risky, but he kept assuring me that nothing bad was going to happen to him or anyone else. I felt it was riskier than he did, but I understood he and our allies could use this against the Sky Lords somehow and seal them off. I was not happy but had to trust them.

The next day was normal. Later I was outside with Isabel and saw Sen walking toward us. I smiled and told Isa to come with me to tackle him -

Oh my god, oh my god, oh my god; panic raced through my mind as I sprinted to pick up Isabel and run with her to drop behind the nearest enormous tree trunk. Everyone else was doing the same, hiding after the incredibly loud gunshot. Senecus was dead, and I had just witnessed it. Henry came up to us quickly. He looked at me as he squeezed my shoulder and gave me a quick smile, gave Isabel a wink, then ran off towards Kal. I could not even process that strange behavior.

I looked down at Isabel, expecting her to be upset. But she was not; in fact, she was looking very thoughtful and appeared to be concentrating. I was about to ask her what she was thinking when the scene flashed through my consciousness again, searing my eyes. Senecus' head exploding in a cloud of red mist, his body still, then toppling over as the report of the gun echoed through the valley. I closed my eyes and tried to shut out the scene. But Isabel reached up and grabbed my face, gently but firmly. I opened my eyes to see her staring at me.

"Mom don't worry. Dad just told me the threat was gone, so we are safe, and he is fine. In a minute, he will check on us. He also told me to tell you he loves you very much. He will see you tonight."

Her calm words were so disconnected from what I had just witnessed. I could feel a warm power coming through Isabel's hands and into my head. It was strangely calming, despite everything going on. "Are you sure? Is he talking to you right now?"

"Yes. He is just right there." She pointed to the edge of the tree trunk. There was a chipmunk looking at me. On a closer look, it had a silver eye. It raised one tiny paw to wave at us. Then it turned into a bobcat and sprinted off through the woods, away from everyone.

When he came back, I was going to kill him for making me witness what had just happened, with no warning. He had told what was going to happen in general terms, but not when it would happen. And he had certainly not told me how gruesome it would be. What I was expecting was for him to get shot in the body, with no blood, and for him to fall over. After the threat was over, he'd just stand up like it was a movie. Never had he said his head would disintegrate in a cloud of blood. And he damn sure should have given me a moment's warning. Even if it was part of some secret plan that only he could know. That made it even worse, and now that I knew he was fine, I was definitely going to kill him tonight. My god, who but Sen would let his head explode, and then turn into a chipmunk with a silver eye? At least Isabel already seemed to know about it and was expecting it. My god, what was wrong with that man? That was a hell of a grand and dangerous gesture just to fool the Sky Lords.

Henry yelled to everyone that it was safe and go back to whatever they were doing. Everybody was good and he would explain everything back in town in a few minutes. Him saying that as he dropped a sheet on Sen's body seemed so incongruous. Isabel grabbed my hand and led me back to the house, speaking normally and talking about anything but what we had just seen. I realized she was keeping me calm. For the thousandth time I understood how special she was.

Henry told everyone in town what was going on. After that a few drifted over to our house to chat. They were tentative at first, but they really wanted to talk and keep me occupied. Anna and Kate, Simon and Jen, Thomas and Willem, Zena, Henry and a few of the younger crowd were the first to show. What the hell, I decided to make it a party, or maybe the strangest wake in memory. Senecus is dead, long live the chipmunk. I was getting loopy, then Isabel came inside and righted me again.

A bobcat jumped through the window and sat on the sofa. Isa screamed in delight and yelled, "Daddy! Kitty! Daddy!" I was still mad, but the sight almost made me laugh. And I was relieved to see Sen, or rather a silver-eyed bobcat, was unharmed.

Henry laughed, then loudly said, "Hey everybody, Sen's back. He ain't dead, he's just kitty. But he can't turn back yet, too soon after all that changing."

Everyone else was still in mild shock. A few had seen what happened, the rest had heard the gory details, so I understood their confusion, as more than half the Valley had not been clued in before the event. I told Isa she should explain again.

"It's just like Uncle Henry said, the whole thing was a play act to make the Sky Lords believe Daddy is dead. He changed to a chipmunk before anything happened, then to a big kitty. But now needs another half hour to change back to normal. Meanwhile, I'm the only person who can pet him. Uncle Henry can answer any questions."

The room erupted with noise and questions. Senecus the bobcat was loudly purring as Isa petted him with both hands. It was just another day in the Valley.

Thirty minutes came and went, and the bobcat was still on the sofa. I made sure he saw me looking between him and the clock. He must have gotten the message as he got up and padded into the bedroom. I followed him in and closed the door. He changed back to human, put on pants, and came over to hug me. Nice try.

"Jo, I know you have to be upset," Sen said. "But this entire plan had to happen as it did to keep the Sky Lords fooled. They believe I'm dead, which was essential to the plan."

"Plan? You mean the plan where you didn't tell me all the details? The one where your head explodes in front of me?"

"Yeah, that plan. The terrible one that Kal told me not to tell you about."

"Oh no, you don't get to toss him under the lorry."

"Uh, I think that's bus, not lorry, but close enough. And you are right, I should have told you. I'm sorry and won't do that again."

"I understand. But you need to understand that I am mad and will be for some time."

"I get it, I really do. I'm sorry I won't be here for the make up part."

"What? Where the hell are you going? You don't get to do this and then disappear."

"I kind of have to. That was the whole point. Now that I'm dead, I'll take the fight to the Sky Lords. I'm the only one that can do it, and none of us will be completely safe until we eliminate that threat. Next time, we might not have any pre-warning, and some or all of us could get killed."

"You can't. You just… can't."

"I will travel there and handle that problem. I won't be alone, since Asif, Michael's son, is there and already leading the resistance. You know we have to take these people down. I just don't know when I will be back."

I was shell-shocked by all the everything today and now this conversation. Then I realized what he was not saying. "Are you coming back?"

"I plan to, despite the naysayers, as I can't imagine giving up this life now that I've found it. I'm finally feeling alive, and happier than I ever have. You and Isa have given what I thought I would never have. But if I don't return, yet I have taken out the Sky Lords, it will be worth it, since you and Isa will be safe."

"I just don't believe it, not any of this."

"I know. It's a lot to take in, but once you think about it, you'll see it's the only way."

"When do you leave?"

"I need to get with the brain trust, but probably tomorrow."

"I understand your logic, but I still can't process it. After this past year I can't... I don't want this to end."

"Me either, but I don't know another way."

We walked back out of the room, and the house was empty. I guess everyone realized there was a tough conversation happening. Isa and the other kids were playing in the yard.

We sat on the sofa, as Sen kept apologizing. Both of us cried a minute but then I knew I had to straighten up. We both needed to spend time outside with Isabel, so we went out and stayed until sundown. Sen went to meet with Kal and the others while Isa and I made a light dinner and ate, although I wasn't hungry. We were both sad but kept each other company. She did tell me, in all seriousness, that he was coming back, I just had to be patient.

Sen came back and we laid down together just to hold each other. Despite what Isabel said, I kept thinking this might be the last time. Sen asked me about Isa staying with us and I agreed. She came in and we all three spent the night dozing together. Morning came too soon. We said our goodbyes and Sen disappeared with Kal and a very large crow.

CHAPTER TWENTY-EIGHT

I could sense when the crack opened in our place-time as I walked toward Jo and Isa. It was what I had been waiting to happen for several days. When the trigger engaged, I began my transformation, as I knew I only had a split second before the railgun slug would vaporize my head. In the middle of the transformation, I also opened a small window to let the railgun slug exit the world to prevent any chance of it continuing through the Valley and hurting anyone. My little window exited onto the far side of the moon, a meter from the hull of the spacecraft parked there and acting as a communication station for the Sky Lords. They thought themselves well-hidden and out of any danger. They were wrong.

It impacted the ship and passed through the bridge. I thought the event had a certain symmetry, as the captain's head exploded before it passed through other parts of the ship, including flight control and life support. He might have been the lucky one as the rest of the crew probably had a few days to live while it sat disabled above the moon. Just another meteorite, they would likely conclude, although a particularly well-aimed one. There would not be time for a full investigation before they died. Smokey's surveillance system, that he had shown me on the moon, made it all too easy. I now could access it from earth in my mind, so I knew where the ship was. Now the ship that had almost fried Michael and me on the island and crimped the use of the moon base were neutralized.

I had donned the old chipmunk guise and ran like hell just behind Jo as she carried Isabel. When they noticed me, I waved, turned into a bobcat, and got out of there. Everyone knew, or soon would know, that I was dead, and now I could disappear forever. Or at least long enough to travel into the future and destroy the Sky Lords. Now even they thought I was dead and no longer a threat.

Of course, Jo was likely to kill me when I got home later. I was going to tell her all the details beforehand, but Kal had talked me out of it. He believed it better for everyone to show authentic shock in case there were any observers. I'd say it worked probably too well. I was definitely going to blame him, but that would not get me off the hook with Jo.

Then Kal had completely ratcheted down all space-time channels and activity in the valley, so there was no chance that anything would get in or out. The only person not fooled was Henry, as it was his trick, but he played along.

The rest of the day was tough. I had to tell Jo about going away to the future and the truth that it may be one-way. Then Henry came to get me, telling me that the brain trust was ready for planning. I reluctantly left Jo and Isa to attend the meeting room in town. We talked as we went.

"I knew I would use that trick someday," I told Henry. "Sure glad it worked. I think it's time for you to transfer that legacy to the younger ones."

"Boss, where are you going this quick?"

"I'm going to the future to rid of us of this risk from the Sky Lords. I feel like if I don't do it now, I might never go."

"You don't seem like you plan to come back. This must be the journey the spirits foretold."

"I do plan to come back, as I've got too much here to lose now."

"But you are setting things up in case you don't. Never seen you do this before, so even you have some doubt you will get back."

"Some, I guess. But I have to do it. These people have to be protected, and I think Isabel is the One the spirits mentioned. Makes my decision simple."

"I got it. Good luck. I'll keep a close eye on the little one."

"Thanks for everything, Henry."

I sat down with the group of Smokey, Kal, and Odin. Kal did all the talking, as the other two would provide some guidance for the trip, but no operational input. It was a brief meeting as Kal could only provide me with how to protect myself, and what I should consider as proper forms to turn into once I arrived. The best news was that they had found out where I was going, as they had figured out where Asif was, and the 'when' that would make the most sense. I did not ask questions about that, as I had the impression that they didn't want to tell me how they had discovered that information. I'd leave the next morning, so at least I had tonight at home. They left, and I went home. The evening was no better than the afternoon, but I spent it with the two I cared about the most.

I walked outside the next morning to find Kal waiting, along with one enormous crow, courtesy of Odin. They would accompany me most of the way to steer me around any surprises. I carried only a small bag with a change of clothes. Kal said nothing as he touched me on the shoulder, propelling me into my journey to the future.

We entered the linkages, and it felt different the longer I stayed in. Instead of a second of darkness and then appearing somewhere else, I was moving toward a light nexus. As I got closer and the light was brighter, I could tell the big black bird was ahead of me. I turned my head and glimpsed Kal behind me. We hit the nexus and kept moving, and though I didn't feel a physical change in direction, my vision told me we were going off at a different angle.

That happened several more times, then the raven in front disappeared as I slammed, feet first -

Into a small courtyard, outside of what appeared to be a house. Most of the greenery was fake, a mixture of synthetic materials and holograms. Even the fountain tinkling in the corner was a hologram. I flashed into my chipmunk state and sat in the corner to watch the area. The flagstones were some type of epoxy. Hell, everything in this place was fake. I crouched on all fours, since that is what I had as a chipmunk, and waited.

An hour later, Asif walked into the courtyard with a drink in his hand. He looked just the same as I remembered him. "Senecus, I have you on my sensors. You are really cute, but I have no nuts to feed you. I have all the sensors blocked, so you can come out now."

I did not sense any danger, so I turned back to myself. We stood looking at each other, then grinned at the same time. "Give me a second to get dressed," I said, then did. We embraced for the first time in a thousand years.

"I didn't expect to see you here. How about a drink?"

"Sure. It's been a long, strange journey. I guess you can say the same."

"Stay here a moment and I'll be right back. I don't have the house sensors set to block your presence yet."

He left and came back with another glass. It was a passable cider drink. It's good to have friends that remember those things.

"I really don't think you are supposed to be here. You know this was a one-way trip, right? There is no longer any chance of going back."

"We'll see about that. I kept getting that same comment before I came, but I have some alternative ideas to get us home."

"We can get into that later. Nice eye, by the way. Mechanical or synthetic?"

"Nope, still natural. Came through Odin. Or rather, his gifts."

"Oh, well, I guess you are no longer keeping a low profile back home."

"I'm about as out there as it is possible to get these days. At least until yesterday, when you guys killed me."

"Did we? I should get the report tonight or tomorrow. Apparently, we are just as incompetent as always. Of course, in this case, I'm glad we were incompetent."

"Well, they shot me this time, and it was a kill shot. But it wasn't me, at least by the time the railgun slug dissolved my head, and they didn't bother to check afterward. By that account, they are still incompetent. Nice place you got here. Does the future not have live plants anymore?"

"Not as many as there used to be. Things changed drastically over the years. But this was a choice, as most everything you see blocks the sensors or feeds false data to them. The flagstones are a special material, and all the holograms do double duty to confuse the sensors."

"Sounds like somebody doesn't trust you."

"These people don't trust anyone. But I'm one of the highest-ranking scientists, so I get special scrutiny. Most of my colleagues over the years have already been 'reassigned' to oblivion. I'm sure I'm also on that list."

"Nice job perks. I guess your retirement plan is death."

"An apt description. This is a dismal place where one fascist paranoid group runs what remains of the world. Sometimes I think a premature death to get out of this wouldn't be so bad."

"No reason to fret. I intend to get us home. But what is your story of how you got here?"

"I remember the shipwreck, being captured by the pirates, then that mob attacking us for no reason. After that, I woke up on that barren island in what looked like a tomb. I left my mark on the cover stone and crawled out of the rocks. There I found a small group of people in weird clothes waiting for me.

"They told me my family had betrayed me and left me for dead. I would be safe if I went with them and would learn great things. I never truly believed them but went with them to see what their game was, and I have been here ever since, working on projects, learning everything about them, moving up in the ranks, and plotting how to disable their systems. Recently, I have put everything into place to shut down their ability to time travel. The only problem is that we will be stuck here as well. Although, if they discover us, we won't have long to worry about it."

"I have a couple of plans to get back."

"Well, if one of them was to travel the same way you arrived, cross that one off of the list."

"How's that?"

"They put up a satellite system that uses a variable resonance that blocks all travel in and out."

"Then how did I get here?"

"Systemic incompetence. They kept playing with different systems that would suppress time travel and eventually came up with something. Their test was to see if it blocked outgoing travel, and it did. They just assumed, wrongly, of course, that the same resonance patterns would block incoming travel. If they need to send something in or out, they can turn it off for a second. They are clever, but not smart."

"They must have been relatively smart to build the limited travel system that they have."

"Well, I believe they didn't build it. I don't know where it came from, but they didn't develop it. They suffer from a syndrome I call 'dethink'. They make progress and get to a certain point in a lot of different paradigms, then quit thinking. It's hard to explain, but the time travel suppression system, or your shooting, are good examples of that."

"So, I might have to change things a little. But how do you plan to destroy their systems?"

"It's not as hard as you think. Advanced computers run everything here. But they are so paranoid, there are only a few computers with no backups. And they have not trained the computer techs in a century in maintaining or improving those systems. Once the computers are down, along with some pieces of hardware, then they are stuck. They didn't invent the systems, and I am confident they can't reverse engineer anything to get it working again."

"Well, there is your systemic incompetence, making your job easier. How are you taking the computers down, and what hardware are you taking down?"

"I have written some simple code that will infect and wipe the computers. They are so 'advanced' here that they no longer guard against that. I also have mini-EMPs set on all the server sites. I'll set the computer program so the satellites will continuously broadcast the outgoing suppression wave. Plus, I'll program in the right frequencies to prevent anything from coming in as long as the satellites stay in orbit. Once I program the satellites to become autonomous, then I take the computers down. Anything the virus does not wipe will get fried by the EMPs.

"The hardware comprises two travel portal generators, one small and one large. Those will require some explosives. The small one is easy, as they scaled it to transport humans. The other is a problem, as it is massive. Many years ago, they built to send modules to old time to build a spaceship. They have used it rarely since it, but it needs to be destroyed. With all the computers gone, the hardware destroyed, and no way for others to travel in or out, I should be able to cut this society off from time travel for centuries, or possibly forever."

"Sounds like a good plan. I might ask to tweak it a little so we can leave."

"We can discuss it later. But right now, I don't see a good exit plan. Earth also has put up substantial defenses, so time travel on that end is also nearly impossible."

"I'm used to impossible. We will figure it out and leave this place. I now have people I need to get back to."

"Good. And you needed people to get to. I have to say, you look happy, and have not aged since the last time I saw you."

"I don't know about that. I have aged some fifteen years at least, over the past thousand years, since you saw me last."

"Oh no, I saw you just over three hundred years ago. You don't remember since you were unconscious."

"You mean you visited during one of my blackouts?"

"Those weren't blackouts. We retrieved you and induced a medical coma quite a few times."

"Oh hell, of course they weren't blackouts. Apparently, everything I thought I knew about my condition was wrong. And all those doctoral research programs were a complete waste."

"Well, mostly, except for the microbiome idea. We had to stabilize you and keep you alive, as your body was not capable of surviving without help. The microbiome adapted to all the inputs and changes. Because of how we did it, plus some luck, as your microbiome grew sentient and powerful, it let you stay in control. You get all the benefits, except you also get to make stupid Senecus decisions. Then the microbiome tries to keep you from getting hurt, or more often gets to heal you afterward."

"Now I'm part angel, part Danu incarnation, and a Sky Lord lab rat. Oh, and thanks for letting me know I'm dumber than a bag of gut cells."

"You are welcome. But with all those degrees, you got to meet college girls, didn't you? Are you just now finding out about your past?"

"I didn't meet nearly as many girls as you might think. Those programs were in science departments, where the old professors ran the female students off. But yeah, the past few months have been most enlightening, including today. What exactly were my blackouts?"

"A lot of them involved time traveling, but of course you were unaware, as you were unconscious. But I should start from the beginning. You now understand that time travel almost always involves paradoxes?"

"I'm slow, but I picked up on that one."

"Excellent. The first time we met, really was the first time we met, when our two ships battled in the Mediterranean. But over the next few years, I came to learn that you were different, not just from us First Peoples, but literally from everything else on the planet that I had studied. Many years later, as I became a trusted scientist here, I could time travel for research. One of my personal projects was to go back and see your origins while keeping it a secret from my employers. Imagine my surprise when I saw my father take a running swipe at your neck with the family heirloom dagger. Then you fell and landed on that monstrosity in the river that killed you."

"Uh, wait, I obviously did not die."

"Yes, the first time you did. I came back again, just before you died in the river, and plucked you out of there. Brought you back here to save your life. The trauma was not that great, but all the material you ingested and absorbed from that thing in the river overwhelmed your body. My team spent two weeks adjusting and changing palliative therapies to keep you alive during the transformations to your microbiome and DNA. Without the extra boost from the knife, I don't think you would have survived even then, as mortals can't withstand those changes. You said earlier that it was Danu?"

"Yep, and just found that out recently. Somewhat a shock to be related to the fairies. Then what? I remember waking up further down the river."

"We finally stabilized you, then took you back and put you on the riverbank, but some years after that episode. We kept a close eye on you, and each time you destabilized, we came back and restored you, then left you outdoors again some years later, after each of those episodes. The time we kept you varied depending on what was happening in the surrounding countryside, as I did not want to drop you back in a war zone, and it also kept my superiors from tracking you. Although they never seemed too interested, once I told them I was doing a long-term viral follow-up study. I switched out my assistants often so they would not know I was going back to work on the same person. Later, it got easier, as I did not have to bring you here for extensive treatments. There was a spaceship near the moon that I spent a lot of time on, tracking and picking you up, then treating you on the ship for the last few episodes. I suppose you did not even notice that a few times you did not wake up in the same crypt you initially crawled into."

"No, I did not notice getting crypt shifted. Give me a minute to wrap my head around this. We met, you heard my stories, then once you became a Sky Lord, you went back and saved me from the river, then picked me up and saved me many times after that, without my knowledge?"

"That is an excellent summary. Welcome to time travel paradoxes."

"Damn. So that really changes everything I thought I knew. I've been time traveling the past fifteen hundred years and didn't know it."

"Funny how things work out, isn't it? Now, tell me about your life the past few hundred years, including the part of how you are now a shape shifter. And how is my father doing?"

We spent some hours talking, occasionally breaking for drinks and snacks. I told him everything I thought was relevant about my life and all the details I knew about Michael. Asif told me about his life, and how strange the future had become. A lot of global warming had changed coastlines and inundated entire countries, leading to wars, pandemics, and famines. The population had significantly declined, then the initial fascist government took over and killed another two billion. Of course, they kept the useful people and all the money and resources. Two centuries of rule had consolidated their power and led to a tightly controlled police state, with perks only for the upper class. I thought that this group of humans was unlikely to ascend, as Smokey had mentioned. Just another reason for them to hate us.

Chapter Twenty-Nine

We finished talking as the morning came and Asif needed to leave to put in an appearance at the research facility he operated. He told me to stay in the courtyard or house, and not to leave for any reason or the sensors would expose me. I asked about going out shifted as an animal, but he was not sure how the sensors would react. They would automatically zap any detectable vermin, to keep rats and strays to a minimum. There were very few pets in this society and only allowed for the uppers to own. My ability to leave was not looking promising. One remaining possibility was going as a bird. But there were few left and were considered pests in certain areas. I stayed in until Asif got back.

I could not access any external information for security reasons, but Asif had an extensive library of written books, holograms for both entertainment and research purposes, and various games. I settled in the library with actual books, as I worried that my use of technology when Asif was gone could set off alarms somewhere.

When he returned, we went through all the scenarios of what I could do versus what might get me, and Asif, caught. We decided I would stay off the technical grid completely. If I wanted to leave the property, my best bet was to turn rat and stick to the sewers or take off as a bird from the courtyard. But I had to avoid any major buildings as they might have pest deterrents. That was a catchy phrase for a sensor-operated laser, and I had no desire to impersonate fried chicken. Meanwhile, Asif was producing credentials for me for the day of our escape. Traveling the links was too dangerous, as just about everything on this rock was suppressed, guarded, or both. The first evening, we went through the plans and caught up on each other's history.

"Contacting the jinn and directing him to shadow the one you know as Caius was a project to determine if or how long I could direct efforts from here without getting caught," Asif said. "It was also useful to sending a warning to your time. I barely knew him, but my family did, and he wanted to help. I understand Caius and his men caught and killed him. That was a tragedy since the jinn are so few. I had no intention of that happening and normally I would not have employed him for that, but I had to hurry my plans. My employers have a new virus that will end the other half of the human population not adversely affected by their previous viruses. It immediately causes infertility and multiple types of cancers and illnesses, as the idea was those people need to die off and not reproduce. But it must happen slowly as not to cause a global panic that might cause any harm to the remaining fifty percent of humans, their intended zombie horde. I believe they decided that with nearly 9 billion people, they could slowly kill off half and still have plenty left over to harvest for food and a labor force."

"Food?"

"Yes, they drop human bodies into the replicators and out comes all types of nutritious goodies. Of course, the master vampires just eat them raw while alive. The remaining couple of billion not turned into candy bars and beer get to be worker drones producing things for them, plus reproducing worker drones for untold generations."

"That is cold, and a hell of a future for humans."

"Exactly, and why I needed to get things moving."

"Well, if it is any consolation, I killed Caius, who had the jinn killed. Then we destroyed Caius' entire organization. But I doubt it caused much of a problem since this new virus was coming out. But I did try to shut off one portal."

"I heard about that. The bomb that came through the portal took out several higher-ups and damaged the equipment. That, plus killing off those two things they had invested so much time in, was what kicked off their newest effort to produce a killer virus. It also prompted the retaliatory strike against you. There was a special project in the intelligence department around that time that I heard about it because they needed both the travel portal to run a fast project here, then finish it on the ship. That had not happened before, so people leaked some if the information. I found out enough to realize who the target was, and that you were next. They deemed the project successful, so I sent the hologram warning. From what I understood of the project, your mate would not survive capture or intervention. Did she?"

"Jo was the original target, and she is now my mate, after a long recovery."

"Sen, I'm sorry. I know that must have been difficult. I'm glad to hear she made it."

"Thanks. She is fine now, actually better than fine. I think you will like her and our daughter."

"Congratulations. I'll be happy to meet them both. I like your optimism, the faith that you can get us there."

"Good, because I know now how to get us out of here. But we will need a few things, including luck, and precision timing of your sabotage events."

"I like it. Let's get started."

The plan was fairly simple. Asif had done the hard work and planted the virus code and multiple EMPs at the computer sites. One EMP should be more than enough, but he had put additional EMPs in each location as backups. He really did not want these people to have any access to time travel again. The physical destruction of the small travel portal was more difficult, but he had already planted charges on and around the device. The last one was the most difficult. It was the large portal that had sent the parts of the spaceship. It was lightly guarded, but the device and facility were massive, the size of a warehouse, and required many charges, set in locations that were difficult to reach, to demolish it. Asif had the charges but had not placed them. I thought I could speed that up significantly when it was time for us to go.

"Asif, is there is any difference in the capabilities of the two portal facilities regarding how many people or the amount of material they can transport in one trip?"

"The small portal is only one person or one fairly small object at a time. The large facility is for groups of people or large objects, which can be quite large."

"And both are operational?"

"Yes, they can send or receive, as the satellite suppressors automatically cease for a second once they detect a signal from either portal. The small one is still used frequently, and the large not nearly as much. It has been some time since a group or anything large has transported out."

The large facility could send both of us out together, and the charges, EMPs, and virus code all set to go off immediately after?

"That should be feasible. But Earth is closed to this portal, as is everywhere else in the solar system, for either anything coming from this future, or coming from the past, in case someone tries a boomerang shot."

"Understood. And even if we got into the solar system, teleporting channels into Earth has also been closed or limited, correct?"

"Yes. Maybe not completely tight for some things, but enough to keep us out."

"That's OK, because we are going to bypass all that, anyway." I told him the plan, supplying a crucial recent detail he didn't know, and then he got it. We decided to implement the plan in two days. Asif kept to his schedule, and I stayed at his place reading books and waiting.

The day of our escape, I turned into my chipmunk form and Asif put me into a shielded case that should have plenty of air for the brief trip to the facility. Once there, he would release me as I turned into owl form, but he would need to change the pest control settings to keep me from getting zapped. Everything went according to plan. As an owl, I flew the small charges to the places that Asif and I had gone over many times with diagrams and photographs. It took thirty minutes to get them all in place. I landed on the platform beside Asif, as he had just finished the last part of the computer programming and beckoned me to come down. I landed and switched to myself. Asif handed me coveralls and an oxygen system, and I put both on. He was carrying an unusual black box.

"What is that?" I asked.

"It's a case made of a special alloy to carry data through time travel, and inside is a copy of their server that contains all their genetic information and experiments. All the viruses they created and released in the past and all the new stuff they are working on. Even better, that server is about to blow up, putting them out of the genetics and virus business. They have no way of replacing this information, since they were so paranoid and only kept it in one place. They killed off most of their scientists and all the people that are left have devolved into machine operators, so they can't easily begin new research. But our scientists can use this to study and either reverse or repair the damage to DNA from their viruses."

"Damn, that is quite a blow to them and help to us. When are we getting out of here?"

"Ten seconds and we are gone," Asif said.

Three security guards barreled through the door. I suppose we had set off alarms somewhere during our visit. They yelled at us to leave the platform. We looked at each other and simply raised our hands. They yelled again, but I ignored them as our time here was done. I reflexively dropped my left hand and sent out a force pulse to knock them over. Not sure where that came from as I was not even aware I could do that. But it was a second too late as they fired before we winked out.

The laser weapons they held had two settings, a single powerful beam for precise shots, and a spread shot setting that sent out multiple small beams. Those spread out to a three-foot diameter at a distance of thirty feet. It was like the difference between a rifle and a shotgun.

Untrained guards usually used the spread shot as they didn't have to aim, and the lasers still caused enough damage to stop whoever they fired at. A few of the tiny lasers still punched through you like an ice pick, but at a distance, you might only get a few and would likely survive. Up close, they were lethal. We were lucky the security guards fired from a distance, but we were unfortunate that there were two of them firing lasers, and a third had some sort of energy weapon that sent out what appeared to be a strong electrical charge that missed us both. Asif was closer and between them and me, so he got a double dose of the lasers, while I took three on my right side.

A second later, we blinked into a dark metal room that was freezing cold. I suppose the Sky Lord ship was in worse shape than I had expected in the few days since I had sent the railgun slug through it. There should have still been power and lights, at least. I didn't know if there was oxygen or not, but we were wearing oxygen masks and systems and had lights on our vests. My oxygen was working, but I could not tell if Asif's was or not, and he was unconscious and in a bad way, with multiple charred spots burned through his body. From what I could see, the metal box had taken several hits that otherwise would have zinged right through his torso. I grabbed him as he collapsed, then I did the only thing I could think of, and I blinked us out of existence.

We were now in a slightly familiar place, and I picked up his lifeless body and ran toward the wall. Hoping it was still a hologram I ran straight at, then through it. I threw Asif in the regeneration chamber as it immediately came to life and started its work. I jumped into an adjacent chamber since I might have a nicked right lung from the lasers. I would probably heal just fine, but I had no experience with laser wounds and saw no reason to take a chance.

Ten minutes later, my chamber was done, and I had no pain and no sign of wounds other than three pink skin dots. I sat beside Asif's chamber to wait. Eight hours later, his chamber stopped, and I saw he was awake and alert.

"I don't know what this is, but I really like it," he said. "I don't feel any pain or sense any wounds."

"Yeah, I want one in my spa room. I didn't expect to divert us here, but I felt it best to get those laser shots treated."

"Thanks for that. That really hurt and would have taken days to recover. Although since I have no experience with laser wounds, perhaps I would not have recovered. Regardless, I appreciate the treatment."

"No problem. Something else that helped was your metal box with the computer data caught several lasers meant for you."

"That was good for me, but I hope the data survived. Otherwise, we won't be able to undo the viruses."

"Well, we won't know for a while. Now I need to contact a friend to make sure the straight link from here to Earth is still available. If so, we should be home in a few minutes."

"I'm looking forward to it."

I got the go ahead from Smokey. The base was considered so secret that he had kept the link to Earth active in case I or my group needed it. Smokey seemed oddly relieved to hear from me, which I did not understand since it had been less than a week since I left, and I had told him I was confident I could get back. He was a little confused about why I was at the moon base. I told him I'd get him the details later.

We popped into existence in North Carolina, at the Farm site. I needed a way station, as even I could not directly access the Valley without advance notice. I also needed to get my bearings, as everything had been so rushed since the botched departure. Now the Farm was empty and lonely, and surprisingly cold. It felt like December rather early fall. It looked mostly the same but was rundown and too quiet. Asif looked around and said, "I assume this was once a nice a place, but I'm hoping not our ultimate destination. These mountains are unfamiliar. Are we in America?"

"We are at the site of our original training area, abandoned a while back. How are you feeling?"

"Since the regeneration chamber, I am feeling excellent. Being back on my timeline, with no worry about my former society about, feels even better."

"Do you think everything went according to your plans and we are done with them?"

"I hope so, but you should send scouts out into the links to see if there is any activity."

"Let's hope for the best. Now I need to contact an old friend and get us where we need to be."

I reached out to Kal and got a mental reply. A moment later, he appeared beside us. Asif flinched but made no other moves. A nine-foot Sasquatch materializing beside you has that effect.

"Hi Kal, how are you?"

"Excellent, I am. Once again, you did what many of us had determined you could not do."

"I want to make less of a habit of doing those kinds of things. You came quickly."

"A most precocious child of yours notified me."

"Guess that would be Isabel. I know it's only been a week, but I'm looking forward to seeing her and Jo."

"Hmm... you seem to have your times confused?"

"How's that?"

"You have been gone two years. We were becoming concerned that you could not return."

"Two years? What the hell?"

"Sen, when we took the laser and energy blast, it could have affected the machine settings," Asif said. "We've seen that malfunction before with electrical surges."

"Crap. I suppose it's too late to worry about it. Just another piece of my life missing. Oh, Kal, this is Asif, my old friend, literally. I believe you know his father."

"It is most pleasant to meet you, Asif. We are in your debt for what you did to protect our time. I am sure Michael will be most happy to see you. I have already sent a message to him."

"How do you already know about that? Oh, right, it has been two years," Asif said.

"Yes, and from monitoring, we know the world of your time is now cut off from all travel in or out. That has been a great help."

"So, Kal, is everything fine here?" I asked. "Can we continue to the Valley?"

"Everything is fine, Sen, other than your prolonged absence. There have been some altercations with remaining adversaries, but Jo has dealt with those. The Valley and all within it remain well and are still protected. We can go now, since Isabel has had time to set up the festivities."

Chapter Thirty

The three of us stepped into the links, and a second later stood in the Valley. Almost immediately, a little blonde bundle of beauty leaped on me from a dead run. For the partial second I glimpsed her, she seemed considerably taller than the last time I had seen her. Standing by were Jo and Michael. While carrying Isa, I walked over to give Jo a big hug. Michael and Asif were also embracing. A sizable crowd was advancing toward us, filled with people I knew and lots of young children I didn't know yet. It was good to be home.

A celebration quickly began with the excitement spreading as soon as we arrived. Everyone was ecstatic that the principal threat to us, and by extension, to humanity, had been extinguished. I was happy as well, but not as much as everyone else. I noticed Henry with what I thought was showing a similar attitude. He had a slight smile but wasn't celebrating like everyone else. I guess that as the world's oldest man, he'd seen plenty of victory parties, followed sometime later by the next adversary or disaster show up. He nodded when he noticed me looking at him. I returned it, and went to enjoy tonight, and hopefully the next few decades, with my family and friends. I had been blessed beyond measure and intended to revel in the glow these people put out. But I really just wanted to take Jo and Isabel home and catch up on two years.

Days later, I was doing what I planned to do for as long as possible. I knew it was naïve to think I could get away with it forever. But for now, I was content to spoon with Jo at night, and by day, sit in the sun and watch Isabel and the other children play. Meanwhile, Jo and Michael were already strategizing to go after the pair of master vampires from Minnesota, now living in Russia. I would always support Jo, and fight with her or for her as needed, but right now my support was as a househusband. I used my martial instincts by filling water balloons for the young kids, and I taught classes for all the new people coming in for training. Our first two classes of kids had been recruiting. Another group of young people were coming in, including some that were family from North Carolina. A kid named Nick was highly recommended and I looked forward to meeting him and the others.

There had been no visits from or word about the Sky Lords in the two years that Asif and I had burped into the time warp. No one thought they were still a threat. I would continue hoping for the best and preparing for the worst.

I had gotten in touch with Monk, who was back in the real world and doing amazing things with the early prototypes of his new quantum computer systems. He had taken the black box Asif brought and was able to salvage most of the data. A copy went to Michael and the Center was working on it full time. The Center thought that with time they could not only decipher the viral puzzles, but possibly come up with countermeasures to stop or even reverse the worst effects. There might be hope for humanity yet.

I heard that Monk's leaving had left Nan sad, but Monk was doing what he did best, and despite his words, I knew those systems would always be his first love. Since the party the day of our return, I had noticed Nan and Asif eyeing each other. There could be a story developing, but I was staying out of it. At least until I could privately embarrass Asif. I knew better than to say anything in front of Nan.

Jo and I were good, but it was still strange for her. My reality was that I had only been gone and not seen Jo for a week, but she had lost me for two years, and it could have been forever. We were going on dates.

"Are we still good?" I asked Jo on our first date.

"Of course, you moron. But I'm still getting used to you being back. Everyone was positive about your return, but I could tell even Michael and Kal had some doubt."

"Awful nice of you to wait for me."

"Who said I did?" Then she jumped on me. It is possible we broke some furniture the next couple of hours.

In contrast, Isabel never missed a beat. It was like she had already known what was going to happen and was confident that everything was fine. She was growing up fast, but then she had been born with abilities that no humans had.

I was sitting in the sun with Jo, watching Isabel's group play football in a field of mud that they had conjured. It looked like a lot of fun.

"I know you well enough that you have troubles brewing in your head," Jo said.

"Maybe. I'm probably overthinking stuff, though."

"Tell me, you lug. Otherwise, you will keep brooding around when you think nobody is watching."

"Hey, I don't do that. At least not much. Anyway, it's probably nothing. But Asif told me that the most advanced technology the Sky Lords had, including the spaceship and the time travel system, came from elsewhere and they did not develop it. They really could not even take care of those things."

"Where did they get the systems?"

"Asif doesn't know."

"And you are worried that whatever advanced group gave that to the Sky Lords could reappear, and fix things for them?"

"Something like that". The other thing I did not tell her was from another conversation with Asif. There was a figure behind the government of the Sky Lords, and the rumor is that it was a master vampire that frightened the entire population. Asif had never met anyone like that, so it could have been a useful myth to keep people in line, like using the boogeyman to scare children. Problem was, I knew Michael believed there were master vampires among the Sky Lords. My fear was that if the Sky Lords came back, they'd unleash the wrath of the worst master vampires on us. I was confident we'd prevail, but I worried about the cost. Meanwhile, I'd let those thoughts stew and try hard to enjoy myself.

"There is something you need to know," Jo said. "Actually, two things, and both are non-negotiable."

"OK, I can not negotiate better than anyone." That earned me a side-eye.

First, I know you worry too much and will eventually get back to doing something stupid. When you do, I'm going with you.

"I'm not sure-

"Just be quiet. We both know you will do it. But I'm not going to lose you again. You plan it, set it up, then we go. I'm stronger, faster, and smarter than you. We will go, and you will be my sidekick. So, that is the first point."

I just grinned. I could get used to being a kept man. "What is the second decree?"

"I want to have a child, and Jo can be a sister."

"Uh, well, you don't exactly need me for that."

"Yes, I do, I want this to be our child. The old-fashioned way."

"Oh, sure, I can do that."

"Yes, you can; and we will, after more practice."

We went and practiced. Afterward, I asked Jo something else I'd been thinking about.

"How was Isabel while I was gone?"

"She was the only one sure you were coming back and was a real rock for me. She and the other kids, of whom she has become the unofficial ringleader, travel all over the Valley looking for adventures. I don't know for sure, but I suspect she had also been traveling the links."

"Hmm, I don't think that is safe."

"Me either. I voiced my suspicions to Kal, and although he did not deny it, he said he would keep an eye out. Otherwise, he was not concerned."

"That is even stranger. I'll talk to him about that."

"I was hoping you would. I never worry about Isa here in the Valley, but the idea of her in the links really bothers me."

Two days later I met up with Kal. We were going mushroom hunting as it was a good season for them. Of course, in the Valley it was almost always a good season.

"Kal, Jo told me that Isabel may be traveling in the links."

"We have observed that and were also concerned at first. But she does not go anywhere dangerous. In fact, she tells us where problems may be. We have investigated her warnings and found she is right."

"Because she went somewhere and almost got caught or hurt?"

"No, she knows before she travels there. We cannot explain it, but she has an instinctual foreknowledge. That should be impossible, and our only explanation is that she somehow sees the future, similar to remote viewing within the links. If so, she is much more advanced than we are."

"Kal, that is incredible, and it's great that she avoids problems. But it still worries me."

"I understand. Yet I advise that you not discourage her too strongly. I feel she would continue her explorations regardless, but subsequently be reticent about revealing her experiences."

"Great point, Kal. Well, maybe I will get her to report to me and Jo. That might make Jo feel better. Possibly she could take Jo or I with her on some of her trips; that might relieve some of our anxiety."

"That is a wise course. You can't stop her, but you could make yourself feel better once you see she is doing it safely and responsibly."

"I'll try that tactic. But not sure I can sell Jo on the idea."

I headed back to cook up the basket of mushrooms for dinner. As I walked, I realized I could not sit still here in the Valley forever, playing and teaching. But I did not have to go straight back to fighting either, so I already had an idea. I needed Asif to help me with an adventure for the children. They were learning astronomy, so perhaps a trip to the moon was in order. It might be a little dangerous, but then it had to be, for it to be an adventure. I probably would not tell Jo about that part.

I also needed to get with Henry about the waterfall at the top of the Valley. It had been showing rainbow hues instead of the usual white mist. I doubted it was anything important since the Valley was so well protected, but it was odd.

I went to chat with Isabel about the link travel, but I just saw her leave the house. It was getting dark, and she was a stargazer like me. I'd let her enjoy another quiet evening, then talk to her tomorrow. I was looking forward to a lot of tomorrows.

Epilogue

I sabel slipped out of the house as she often did at night. She loved to listen to the creek, all the insects, and lie down to watch the stars move through their slow circular dance in the sky. As she approached the creek, she saw something different tonight. A shape, appearing as a human female, but composed more of thick, glowing rainbow-colored smoke rather than flesh.

Isabel ran to her, exclaiming, "Grandmother! I thought you had left forever. I'm glad you are back."

"Oh Isabel, you are so lovely. Yes, I have been gone for longer than I can imagine. But you brought me back. Thank you, child. Let me look at you for a moment."

Isabel stood in the rainbow glow with a smile. "Oh, grandmother, how did I bring you back?"

"When you were conceived, a signal went out that triggered my coalescence from all the waters of the world. It took some doing, but now I have pulled together enough form to make this journey and meet you properly."

"That's great. I remember you visiting mom in her dreams before I was born."

"That was me, responding to you and trying to reassure your mom. She was a little worried about what was happening."

"I remember that, and it was OK until bad things happened right after. But everything turned out great once dad brought her here."

"I know, and I'm so happy for all of you."

"Let's go meet mom and dad."

"Yes, I believe it is time to meet my children."

Isabel grabbed the glowing woman's hand. It was warm and soft, and Isabel led the way back to her house. She was shivering with excitement. Mom and dad were going to be so surprised.

Isabel hoped she could go along to visit Auntie Morri for Christmas. She looked back as she walked, and noticed the creek was giving off a slight but beautiful rainbow glow. Everyone in town was going to enjoy that. Everyone was finally going to meet Grandmother Danu.

Author's Note

All the physical places described in the book are actual locations. At least, all the ones described in the current century. And most of the more ancient places exist as well and can be visited today. Take a trip, especially outside your home country, and visit some place you may write about someday.

All characters in this book are fictitious. Any references to actual historical figures were also fictionalized to fit the story. Of course, I had to say that for legal reasons. But just how fictitious are these characters in your imagination?

Watch for the next two releases in the Fisher of Time world. *Tourmaline Skies*, a semi-standalone novel written slightly more as a fantasy romance, introduces new characters. One is a Nunehi shapeshifter, the other a fae werewolf. Their relationship begins just after the events in *Danu Valley*, and soon veers into the worlds of Senecus and Morrigan.

The next book in the series is *High Lands*, continuing the stories of the characters in previous books.

ABOUT THE AUTHOR

Doug Smith, PhD, is a former science non-fiction writer, producing obscure texts immortalized nowhere important. But he is now writing what he loves to read: science fiction and fantasy stories. When not writing, he functions as a can opener for a cat that is not his.

Formerly a resident of The Netherlands, he is now living near Asheville, North Carolina. Visit his website at for more information. If you enjoyed this series, please let him know as he prepares for the next episodes, featuring Jo and Isabel. Also, please take a moment and leave a rating or review. Those are sustenance for the writer's soul.